Alberta C. King
224 N. Chapel St.
Baltimore, 31. Md.

December 1945.

THIS NIGHT CALLED DAY

This Night Called Day

By

E. J. EDWARDS

THE BRUCE PUBLISHING COMPANY
Milwaukee

"Work and worship. These are the watchwords of that night which we call day. They are certainties. . . . Speculations are only useful inasmuch as they lead on to work and worship. . . . We have a kind of creative or conserving force within us. And we have to evolve order and beauty out of our surroundings — the brown earth, the barren sea, the souls of men; or we have to help in keeping intact such work as the progressive centuries have wrought for mankind, and to keep earth, and sea, and human lives from reverting to primitive chaos."[1]

---

[1] Taken from *Under the Cedars and the Stars,* by Canon Sheehan. With the permission of Benziger Brothers, Inc.

PROLOGUE

A line of gaily honking autos came down the road from the Catalina foothills. The wheels of the leader churned up a cloud of powdery dust as it swept around a bend and headed for the city of Tucson. Like a puff of incense the dust billowed up and hung for a peaceful moment, sun-gloried, in the May-day's clear, warm air. And then the next car, and the next plunged into the cloud, each adding its contribution to the whirling powder that drifted upwards. There was exhilaration in the way each gleaming vehicle flashed through it, careening recklessly around the bend, and then gliding onward to the city.

The very last car was different. It alone did not seem to share the gay mood of the others. In a cautious manner it approached the bend, slackened its speed and then came to a quiet stop. The wall of tamaracks that sentineled the bend hid it from the view of the preceding cars. A bronze-faced young man in a trim tuxedo hastily alighted and then assisted a young woman in bridal dress from the car. The man turned to the chauffeur. "O.K., Mike," he ordered. "Run along now."

"And what do I tell Doctor Bashford?" pleaded the worried man at the wheel.

"That we changed cars on the Sabino Canyon road," laughed the groom, and he pointed toward a roadway that forked away in an easterly direction. A small roadster was drawn up alongside it.

Mike shook his head. "All those people at the Pioneer Hotel for the reception — and no bride or groom. Boy,

I'm a dead duck!" He meshed gears and swung the car around the bend.

Like two mischievous children the couple carefully made their way to the bend and peered around it, watching the car until it had caught up with the others. They looked at each other, their faces filled with the glee of their successful plot, and then they scurried over to the roadster. The young man backed the car and sent it rolling along the way they had just come, out into the Catalina foothills.

"Gayle," said the girl, a faint shadow of doubt in her voice, "what will Doctor Bashford do when he finds out?"

"He'll roar right out to Sabino Canyon — that's a good forty-five minutes drive — and when he doesn't find us he'll rattle his hocks over to our house. That's a good hour's drive. We've got several hours, Marilyn."

He slid one arm about her waist, drawing her close, as his foot pressed down on the accelerator. The car leaped forward, and filled their ears with the roar of the rushing wind. Something of the exultation of the hour was in Gayle's driving and the car skimmed over the roadway like a swallow in flight. The warm dry air flowed over their faces, a boundless blue sky vaulted above them, the desert rolled onwards clear up to the crumbled peaks of the eastern Catalinas. All of it was vast and good and endless — like their love, on this their wedding day.

Gayle slowed the car down and turned it westward into a side road. Peacefully the car purred along till it came to rest before a spacious one-storied, Spanish mission style dwelling. The white of its snowy walls was in dazzling contrast to the dark green of the garden all about it. There was one porticoed house near by, the only neighbor. A low, white, paling fence left the view open to the four corners of the compass.

They pushed open the gate and walked through the garden up to the door. Gayle rang and a maid appeared.

"Why — Doctor Wade!" she exclaimed. "I — I thought — the reception at the Pioneer Hotel. . . ."

Gayle laughed. "It's all right, Nora. We'll be going there — later."

"When Doctor Bashford finds us," explained Marilyn, her eyes twinkling.

"We didn't want the crowd around," added Gayle. Nora's maternal face lit up with sudden understanding. Gayle turned to his bride. "Are you ready, Mrs. Wade?"

She nodded, her eyes sparkling. "I'm dreadfully heavy," she warned.

He picked her up in his arms. "You don't weigh more than a whisper — an angel's whisper," he said, and stepped across the threshold. It was pleasantly dim and cool in the white-walled living room, with its Venetian blinds drawn against the Arizona sun. Gayle walked slowly across the room, tinglingly aware of the exquisite softness of his burden and of the faint flowery perfume enveloping him in a delicate fragrance as Marilyn clung to him. He paused before a snow-white fireplace with its gleaming black flooring and polished brass andirons.

"This it?" he asked.

"Yes."

He set her down and she went quickly to the wall and pressed a button. Fluorescent light flooded up from a hidden recess in the mantelpiece and illuminated a picture. It was a simple reproduction of a landscape. There were two trees at the left and in the distance some hills. A wayward little footpath straggled forlornly through the center of the picture, seemingly headed for the distant hills, but the profusion of blue flowers carpeting the ground soon swallowed up its wistful wanderings. It was not a valuable picture. Even the original could not have been worth much. Yet here it was lording it over a room filled with furnishings that were exquisite, choice and costly. And strangely enough there was no incongruity. In its gilt frame above the white mantelpiece, bracketed by pieces of gleaming crystal, it looked singularly appropriate, complacent, restful.

She did not ask him if he liked it. Her face was lifted to

[3]

the bright-colored scene and a satisfied, relaxed look covered her delicate features. "It's nice," she murmured.

Gayle turned to her, an amused tolerance in his gray eyes. "It's just a crooked old cow track."

"Winding roads lead to the happiest lands." There was a musing far-away note in her voice. "The blue bonnets, and the clouds, and . . ." The sentence trailed away into silence, and Gayle looked down at her.

"Blue bonnets? Is that the name of the flowers?"

She nodded. "Little ladies in blue bonnets." She looked at him. "Lupines to you, Mr. Scientist."

He took her hand. "I like it."

She smiled. "You furnished everything, Gay. I had only this to bring to our home."

"I'll furnish everything you want or desire, from here on out."

"You are all that I really want, dear. It's all that I can give in return — myself."

He lifted her hand and kissed the wedding ring.

Nora came in. "Did you like it, Doctor Wade? The picture?"

Gayle looked at her a moment. "So you're the culprit that had it installed. A conspiracy."

"Nothing of the sort," said the maid. "We just talked it over like." She looked at the picture. "It is a restful looking bit of color. Knowing Dr. Bashford as I do, I'm thinking a look at it right now would do him a lot of good." She turned to them. "Don't you think you — "

"Oh no," cut in Gayle. "Not for an hour or so yet. We are going to sit out there in the garden till they find us."

"I know it's not going to help Dr. Bashford's blood pressure," commented the maid.

Gayle was indifferent to that fact. "I don't like that veil, Marilyn. It hides your hair."

She unpinned the veil and handed it to Nora. For a moment his eyes were filled with the sight of that cloud of golden red hair framing the delicate oval of her face; then she moved over to him and arm in arm they went out into the garden.

"The palo verde is in full bloom," he said as they walked down the path. All the rugged strength of the rolling foothills was outstretched before them, climaxed by the towering wall of the distant Catalina Mountains. "Most people would put a wall about a place like this," explained Gayle. "But Dad was a real westerner. He had to have distance in his landscape."

"I like it this way," replied the girl. "The mountains, the far horizons. . . ." Her gaze swept around to the west, and noticed the near-by porticoed house shaded by pepper trees. "Who lives there, Gay?"

"An old gent and his sister."

"Do you know them?"

"Just to say hello. He's a retired preacher or something. We haven't much in common."

They went down the path to the far corner of the garden where the palo verde stood, decked in gold. The blossom-laden branches bunched out from the low trunk like a nosegay of flowers. Gay drew the girl beneath the branches. "Look up, angel, and tell me what you see," he directed.

Her response was a single, breathless, "Oh." Against the vivid May sunlight all the myriad tiny blossoms shone transparently golden. A faint scent sweetened the air and the soft low hum of a few bees added melody to it. All about them the branches drooped, slim, smooth, green withes, unleaved, but bending downwards with the weight of their ophir-petaled blooms. The couple seemed housed in a cloud of gold.

She put her arms about him and laid her cheek against his. "It's heavenly, Gay," she breathed.

"And it's just the beginning, dear," he murmured, moving his head slowly till his lips found the cool smoothness of her cheek.

They stood in silent happiness and aloneness, the inner joy of their wedding day merged somehow into the delight

[5]

of this tree in flower, till the westering sun began to lose its alchemistic power and the blossoms were no longer transparent films of gold but solid little armies of buttercups clasped to the slim green strength of the boughs.

As though directed by one will, they moved out from beneath the tree, and made their way to a glider drawn up on the lawn. Gayle sat down, leaned back, stretched his legs, and Marilyn perched on the edge beside him, her cloud of white skirts fluffed out about her. She leaned back slowly into Gayle's waiting arm.

A long chittering trill kept spilling from a bird throat. There was a clocklike invariableness about its simple song. It broke up the languorous stillness yet was perfectly one with the pattern of peace. Serene sky above them, mellow sunlight, velvet air, and this ever-recurring, down-flowing tinkle of bird song. The sound was like the caressing stroke of a soft white hand, firm, then fading away into complete quiescence.

"I know now why they call it God's country," said Marilyn. A great contentment filled her voice.

Gayle looked at her with patronizing amusement deep in his eyes.

"I can almost feel Him," she said with deep seriousness.

"It's easy to — with you here," replied Gayle. "I could almost believe in Him myself."

She pressed her cheek against his, but her eyes, misted, trance-like, stared off at the distant bulk of the Catalina Mountains. "We are one now, Gay," she murmured.

"And that makes us part of all this. We are complete. I feel right. Although I've lost myself."

"You will be that way — for always."

" 'Till death do us part,' " he quoted softly.

Her eyes turned slowly toward him. The tinkle of bird song suddenly stilled. Over everything was a hushed expectancy. "No, Gay, not till death do us part," she said with solemn assurance.

"Isn't that always?"

"That's only this life. It's so short a time — till death."

Gayle's eyes looked deep into hers. "It's forever, dear. For life, through death, and — whatever is beyond."

"I believe that, Gay, with all my heart. Life does not stop with death. Death does not take life away. It just changes it to another one, a better one."

"When you say it I can believe it."

"What is heaven if you can't find your love there?"

"Isn't this heaven now, Marilyn? We two, alone?"

"Yes, Gay. Heaven for a little while. It has to end. The real heaven will be when we are together and no possibility of parting."

The sun was down below the western mountains now, and a faint shadow fell across her face.

"You're very solemn, Marilyn," protested Gayle. But he caught his breath at the sight of the grave beauty in her face.

"I feel solemn, dear. Ever since that moment this afternoon in the chapel. I was looking out through the huge window that makes up the whole rear wall of the sanctuary. The Catalinas stretched out like a picture and the minister was saying 'till death do you part', and suddenly a strangeness came over me. I knew it was not true; I mean, what he was saying. Something inside of me told me that it was not so. My love for you would be like those ageless mountains. It would always stand. My love for you would have no end." Her voice was low, vibrant, filled with a soul's complete conviction. "I knew that I would love you, Gay, always and forever."

The intense sincerity of her words struck Gayle dumb. For a moment he was beyond his depth; she was away from him in the world of the spirit and he could not follow or touch her. He was an earthy, matter-of-fact man. It was a disembodied spirit talking to him now and it left him suddenly chill. As a rule his mind followed or anticipated her in all her likes and dislikes. It had been like an instinct between them, but now for the first time he felt as though he was an outsider.

[7]

And then, turning, she read in one swift glance the bewilderment in his mind and pressed her lips lovingly against his. Perplexity, fear dropped from him. His Marilyn! Dainty, *spirituelle,* yet understandingly feminine. Love for her drowned his brief bewilderment in a passionate tide. His lips returned the pressure of hers; then he buried them in the fragrance of her hair, and whispered, "That's the way it will be, Marilyn — forever."

She smiled, then, confidently. For them love was a timeless summer, with no shadow of change or variation. For one brief moment they had touched an eternal truth . . . that we were made for bliss, an endless ecstatic bliss; and with the sublime confidence of youth they laid hold of it.

Long they sat in silence, the twilight deepening about them. A murmured thought, a quiet kiss, while their eyes feasted on the interplay of colors on the mountains. They watched the ensanguined cliffs of the Catalinas and the canyons hollowed with penumbrous gloom. The reflected light of the dying sun spilled a tide of loveliness over the mountainside, and gradually the whole stretch of crumbly dun rock took on one vast wash of crushed-grape color, glowing, fusing, fading into pastel pinks, into purple shadows and then into darkness. For a while a cloud overhead still held the vanished sun's smoky effulgence, then this, too, chilled into a slate gray. The aquamarine of the horizon merged into a deep blue, a purplish gloom; and then, over all, was night.

Cheek to cheek, they watched this panorama fade. Centuries of sun, seas of sand and towers of jutting rock, eternally beautiful, recurrently shadowed by night, but immutably beautiful, strong and joy-filled. So, too, they felt, would they be. For tomorrow always brought the day, and there would always be a tomorrow.

And then the glare of automobile headlights invaded the garden. With a squeal of brakes a car ground to a stop before the gate and a ball of a man bounced out. He banged open the gate and started up the walk. "Gayle!" he shouted. "Hey, Gayle!"

Gayle turned to Marilyn. "It's Doctor Hiram J. Bashford," he announced and the slight pause after each of the words conveyed to the girl his dissatisfaction. He sighed. "The honeymoon is over." He stood up. "Here I am," he called.

The fuming doctor stalked over to them.

"What the devil kind of a kid's trick is this?" he demanded. "I've been chasing you all over the landscape."

Gayle's voice had a hint of repressed laughter. "We got lost."

"Lost? My foot!" snorted their pursuer. "Marilyn, they're waiting at the Pioneer Hotel. All those people. Come on."

"My veil. Wait a minute." She made for the house.

The chubby doctor turned on Gayle. "Now just what was the fool idea?" he demanded. "You can't treat people that way."

The laughter went out of Gayle's voice. "It seems to me I have. After all it's *our* wedding. We don't need them around."

Doctor Bashford looked at him aghast. "That's a selfish thing to say, Gayle."

"Maybe it is. But then, I am in love, and I guess love makes you that way."

Doctor Bashford stared at him a moment, restraining his rising anger with difficulty. "I see you know all the answers."

"Is that bad?"

"It's worse, it's stupid, it's . . . it's tragic."

Gayle laughed good humoredly and put his hand affectionately on the older man's shoulder. "But that's the way I was brought up, Hi. You ought to know. You've had a hand in it." Hi gave an angry grunt of amazement and twisted his shoulder away from Gayle's hand. "Tuck in your shirttail, Hi," soothed the younger man. "A fellow doesn't get anywhere nowadays if he doesn't know the answers."

Hi looked at him a moment hardly able to credit his ears. "Are you telling me you know all the answers, son?" His voice was deceptively soft.

[9]

"Sure. At least all that I need to know. Anything wrong with that?"

"Plenty. You know too much and — not enough." Hi's voice was cold and hard.

"Come on, Hi, don't get your hackles up," said Gayle. "We just wanted to have the first few hours for ourselves. I — well, I guess you wouldn't understand."

"No; I wouldn't. I've buried two wives and married a third."

"Well, we just wanted to be alone."

"Alone? You'll be that for the rest of your lives. Man, you'll have more than enough of that, I'm telling you."

Marilyn came up just then and Gayle put his arm around her drawing her close to his side. "I don't think so, Hi," he said with deep seriousness. "I don't think so."

Unhurriedly Gayle and Marilyn went down the walk, entered their car and drove off. Doctor Bashford walked over to his own car, slowly, tiredly, like a man bent beneath a burden. Thoughtfully he opened the door and sat down, his hands lying limply on the wheel. The long anticipated joy of the wedding banquet was forgotten, his eager interest in the conviviality of fore-gathered friends and abundant hilarity drained suddenly from him. It was not the fret and fury of chasing the fugitive bride and groom for two hours that had occasioned this sudden change in his disposition, but the cool insouciance of Gayle's replies opening up to him in one startling glance the bed rock of the boy's character and the wellspring of his motives. He loved Gayle, but his affection did not blind the clearness of his judgment. Slowly his hands tightened about the wheel. "The answers . . . all that he needs," brooded Hi in a somber voice. "A fool . . . like the rest of them . . . self-sufficient."

A sense of hopelessness enveloped him as he spoke, for he knew, as no other one did, the hard independence of Gayle's make-up, and how devastatingly intolerant he could be of what he considered interference in his own affairs. He had gone as far as he could in trying to tell

Gayle the idiocy of his self-sufficiency. That was clear to him. The boy had grown up and away from him in one brief interchange of words. And yet looking back, he saw it had been a gradual process. The girl . . . his marriage to her . . . that had been the supreme and final link in Gayle's chain of achievements. It confirmed the truth of the theories which the boy had been evolving in his soul. It put the crown on his egoism and self-sufficiency. Gayle was riding the crest of the wave, he was successful in all that he had attempted, and a successful man is the hardest person on earth to convince of the error of his ways.

Hi's mind swung back to the picture of Gayle with his arm about Marilyn. "At the very moment he is telling me how self-sufficient he is he shows his utter dependence on another! He's heading for the rocks."

Irritably Hi switched on the ignition. "I can only stand by. He picked his path, he'll have to follow it himself."

Automatically he shifted the gears and the car lurched onward in an aimless hesitant way as though affected by the mood of its driver.

Chapter 1

FROM its perch in the pepper tree a twitchy-tailed bird cocked its head and gazed at Manolo. Manolo sunk his trowel in the loam of the garden bed and eyed the old man in the wheel chair. The old man stared across his garden fence at the young man and girl.

The bird was unmindful of all else save the freshly-turned soil beneath Manolo's hands. Manolo had forgotten his work in his interest in the old man's absorption. The old man was heedless of everything except the happy young couple. And the boy and the girl were totally oblivious of the whole wide world.

Manolo chuckled and the old man slowly turned his head. *"Miel de la luna,"* said Manolo, his face upended in a grin. "Always honeymoon with them, eh, Padre?"

"Yes," replied the old man. "Strange isn't it? They are married almost three years, have a little boy — " His voice trailed off.

"Caracóles!" ejaculated Manolo. "One boy. *Un niño.* What is that? I have six niños."

The old man made no reply. There was a splendor on the girl's face and a glow on the man's countenance. "It's almost mystical," muttered the old man. "It doesn't change, it doesn't tire." There was not just curiosity in the gaze of his kind blue eyes but a wonderment, and in his whispered words a gratefulness to be able to witness such a thing.

Lingeringly, the young man's arm came away from the girl's waist and he entered the car. The girl put her face in through the open window, tilted her chin and closed her eyes. The man leaned over and kissed her lightly on fore-head and nose tip. She reached in, took his right hand and imprinted a kiss on its palm and then folded the fingers of his hand over it. His eyes shining, he held the tightly closed fist aloft as he settled back in his seat. His left hand took hold of the wheel and the car awoke to sudden life.

She followed it with happy eyes till it swung out of sight, and then, reluctantly, she turned back up the walk. Over the low palings of her fence she encountered the old man's interested gaze. She walked over. "Isn't the sun lovely today?" she called out.

"It is indeed, Mrs. Wade. Only Tuscon could have sun like this in January."

"Arizona, the Sunshine State! I'm happy about those poinsettias." She gestured at the blossoms against the side of his house. "May I come over and look at them?"

"All you want," offered the old man.

She paused a moment at the mailbox before his gate. In black lettering was a single name: Paul Hutchinson.

She gave a smoothing touch to the immaculate white house apron that covered the front of her bright gingham dress, then ran a hand beneath the wealth of burnished red hair that fell to her shoulders in such abundance. She pushed open the gate. There was a lilt to her walk, a gay uncon-sciousness of the fact that people had been spectators of her endearing farewell. Manolo's eyes came up from his work and followed her with appreciation — in spite of his six children.

"Your flowers are a delight, Mr. Hutchinson," she said putting one slender white finger on a flaming poinsettia petal. "That man of yours is a wizard. I can't get mine to bloom like this."

The old man smiled. "Did you hear that, Manolo?"

"*Seguro, Padre,*" replied the Mexican, squatting back on his heels: "*Tengo bueno mano.*" He held up a grimy fist. "I have good hand, Señora. Everything I plant grows good."

"So that's the secret. She held up her hands and looked

at their soft gracefulness. "Maybe if I didn't wear gloves?"

Manolo looked dubiously at his begrimed hands then at her white hands. "Gloves! *Caracóles!*"

Her laughter spilled out. It was a bright, companionable laughter. Manolo grinned and a twinkle came into the old man's eyes.

"Would you like to take some flowers with you?" he asked.

"Oh, dearly. But I'll be greedy. I'll never stop." She went closer to the flowers. "How many may I have?"

"As many as you want. They are there to make you happy."

"Oh, but I am happy."

There was a pause. "Yes, I observed that," commented the old man slowly. "You *are* happy. And it is good to see one as happy as you are." For a moment his eyes clouded as though memories of pain and sorrow had welled up from the caverns of the past. His expression cleared. "May your happiness not only stay but grow."

She looked at him with a quizzical smile. He was so formal, yet so sincere. "What a lovely wish! Thank you."

"And that goes for your husband too, the doctor."

Her smile deepened. "Gayle will always be happy if he has me," she declared with charming assurance.

"And, of course, you will always be happy as long as you have him," he added with shrewd solemnity.

Her eyes lit up with sudden laughter and acquiescence as though he had discovered a close-held secret. "Gayle's the dearest thing. He looks awful solemn unless he's laughing, but he's just as true and steadfast as — as — " She faltered for a comparison and then her hand swept out in a wide gesture — "as those mountains."

The old man's eyes took in the ancient Catalina Mountains, their splintered skyline, the deep-cut cavernous sides, a bleak, burnt-out tremendous mass, pitilessly clear in the revealing bright light of the sun.

"They have been there a long time — those mountains," he said.

"Gayle has a ranch further out there in the foothills," she went on. "He's still half a wild cowboy. Every once in a while he goes on a rampage."

"Until you get the halter on him again?"

"Oh, it isn't that bad," she protested. "He's just sort of sudden in his decisions. It's the way he thinks, you see. A thing is good or bad, black or white for him. He's a dear, but a very downright sort of a dear."

Her eyes grew reminiscent and a light transfigured her face.

There seemed no place in her whole composition for anything except this love, and the old man, whose three score and more than ten years had seen too much disillusionment, felt tempted to drop a word of warning, but in the face of such a joy it would have been unforgivable.

Her eyes came back to the old man, his patriarchal face, his bulky brown loafer jacket, his dark trousers.

"Can't you leave that wheelchair ever, Mr. Hutchinson?" she queried.

"Just to get in and out of it," he said ruefully. He pointed to his knees. "Arthritis."

"Oh!" Her voice was deep with sympathy. "Arizona seems to be the last resort for us sick ones," she said with a sigh.

"Us?" He raised his eyebrows questioningly.

She nodded. "Asthma. I had such awful attacks back East, but Arizona's dry climate is really making me well. I had only three attacks in the past two months.

"Well, with a doctor for a husband — "

"Gayle doesn't take care of me. His partner at the clinic is my doctor. Doctor Bashford."

"I know him. He's caring for me too."

"Do you like him?"

"Very much."

Manolo had finished cutting the flowers. He placed the vivid red blooms in her arms. "I love the coloring on these poinsettias but my real favorite is a lovely, fragrant little flower — mignonette."

[16]

"Mignonette. Well, well; I know that flower. It's a delicate thing. Arizona is a trifle too harsh for it."

"Isn't it a pity?" She studied his face and her eyes were the eyes of a child. Her next question had the abruptness of a child's query. "You're a priest, aren't you, Mr. Hutchinson? Manolo calls you Padre."

He nodded. "An old, broken-down one."

She came up to him and extended a hand. "Marilyn is what my friends call me. I'm not a Catholic. May I call you Padre?"

The Padre took her hand. "Delighted," he said. There was a little golden cross swinging from a chain about her neck. "Marilyn," he mused, "and she loves mignonette."

She liked the way he said it. There was such a candid simplicity about him. He was as plain as bran bread. Yet at first glance he produced a venerable, almost awesome impression. A massive forehead with a little tuft of white hair in the center. The bridge of the nose was a straight line but the nostrils broadened out at the base. Two deep lines calipered down about his mouth. Though the chin was firm, it looked curiously small beneath the scholarly brow.

"I'm going to ask you a question," she suddenly announced.

The blue eyes twinkled. "I've been answering them for the past twenty-five years," he replied.

"Oh?"

"At the University."

"What did you teach?"

"Various things. My last years there I lectured on Ascetic Theology." Her eyes grew round. "It isn't as dangerous as it sounds," he said comfortingly.

"It sounds formidable." She hesitated, suddenly embarrassed in the presence of learning. "You wouldn't mind answering my question, would you?"

He shook his head.

"Even if it seemed rather childish?"

" 'Out of the mouths of children, O God, Thou hast

perfected praise.' " He said it in such a sonorous preacher voice that she was forced to smile. Her hesitation vanished and she confidently proposed her question.

"When Gayle and I were married the minister said that we were to be man and wife 'from this day forward, for richer, for poorer, in sickness and in health, until death do us part.' Do you believe that? — I don't."

The Padre looked up. "I do," came his quiet reply.

A silence fell between them. Marilyn's eyes studied the flowers without seeing them.

"What is it that you don't believe about that part of the marriage vow?" probed the Padre.

Her eyes came up to his, not troubled but full of an exalted assurance. "The last part," she said simply. "I told Gayle after the ceremony that my love for him was not going to last until death parted us — it would be for always, even after death, forever."

The Padre's eyes did not leave her face.

"And Gayle agreed with me," she added as though that clinched the matter, but her eyes were questioning his.

"There is an old, old line," came his quiet rejoinder, "that 'true love never dies.' But the curse of this weary old world of ours is that there is so little of true love in it."

Marilyn's face became radiant. "Oh, but ours is true. It will go on and on and on."

"You have me convinced," smiled the old man. "Even the heavenly hosts would have to bend an ear and believe when you put it that way."

A strident voice hailed Marilyn from across the garden. "That's Nora," she explained to the Padre, inclining her head toward a bulky woman who had suddenly appeared on the porch of the Wade home. "Bucky, the other member of the family, needs attention." Her face suddenly crinkled in a smile. "You know I have a little sister back east. Ruth is younger than I and very practical. We used to discuss such unmaidenly topics as the rearing of male offspring. I very much fear that I'm too much on the idealistic side. When

[18]

Ruth sees Bucky I know she will say I have spoiled him."

She held out her hand. "I like to talk to you. May I come over often?"

"And steal my flowers?" he said with a mock rueful face.

"You want me to, don't you?"

"Indeed I do."

Her hand slipped away from his. "I'll be back."

She left him strangely happy and content. The warmth of that loving happiness within her had reached out to him. It was something vital that flowed from her. She was surcharged with the joy of her love and it imparted itself to others. "*Bonum est sui diffusivum,*" he muttered. "She rather puts reality into the old scholastic axiom. Gives it form, so to speak."

He watched her going up the walk. A picture composed of gingham, flowers, sunshine on glistening red hair, and a face lit with joy. He was never to see it again.

Chapter 2

FAR out on the Fort Lowell road, in a little
adobe cabin, a phone rang insistently. It would not be denied. The tired woman left the bedside of her ailing child
and lifted the receiver. . . . "Who, Doctor Wade? . . . No.
He left a few minutes ago. . . . No, I wouldn't be able to
reach him now. . . . Uh huh. I'm sorry."

She hung up the receiver. Even doctor's wives got sick.
Well she had enough sickness on her own hands. She went
back to her ailing child.

Gayle's car thrashed noisily along the road. It was a
strange and chilling day for Tucson. Blustery with rain and
a bleak rawness. Every January brought several such days.
They were the climax of the winter. Tomorrow morning
the surrounding mountain peaks would be dusted with
snow, and when the sun broke through the clouds the rugged
old ranges would be glorious in sun-capped splendor. Gayle
knew Arizona and loved it. Something of its hardy severity
was in his make-up. His upbringing at his father's ranch had
bred in him bone, muscle, and self-reliance. The things he
wanted he went after with a quiet determination that would
not brook defeat. He had achieved them all. Money, independence, a position of respect and local importance, and
eventually a beautiful wife. There was nothing he could
not have if he set his mind to it. But just now there was
nothing that he wished for. He had filled out the horizon of
his desires and was content. But the consciousness of this
ability, this self-sufficiency, this personal drive within him
was always there; and the knowledge that he could at a

moment's notice turn it loose, converge its efforts about a task, filled him with an elan that at times was almost arrogance. But outwardly this never showed. He himself had never attempted to analyze this trait of his character. It was a confidence in his own ability, his independence of outside aid, a consciousness of his power to bend other forces to his will. Life had no secrets for him. At least no secrets that he could not discover if he wished to. A rather taciturn air covered the actual depths of his nature. Since his marriage much of his external seriousness of expression and economy of speech had disappeared and his acquaintances had commented on it. To their way of thinking Marilyn had enlarged him into a very companionable, social sort of being.

His car entered Miracle Mile, a stretch of pavement running north from the city. People had said it would be a miracle if it was ever finished. And when it was completed it had its name.

From the doorway of one of the "motels" lining the road a muffled figure jumped out into the rain and thumbed frantically toward the city. Gayle brought the car to a stop.

The door opened and a pair of hard blue eyes regarded him appraisingly from beneath a wet turban. They were young eyes but there was no innocence in them.

Gayle laughed. "Well, do I look respectable enough?" he asked.

With one sinuous movement the girl was into the seat beside him. "Have to beware of the wolves," she said and pulled off her turban to shake the rain from it.

Gayle gazed for a moment in quick satisfaction at the shock of red hair that cascaded about the girl's face. Swiftly aware of his silent staring, the girl faced him, her mouth a tight line of sudden misgiving. She did not usually misread a face.

"It's just like my wife's," he said softly.

Her face cleared. "A redheaded wife? Mister, you are to be pitied."

"Not me!"

The girl looked at the sincere joy lighting his bronzed countenance.

"It must have been just recent," she commented.

"Why?"

"Hasn't worn off yet."

He laughed. "Three years."

"Huh?"

"We've been married three years."

She lapsed into silence. Three years and the guy was still in love! She sighed. If he liked redheads, why couldn't he have met her first? She inventoried him in a few swift glances. He looked like the real goods. Broad shoulders, dark suit, a snap brim hat from beneath which a pair of light gray eyes looked out. Against the solid bronze of his face they looked like pale stones. But he wasn't tough. The skin wrinkled at the corners of his eyes when he laughed. The whole face was a trifle long and the nose jutted out with a surprising upturn at the very tip. Somehow he induced in her a sensation of rugged honesty, masculine steadfastness. She sure needed a masculine arm on which to lean right now. A moody look came into her eyes.

"Where you going?" he asked.

She hesitated a moment. "Is the Desert Moon along your route?"

"Desert Moon? That's a night club, redhead. You're a little bit ahead of schedule."

"I'm not a patron," she said, pulling her coat tighter about her to cover her outmoded dress. "I'm looking for work." Her tone was a trifle sullen.

He looked at her kindly. "Entertainer?"

"Uh-huh. — Stranded."

"Need a stake?"

She cast a quick look at him. A right guy, and she needed the money for a lot of things, but —

"No," she replied. "Just a job."

He said nothing and she kept her eyes on his strong hands

as they held the wheel. It would be so pleasant to place herself in the protection of a pair of steady, capable hands like that.

The car pulled up before the Desert Moon. She crushed her hair back under the turban. Gayle's left hand rested idly on the wheel as he watched her tuck in the ends of her turban. He suddenly spoke.

"Look, Red. They have all the entertainers here that they need. I know the owner — Tony. Perhaps if I put in a word for you — ?"

"I'd sure appreciate any help," she cut in quickly.

He pulled out a card and scribbled on it. "Here, ask for Tony and give him this card. I'm not guaranteeing anything, but it will help. Better than going in cold."

"Gee, thanks. You are one right guy." She looked at him wonderingly.

"Your hair did it," he laughed. "It's like Marilyn's."

The car sloshed off into the rain.

It was about ten thirty when Gayle drew his car up to the curb on South Stone. A large opaque window proclaimed to the passer-by that this was the: "Bashford and Wade Clinic." Gayle was halfway across the pavement when the door of the clinic burst open and a nurse rushed up to him. "Dr. Wade, hurry home. It's serious. Dr. Bashford took the call. You're to follow — at once."

Gayle stood dumb.

"It's your wife."

"My God!" He spun about. A passer-by went down on the wet pavement, cursing volubly. Gayle didn't see or hear him. His car skidded like a mad thing around the corner, tore through a red light, and was gone.

* * *

The rain stopped abruptly in the Catalina foothills. Manolo went out in his garden. He had a winter lawn to look after. Suddenly a car came tearing up the road and pulled to a mud-splashing stop before Dr. Wade's gate. Its

[23]

door flung open and a stumpy, barrel-chested man charged up the walk. There was a small black valise in his hand.

"Doctor Bashford," murmured the Mexican. *"Ay de mi!* The baby of the Angelita is sick." He shook his head and sighed. *"Lastima!"*

Some time later Manolo's head jerked upwards from his work. Another car roared up and, with all four wheels locked, slid to a stop alongside Doctor Bashford's. Gayle stumbled out of the car and ran into the house.

Manolo looked at the open door on Gayle's car and then at the gate almost torn off its hinges. "Ay yay!" he breathed softly. "It is the Angelita herself maybe." He thought of their daily joyous leave-takings and then shrugged his shoulders. *"Asi es la vida, no es como se canta."* ("Such is life; it isn't like they sing about.") He went over to Gayle's car and thoughtfully closed the door.

*   *   *

Dr. Bashford was standing before the living room table as Gayle burst into the room. The elder man's grim face held the story but Gayle brushed past him as though he were a piece of furniture. The door of Marilyn's room was open. He fell on his knees beside her bed. Her face was black, cyanotic, a look of fear distorting it. "No, no," he breathed hoarsely and caught her up in his arms. His kisses showered down on her hair, throat and lips. No welcoming light lit up her eyes, no eager sigh of satisfaction breathed from her mouth. She lay limp in his arms. His lips drew away slowly and he let the body slip back on the pillow. Mechanically his finger sought for a pulse. There was not the vestige of a beat. She was lifeless clay.

Frenziedly he snatched at the medical bag on the bedside table. Doctor Bashford's hand came down on his, firmly. "It's no use, Gayle. She's gone."

A wall came down over his mind. There was no thought, no sensation. The fact of her death had suddenly gone into his consciousness like a blade of ice, and it turned his whole being numb.

[24]

His next realization was of a voice talking, talking. It sounded strange and very far away. "I tore out, Gayle, as fast as I could. She was in a bad way. I used adrenalin. It was no go, Gayle. *Status asthmaticus* — you know what that means. God, I'm sorry."

It was Hi speaking — Bashford. *Status asthmaticus.* He knew what that meant — intractable asthma — the heaving muscles, the convulsive choking, the tearing agony of death.

She was gone. Gone. Why didn't he feel pain? Why didn't he cry? He loved her. Stupidly he looked at his hand. He was seated at the living room table. There was a glass in his hand. How did that get there? It was an empty glass.

He did not feel anything; He had no sensation of pain or muscular contraction but suddenly Doctor Bashford's strong hands gripped his shoulders. "Gayle!" he shouted.

He woke for a moment. There was blood streaming from his right hand and splinters of glass on the table. There was a sharp click as Doctor Bashford's medical bag was suddenly opened, and that was all Gayle remembered.

Chapter 3

IT WAS a week after Marilyn's funeral and Doctor Bashford barged about the confines of his clinic like a steer on the prod, as he would have expressed it. It was not just the overwork at the clinic and the aftermath of Marilyn's startling death that weighed on him. — It was Gayle. Doctor Bashford was worried about him. And when Doctor Hiram J. Bashford worried he rampaged.

There had been no tears — that was bad. There had not been a stony calm — that was worse. To others, Gayle was just the usual Doctor Wade. But not to Doctor Bashford who knew him so well. The boy was dead.

He had come back to work at the clinic, and it was pitiable. — Knowing him before and knowing him now. Of course, he did not have to work. There was the ranch left him by his father and there was money in the bank. But it was imperative that he go through the motions of doing things — at least until his heart started to beat again. Doctor Bashford had bullied and cajoled him into taking up his practice again. But it wasn't working. And Doctor Bashford knew it and worried about it. So he tramped about his office, said some very unexpected things to a neurotic patient, and shocked the nurse with a hair-curling cowboy curse.

Gayle came in to his office and took off his white jacket. He shrugged his way into his coat and slumped into a chair.

"Hi, I don't want to let you down, but I can't go on here. Get another doctor in my place."

The worried look did not leave Doctor Bashford's full-fleshed countenance. "It's rough riding now, I know, Gayle,"

he replied, "but can't you hang on? It's what you need —
work."

"I guess it is, but I just can't do it, Hi. There's — there's
no sense to it anymore. I used to come home, you see, and
tell her all about the day's work, people I'd met, things I'd
done. She'd enjoy that. We'd laugh over the funny things
and ponder over the serious ones. And now —"

"Why not go to the ranch for several weeks, Gayle?"

Gayle looked at Hi's pudgy red face in a curious way.
"No," he decided; "not the ranch. She wouldn't be there
either."

Doctor Bashford's lips pushed tightly together and his
brows corrugated. "Look here, Gayle. It's okay about the
clinic. I'll get another doctor to wrangle the stock — pro tem.
But you've got to pull up your socks and snap out of this,
boy. Sure I know you loved Marilyn. But you've got to face
facts. You've got to take hold and start over again. That
part of your life is finished."

"Yes," he agreed dully, "that part is finished. But what
am I to do? I still love her. Always shall. Nothing else counts.
I'm only half here. Man is made of body and soul. That's
what they say. Well, if it's true, then she was my soul. My
soul is gone. It's a funny feeling to be just body. I don't
know if it's worth while living that way."

Dr. Bashford looked at him long and searchingly, a sentence trembling on his lips. This was the hard, firm, confident man who once had told him he knew all the answers.
Was this the time to point out the vulnerability of that
tragic self-sufficiency that dominated Gayle? It would be
cruel to tell him now, but a physician must at times cut in
order to heal, even as a friend must at times be cruel in
order to be kind. His voice was hesitant and low. "Several
years ago, Gayle, on the night of your wedding, you told me
that you had all the answers — all at least that you needed."

Gayle's eyes came up to his. "Did I?" He pondered in
brooding silence for a moment. "There is an answer to
everything."

"But — don't you see, Gayle — in your case you were sitting on top of the world and now —"

"The world has broken into small pieces," cut in Gayle abruptly. "I can build it up again. That is an answer." He stood up. "Only I don't know if I want to — if it's going to be worth it. That's what has me stymied."

He took his hat and walked listlessly out of the office, and Doctor Bashford, aware of the import of his words, could only take his head in his hands, put his elbows on his desk and rock his head from side to side impotently.

*   *   *

Evening had fallen. A vast peace shrouded Tucson, its streets, the white-walled houses, the encircling mountains. Across the base of the eastern Rincon mountains was a murky scarf. One cone thrust clear of it and caught the reflected westering light.

Gayle's car moved slowly along Miracle Mile. Motels, eating houses, an occasional store lined the road. He had no eyes for them. The curious emptiness of the evening was answered by the emptiness of his loss. The motels thinned out. A railing of iron appeared at the left side of the road, a broad driveway. He swung his car into it. This was Evergreen Cemetery.

Marilyn's grave was still blanketed with flowers. He stood looking at them. He did not know what to do. At a near-by grave a black-gowned Mexican lady knelt and made the sign of the cross. Prayer? Marilyn did not need prayer. Of that he was sure. It was just that he wanted to be near her — or what was left of her. He had been lonely, desperately lonely, and so he had come.

The first impact of a mortal blow is painless. It was only now that he began to waken from the numbness that had shrouded him. Sensation seemed creeping back into his soul, and the distracting, ever-driving, mortal pain of his loss took hold of him.

There was no one to care any more how he lived. There

was no reason why he should live. What had life to offer? Honor, recognition, additional wealth — he wanted none of these. They did not fill, they did not satisfy. They were just adjuncts to love. Love was happiness. And happiness was life. And love had been snatched from him.

He thrust his hands into his pocket and walked down the graveled path. All about him were the signposts of death. Death. That wasn't too bad. There were worse things than death. There was life. A life without Marilyn.

He came back to her grave and picked up a flower. It was beginning to wilt. It had been a fair flower. Now it was going back, gradually, into primeval dust. Growing old with Marilyn would have been joy. This cutting off in full flower was cruelty. And one could do nothing about it.

The flower slipped from his fingers and his footsteps dragged slowly away. The tearing desire to be with Marilyn had not been assuaged by this futile visit. His need, his loss burned the more desperately. He entered his car, meshed gears, and directed the car slowly back on to the Miracle Mile. There was no place to go, no one to see. He just wanted one thing . . . Marilyn. The touch of her hand, the softness of her hair. . . . His mind gave an odd jump. The girl he had met here! Her hair had been so like Marilyn's. He recalled their talk, her hopes for a job. The car's wheels began to rotate with greater speed. They set up a drumming, whirring, throbbing refrain in his head: concentric circles of sound, matching the ever widening waves of frustration that filled him. And then a moment of deep emptiness, a strange surcease, laid hold of him.

For an instant Marilyn's dear face was before him, the love-light deep in her eyes. It was but a flashing glimpse, too swiftly gone to be savored, a vague, evanescent image out of the deep dark pool of memory. His life had been a lonely sky with one sweet star to comfort him, and now that radiant star was quenched. He would do anything to bring about its return. More, he would go to any extreme to recall his shadowiest remembrance, to make it live again for him.

[29]

The rhythm of the car's rotating wheels throbbed out their approval and surged and sang her name to him until a garish neon sign at the roadside recalled him to reality. He drew up before the Desert Moon.

A low narrow oaken door admitted him to a bar. Beyond were small booths and a door that opened into the actual night club. It was a curious arrangement, a remnant from frontier days when the first need of the customers was to wash the alkali from their throats. A shrewd business management retained it. The bar served the customers coming and going. There was always a need of an additional "one for the road" on leaving.

Gayle went through the barroom and was assigned a corner table in the spacious main room. A small orchestra was playing a popular number. After a while he saw her, standing at a distant table. The orchestra preluded a song and the leader swung his baton over to point out the girl to the patrons. She began to sing. It was a sleepy contralto voice, lulling, effortless. She finished her song. There was a scattered hand-clapping. She smiled and sat down. A few minutes later Gayle saw her rise and begin to move slowly about, directing an artificial, expectant smile at the various patrons.

Gayle followed her movements, the play of light on her hair. Marilyn's had been like that. She had worn it just like that too, a brushed-out cascade falling to the shoulders. She came to an adjacent table. Her undulating walk was very graceful. She smiled and the diners smiled back. She turned easily and smiled at Gayle. His eyes were focused in a sharp, burning intentness on her. Sudden surprise wiped out her smile.

"Why — hello!" she managed.

"Hello — Red."

She looked at the vacant chairs. "Alone?"

He nodded. "Want to keep me company?"

"I'll have to sing a song for you first. Rules. O.K.?"

"Go ahead."

"What will it be?"

"Anything."

She signaled the orchestra leader. When the song was finished he drew out a chair for her and ordered a drink. There was conversation now to be made. He struggled up out of his slough of darkness and longing and found a casual question.

"This is a new kind of entertaining, Red. What's the idea?"

She looked down at her glass a moment, then up into his eyes. "I wasn't entirely frank when we first met. I'm a table-singer."

"Is that bad?"

"Just now, yes. In most cities the regular entertainers, the floor show, don't want us. We sing request songs for patrons at the tables and they pay off. The floor show thinks it crimps their act."

"No trouble here yet?"

"Not yet." A pair of thin lines appeared between her eyebrows. "Tony gave me a chance, after I waved your card at him." She shot him a grateful glance. "But the patrons haven't caught on yet." She opened her hand and showed him a crumpled dollar bill.

"Tonight's take?" His gaze moved over her face and fixed with an abstracted yearning on the silken radiance of her hair.

She nodded. "And I warbled six times."

"You don't get a salary?"

"No, just what the customers choose to give." Her voice became bitter. "Looks like a hick town to me."

Gayle's eyes left off staring at her hair. A faint glint came into their gray depths. "It's *my* town, Red."

"Sorry," she mumbled. "I'm just down in the mouth. This kind of a job takes clothes to put it over, and clothes mean money. Of which I have the usual absence of." She pushed aside her drink. "I think I'll try another town as soon as I have the wherewithal to travel — if and when." She glanced dubiously at the crumpled dollar.

Gayle's gaze slowly left her face, traveled for a fleeting instant over her outmoded gown, and then came to rest on the glass in his hand. The dejection of her mood matched his own low spirits. Yet in some indefinable way her presence was helping him. The turn of her head when she gestured, that ghost of a frown when the tiny lines appeared between her brows, the wealth of burnished hair. There was a sop of comfort in her similarity to Marilyn.

"I don't want you to go, Red," he said.

The sincerity of his voice startled her. She covered up with a quick, short laugh. "The name is Sheila — Sheila Starr."

"Starr — that's right for you."

She grimaced wryly. "A fallen star," she said and Gayle looking full into her eyes read all the disillusionment and defeat there. His gaze did not falter. Being deep in tragedy gives one certain rights.

His steady look disconcerted her and she stood up. "I'll be back in a little while," she said. "I'm going to give it another whirl."

He made no reply. She sauntered away and after a while he saw her signal the orchestra leader. Gayle went out to the bar and sat down in a phone booth. He called a number. "Tom? This is Gayle. A little favor for a friend of mine." He explained about Sheila. "Round up some of the fellows. See that there's at least one of them out here every night. Five dollars a throw. Yes; for each song."

He went back to his table and called a waiter. "Have that table-singer sing 'Sleepy Lagoon.'"

Sheila came to his table and sang.

Gayle gestured to her glass. "You didn't finish your drink, Sheila."

She sat down and her eyes looked into his. His heart sank. Her eyes — there was no Marilyn in them. He took out his wallet and folded its contents into a tight packet and slid it into her hand. "That's for the songs, Sheila. Get a new dress."

[32]

"Gee, doc," she protested, "that wasn't the idea. I mean, that weepy history of myself. . . ."

"Wear your hair like this, will you?" he interrupted. "Like it is now."

A pleased look flitted across her face.

"I'll be here tomorrow night," he said.

Her hands went to her hair and then suddenly fell away. "Look, doc, this wife of yours — the redheaded one you spoke of — we redheads sort of stick together. . . ."

His face, suddenly bleak and twisted, stopped her. There was a look of tortured self-loathing in his eyes. Marilyn out there in the cold dark of the grave, and here he was in the midst of light and laughter — another girl at his side. His hand fumbled to the side of his face and then tremblingly drew away. This place, this girl — it was sacrilege. He stood up abruptly.

"What is it, doc? What did I say?"

"She's dead — gone."

"Gee, I'm sorry." Her voice was low.

He walked away. She followed him to the door, but he stalked out into the night without another word.

"What a lousy break!" Sheila muttered. "The poor guy!" She opened her hand and counted the money. Eighty-five dollars! A right guy if ever there was one. She folded up the bills and made for her dressing room, and as she went a calculating look crept into the blue eyes.

Chapter 4

~~~~~~

THE door of the Desert Moon thudded shut behind Gayle and he made his way out into the gloom of the night. Sheila was obliterated from his mind. The pain of his loss had come down upon him again and it was an overwhelming anguish. His throat felt clogged. It was hard to swallow, an ache to breathe.

Automatically he found his car and drove home. For a while he sat alone in the dark emptiness of what had once been paradise. Bucky and Nora, the child's nurse, had been dispatched to Doctor Bashford's house after the funeral. He could not have them about. He wanted to be alone.

He got up and went through the rooms putting on the lights as he went. Every piece of furniture called up memories and accentuated his pain. It was more than he could stand. He bolted from the house and strode across the road out into the desert. Clumps of greasewood and cacti and mesquite, scattered blobs of darkness, lurked all about him. He threaded his way among them, walking, walking. Overhead, serene Arizona skies, full of glittering stars, arched endlessly. But Gayle saw only the clay beneath his feet. He knew how to use his hands; there was strength and skill in them. On his father's ranch he had learned the hardy western life and was capable enough with rope and branding iron. His medical training had given a much more delicate skill to his sinewy fingers. But how could he lay hold of this problem?

The west breeds men that see clearly and decide surely. All his young life Gayle had been doing just that. And now he was up against a wall. He could not see. How then could he decide? All he knew was that he had lost Marilyn. Live without her? Remarry? The latter was as repugnant as the former was impossible.

He scuffed along aimlessly, his thoughts whirling about in a frenzied maelstrom. The meaning of possession and the meaning of loss. Mysteries hidden from our minds. Until the reality hits us. Gayle knew that now. The ecstacy of possession was an unknown land until the fullness of it had flooded his being. And the hollowing halls of loss, the desert of desire, were things undreamed of until one had actually walked their desolations. Imagination could conjure up some ideas about these things, but how far they were from the agony of actual fact!

The crisp, dry air of the night was good on his hot face and gradually the congestion left his throat. He breathed more easily. But a pall of gloom settled over him, so deep, so desolate that it was almost as if the dull, persistent pain of breakbone fever had invaded every nerve and fiber of his body. The realization welled up in him that he was faced with a problem with which he was utterly unable to cope. You could not do anything about death. He looked up at a giant Saguaro cactus. It was all of thirty feet high, its pleated sides ridged with spines. Even such a thorny grotesque creature he could twist to his use, extract moisture from its pulp to combat desert thirst. But with death he could do nothing.

It was very late when he turned and plodded homeward. Over the western Tucson mountains a shooting star cut a bright streak across the sky and then was gone. He stool still. A thought suddenly blossomed in his pain-wracked mind. There *was* something he could do.

*   *   *

For several days Gayle stayed shut up in the house and at night he walked the desert. Time had ceased to be. It was just water flowing uselessly under a bridge. The dry fall of sand in an hour glass. Life was an untenanted room. And as he stumbled along through this vacuum, there was only one thing that lived in him, the thought that had come to him when he had seen an eager star abruptly quenched in the night. It was an ominous thought, but it grew bigger and bigger with possibilities.

The conventions, law, what other people might think — these were things to which he gave no consideration. It was *his* problem to solve and they had no part in it.

It was the evening of a day to be ever memorable. Gayle carefully set about his preparations. He brought his medical bag into the living room. The prepared hypodermic was laid on the table's glistening black top. There was a slender stalk of a vase in the center of the table and in it he had placed an artificial rose. It was all he could get, but it was red, and that had been how Marilyn had always liked the table to be adorned. She had attached some symbolism to it. It had always greeted him on his return, a single red rose, fresh, vivid, fragrant — like her love, adorning and pervading the house.

Nervously he tugged at the collar of his shirt pulling it still more widely open at the throat. He rolled up the sleeve on his left arm, well above the elbow. For a moment he gazed about him, then he went to a low sofa set against the window. It was an exceptionally large window, larger than the length of the sofa and commanding an amazing view of the distant Catalinas. He rested his arms on the back of the sofa and watched the vast panorama of mountains. Every day he had done this with Marilyn. Here they had talked and gradually grown silent as the slow shadows of night moved up the mountainsides. The ineffable beauty and peace of this daily spectacle had been so good for them, silently drawing them together in a communion of spirit about which they never spoke. It had been a hard and fast ritual with them. Tonight it was as beautiful as ever but somehow it did not reach him. There was no peace in it for him. It brought home to him again what had become mad-

deningly, poignantly clear — there would be no more joy
for him until he was where Marilyn was. He could not con-
tinue this half-living. He had to be with her. Where she
had gone he would go. It was as simple as that. He had
drawn up a holograph will. Everything was in order.

The sun sank deeper over the western mountains and the
shadows stole over the foothills and up through the canyons.
Long purpureal chasms edged up the gouged-out slopes,
swallowing up the soft rose coloring that had turned the
calcined rock into such unearthly loveliness. His eyes followed it moodily. All beauty had to die. What a useless life
it was. Nothing stayed.

When the tip of the highest crag went into the upward
marching gloom — that would be the moment. A matter of
minutes now. He rose and went to the table. He bent over
it to pick up the hypodermic. His fingers closed on it. They
stayed there. He made no movement. Shock stunned him.
For a split second every vital function seemed stopped. And
then his senses went reeling.

Dazed, he saw his fingers slip away from the syringe and
then he clutched the edge of the table. He leaned over
breathing deeply, life and joy suddenly flooding through
him, incredulity and happiness struggling together in his
face. Then he straightened up slowly and his brow puckered
as though he were trying to recall some elusive memory. He
gave his head an impatient shake and slowly circled the
table, his breath coming in slow deep respirations. He went
back to the sofa, sat down, and brushed the back of a hand
across his eyes. For a moment he held his right hand out
before him. It was filled with a fine trembling. Roughly he
seized it with his left hand. There was the hard comforting
feel of firm flesh and the solid bone beneath it. He stood
up again and went to the farthest corner of the room, his
eyes questing about in suspicious bewilderment, his brow
creased in wonderment. A few quick steps took him back to
the table. He snatched the vase from the table and sniffed
at the artificial rose it held. As suddenly he thrust it back.

A moment longer he stood staring, excitement mounting in his eyes, and then with a mad rush he was out of the house.

*　　*　　*

The Padre was sitting in his wheel-chair beneath the portico fronting his house. His face was toward the shrouded Catalina Mountains and something of the burnt-out strength of the old mountains was reflected in his colorless countenance.

The gate clattered shut and there was a crunch of excited steps on the graveled walk. He opened his eyes. A disheveled figure stood before him.

"I want you to come to my house, right away," demanded Gayle.

The Padre closed a small red-covered address book lying on his lap and placed it carefully in the top pocket of his jacket.

"It's important. Something . . . I need you."

The Padre's gaze took in the rolled up sleeve, the shadowed eyes, the febrile excitement that caused the strong young hands to shake.

"Why yes," assented the old man sedately, "but—"

"Can't you understand?" There was desperation in the taut voice. "It's—it's life and death."

The old man joined his hands and with one index finger pointed to his legs. "I just wanted to say that I can't move out of this chair."

"Oh—" Gayle seized the chair with impatient roughness. "I'll wheel you."

As they passed through the gate the Padre spoke over his shoulder. "Any trouble in the house?"

"I can't tell you—I—I don't know. You just see for yourself."

The old man's hands lay placidly on his lap. There was no sign of any emotion on his face.

They entered Gayle's house. Gayle left the wheelchair standing at the threshold and went to the sofa. He sat down abruptly. The Padre cast a glance about the room and then stared inquiringly at Gayle.

"Just look around," said Gayle throwing out both hands in a nervous gesture; "tell me what you think of my living room."

The Padre's glance at Gayle grew a little more searching. He knew that the death of his wife had shaken him severely. He hoped it had not unbalanced him. The young man sat there watching him. He was breathing rapidly. Obediently, the old man began to wheel his chair about, inspecting the walls, the picture over the fireplace, the graceful arrangement of every exquisite thing. Finally he stopped at the table. His eyes went over it critically and then came up to meet Gayle's. "A lovely room, Doctor Wade." His eyes settled disapprovingly on the flower adorning the center of the table. "The only discord," he murmured. "That rose. . . . It's artificial, isn't it?" He leaned over to peer at it and abruptly stopped. He turned towards Gayle. "You've put perfume on it — the scent of some other flower."

"You smell that perfume?" Gayle was standing, his voice brittle, high-pitched.

"Decidedly. The table reeks of it."

"That's Marilyn's perfume. Mignonette. I paid one hundred dollars to have it made for her. It's exclusive. The formula is on file for my order alone."

"Well?"

A torrent of excited explanation flowed from Gayle. "I didn't put perfume — any perfume — on that table or that rose. I've been home, all day, alone. There was no perfume there on that table, a few minutes ago. I got up from this sofa, went to the table for that syringe — and noticed the perfume. It — it — just came."

The Padre's eyes widened. "Is there any of your wife's perfume here — in the house?"

Gayle thought a moment. "Yes. There was some left. But it's locked in a trunk. All her belongings were placed in a trunk after her death — all except this." He thrust a hand in his pocket and brought forward the small gold cross the Padre had once seen about Marilyn's neck.

"Take a look, doctor. See if that bottle of perfume is still in the trunk."

Gayle went swiftly from the room. The Padre picked up the syringe and noted that it was prepared for use. There was a bottle with some tablets beside the medical bag. He read the label on the bottle and his eyes clouded with deep sadness. He circled the table, then the room.

Gayle re-entered the room. A fragile little bottle was in his hand. He thrust it at the Padre. The old man unstoppered it and sniffed judiciously. "Same thing," he muttered. "Where was it?"

"At the bottom of the trunk," replied Gayle. "The trunk was locked." He held up a key. "This is the only key to it."

"There was no way —?"

"I tell you I've been here all day. Nobody else has been here."

The Padre folded his hands, put the two index fingers together to form a church steeple, looked at them gravely a moment and then suddenly pointed them at Gayle. "And you?"

"Me?" Gayle looked blankly at his interlocutor for a moment and then the meaning of his query reached him. "Of course not," he retorted irritably. "What would I put the stuff there for? I'm not off my rocker. That perfume just came out of nowhere and settled over the table." He paused a moment. "I *was* thinking of my wife," he conceded, "and when I noticed that perfume I thought it must be an hallucination. That's why I called you. It isn't, is it?"

"If it is, we are both suffering from it." He brought down his chin and peered at Gayle through the tuft of his white eyebrows. "And I'm not given to that sort of thing." He looked about him. "We can give the matter a simple test though. Open the door and the windows in the adjoining rooms."

Gayle hastened to comply. A light breeze ruffled through

the room. The rose moved noticeably in the vase upon the table. From his pocket the Padre drew an alarmingly ancient looking timepiece and held it in his hand. After a long silence he snapped it shut.

"Fifteen minutes are up, doctor. What do you make of it?"

"It's still here . . . right over the table. There's not a trace of it any place else. And you?"

"Same as you. You can close the door and windows."

Gayle complied and returned to the room. "I wonder how long it will last?"

"You know, of course, doctor, how the molecular theory explains the transmission of an odor or perfume." Gayle nodded, understanding suddenly the reason of the old man's experiment.

"That syringe —" The Padre's steepled index fingers were directed toward the object. No need for it's being there, I suppose?"

For a fleeting second his eyes were on Gayle's rolled-up sleeve. Gayle caught the glance and blood slowly mounted to his face, giving it a thick, congested look. He passed the palm of his right hand over his left forearm and then slowly slid the sleeve down. He picked up the syringe, placed it in the medical bag and left the room.

When he returned the Padre had moved from the table. Gayle went up to it and looked about blankly.

"The perfume's gone," he announced.

The Padre nodded. "It disappeared as you left the room."

Gayle stood silent, his head slightly bowed. "I can't doubt it," his voice was awe-filled, wondering. "I can't doubt it."

"What?"

Gayle looked up at the flat tone of interrogation and seemed about to blurt out a reply. He checked himself. "You are not aware of the strangest thing about this whole occurrence, sir," he explained. "At the first breath of that perfume a recollection jumped into my mind. It came out of nowhere. The day we were married Marilyn said to me; 'The words that the minister pronounced over us, Gayle, 'till death do you part' — those words do not apply to *us*. My love for you will last even after death, forever.' " Gayle's eyes met and held the gaze of the Padre. "Do you believe that?"

"Love is a spiritual thing, son. Genuine love I mean. And the soul does not die or it would not be a soul."

Gayle nodded his satisfaction. "This — this happening changes everything for me."

"I imagine it would."

Gayle fitted his right fist firmly into the cup of his left palm. "I've got something to go on now."

Two deep lines appeared between the Padre's white brows, they met and formed a triangle. Was the young man going to act on his strange occurrence at once?

"You've been kind and helpful, sir," said Gayle rising and taking hold of the wheelchair. "I'll get you back to your house now. I've got to think this out — alone."

Back in his own dwelling, the Padre looked about the shelves of books in his room. There were more than a few dealing with mystic phenomena, psychiatry, and abnormal mental states. He knew what they contained. After a while he reached into his pocket and drew out a little red-covered address book. The covers were well worn. He read a few lines and then closed his eyes. A look of serenity gradually smoothed out the perplexity that had been on his features.

Chapter 5

GAYLE slept little that night. His mind was a hive of thoughts, but toward morning he fell into an exhausted sleep. A tremendous thumping on the door awoke him. He threw on a lounging robe and went to the door. Doctor Bashford pushed his way in.

"Howdy, neighbor!" he cried.

"Good morning, Hi," replied Gayle.

"I'm full of beans, bacon, and bounce," said Hi.

Gayle's sleepy gaze took in his visitor's tight fitting blue levis, the checkered shirt, the battered ten gallon Stetson. "What is it?" he asked. "Round up?"

"You called it. Get on your togs. We're going to the ranch."

Gayle slouched into a chair. "No. Not today, Hi."

Hi looked at Gayle's pale face, the tired lines about his eyes. "It's Sunday. I've got to get some relaxation, boy. Come on, get going."

"No. Not today."

Hi pushed his fleshy lips tightly together and his eyes narrowed as he fixed a calculating look on Gayle's drooping form. Suddenly his voice rose in loud complaint. "Hilda's got me in the doghouse. I got tight at the Club last Sunday playing pitch. No golfing for the rest of the month. It's the ranch or the rocker." He came over and put an arm over Gayle's shoulders. "Lordy, boy, don't let me down. I need some exercise and a couple of drinks."

Gayle looked up at the pudgy face and the protesting, worried eyes.

"All right, Hi."

He went back to his room to change his clothes. Doctor Bashford's face creased with satisfaction as he scrubbed his iron gray hair a moment with stubby fingers and then thrust an unlighted cigar into a corner of his mouth. The nurse at his clinic would have recognized the signs — another case was on the road to recovery.

Gayle reappeared in high-heeled boots, old shirt, levis, a much-used sombrero. Hi looked at him a moment. "Joshua! I shouldn't have taken you off the ranch, Gayle. There never was a man could look like you do in western togs."

"Saddle-soap!" was the sour retort.

They clumped out to the car. Hi let out the clutch and the car headed for the distant Catalinas. He settled back behind the wheel and then cast a look at Gayle. "Say, that son of yours — Bucky," he began. "How long you figure on stabling him with me?"

"What's the matter? Is he causing trouble?"

"No—o—o. Not trouble. He's just driving me nuts by swift and sudden stages. He runs around the house like a green-bottomed beetle."

"If he's too much trouble, Hi — "

The older man's right hand came down on Gayle's shoulder with friendly violence. "Just trying to get a rise out of you, Gayle. Bucky's no trouble. I do think Nora feeds him mercury, though, the way he wiggles around. But he's welcome to stay as long as you want."

Some of the tenseness went from Gayle's face. "Thanks, old-timer," was his quiet rejoinder. It was good to have friends and there was not a truer one than old Hi. He had been a father to him ever since his own dad's death. Gayle pulled off his hat and faced around. "Hi, I want to tell you something. A strange thing happened to me last night — a very strange thing."

His voice was over serious, and Hi did not want him that way. He let his eyebrows go up a trifle. "You sort of look it, son. If I didn't know you so well I'd say you had inhaled an overdose of tarantula juice. Go ahead. I'm listening."

In a few brief sentences Gayle told him about the mignonette, its sudden appearance and departure. "What do you think about that, Hi?"

Hi kept his eyes on the road ahead and his voice was coldly casual. "It's nothing that a good whiff of the horse corral won't cure," he said.

Gayle, suddenly cold and silent, turned away from him. Hi looked at him speculatively for a moment. The boy was as touchy as a boil. The silence drew out uncomfortably long. Finally Hi spoke again. "All right, Gayle. I was off on the wrong foot. But you know me, son. I always would use a hammer to play a harp." His voice grew kindly. "Now go ahead and talk."

Gayle's voice had a dogged determination in it.

"You know my neighbor — Hutchinson?"

"The Padre?"

"Yes. How does he stack up in your opinion?"

"Well, every time I get a look at him I think of Walt Whitman. He hasn't got all that sassafras on his face like old Walt, but he's got the same wide look in the eyes. Why?"

"Did you talk with him? I mean about other things — not his health?"

"Yes, I did. Just once. I didn't agree with him, but he talked in a straight line. It wasn't calf-slobber, it was horns and hooves. He'll do to ride the river with."

"I'm glad to hear that. He's my witness. I brought him to the house and he noticed the mignonette."

"Huh? You mean that he smelled that perfume too?"

"That's right."

He smote his forehead with his palm. "What a rock hit grandfather! Go ahead, tell me."

Gayle quickly recounted the Padre's coming to the house and the simple test he had performed.

"Joshua!" said Hi weakly. "I don't like fairy tales on Sunday morning." He bit off the end of his cigar and spat it out the window. Gayle's eyes were fixed patiently on him. "Look, son, that stuff was all right for the Middle Ages. Those people were spoon fed on miracles and angels till it ran out of their ears. This is the twentieth century. This is Arizona. We just don't do things like that."

"I didn't do anything, Hi," came Gayle's quiet reply. "This was done to me."

Hi bit off another piece of his cigar. "If it had happened to me, you know what I'd be doing?"

"A binge won't help, Hi. You should be able to see that."

"No; but it would make you forget it."

"For a few hours, yes. But I don't want to forget it. I'm facing it. I've got to figure it out."

Hi was silent for a while. "Well — there's a patient of mine, got a shadow on his lungs, had pneumonia. His name is Doctor Tisorek. A bug-eyed little squirt, but seems to be top hand in this psychiatry line. Has enough letters after his name to make up a tub of alphabet soup. I'll give you his address. Next time this — this eau de cologne goes on a rampage, get him out there to investigate. I'll tell him about you."

"But not about the mignonette," said Gayle quickly. "I don't want any mention of that yet, to him or anyone else."

"I don't usually run off at the mouth."

"Sorry, Hi. I know that. I just wanted to be sure."

"That's one of your failings, son. There are few things in this world you can be sure of — outside of death and taxes."

"I know that now," said Gayle seriously, and lapsed into silence. Hi looked at him covertly, astonished at this concession; then he stepped on the accelerator and sent the car smoking along the alkali-powdered road.

*　　*　　*

Late that evening Hi brought Gayle home. The old man was in a mellow mood. They had ridden hard for several

[46]

hours on horseback and on their return to the ranch Hi had taken down his "few" drinks and now all was right with the world. His hat sat askew on his head as he waved farewell to Gayle. The car roared away and Gayle went in, changed clothes, took a shower and put on his lounging robe. He felt comfortably tired but his thoughts gave him no rest.

Gayle's upbringing had been the virile one of the ranch and his religious training had been restricted to some desultory attendance at Sunday School. His association with Marilyn had not altered the comfortable agnosticism into which he had gradually drifted. She had been deeply religious and anything that she cherished interested him. He had gone to church with her quite frequently on Sunday, but it had been merely as a concession to her and not from any personal liking or from principle.

The appearance of the mignonette was a fact. How it had happened, what was the idea in back of it, the possible religious significance — these things did not interest him in the least. It was a sign from Marilyn. That was all that was clear to him. A mysterious sign but a genuine one. It filled him with joy and yet the joy was pain. He had not lost her. She was alive; she could manifest that fact. But how was he to see her? How was he to get into contact, visual, tangible contact with that sweet presence? And how he longed to see her! He needed the sight of her like a thirsty man needs water. But she did not appear to him. Last night he had not even dreamed of her. Surely science must have an answer for his need. He had a shelf of medical books at the clinic and he felt certain he would find an answer to his problem in them.

Next day he drove to town, parked his car opposite the Pioneer Hotel and walked along South Sixth Street. The mid-morning crowd of people brushed by him, intent on the various affairs of life. It felt curiously good to have people around him. He found himself looking at them, amazed at the ignorance of other people concerning what he knew.

[47]

There was a vague sort of pity in him that they should be denied the mysterious knowledge he had. The policeman at the corner; the barber stropping a razor and gazing at the passers-by with a somnambulistic stare; the little Mexican newsie hawking his papers, the cowboys clacking by on high-heeled boots and tight-levied legs — what would they think, what would they say if they knew what he knew? They would not understand. Probably they would have the same reaction as Dr. Bashford had had at first. And suddenly everything jarred on him, the hurrying people, the bright sun, the noise of traffic. Their complacency with the dull details of making a living was an irritant to him. Acquaintances tossed him casual greetings but he walked in an utter void. He was alone. She was not at his side. That made everything meaningless. He had not known this before, that the presence of one person could populate a place, make of it a singing joy, and that the absence of one person could make thronging city streets into a drab desert. He quickened his pace and entered the clinic. Dr. Bashford was not in. He found a book that promised help and hurried home. At once he sat down and began to read. That was the first step in the wrong direction.

The next day and many ensuing days saw an absorbing change in him. He began to haunt medical libraries, at the hospitals and the university. He sent away for books, he borrowed volumes from his colleagues. His attitude was carefully noted and reported to Doctor Bashford. It all summed up in this: "He's like a research student on the eve of a great discovery."

Love is a very egotistical passion. In the mind of each individual lover is the conviction that there has never been a passion like his before. He revels in that thought, that his love is different from all others, that it is more entrancing, more complete, more perfect.

Gayle could still recall all the details of that utterly incomparable day when he had wed Marilyn. The honeymoon trip had to be canceled because of the excessive work at the clinic. It had not affected them in the least. Like truant youngsters they had stolen away for an idyllic honeymoon of two full hours. Bright pulsations of memory still throbbed through him, carrying all the intimate, tiny details of that happy time. The caresses, the murmured words, the satiny feel of her cheek against his, the blossoming palo verde tree housing them in living gold, the song of sunset color on the Catalinas. Two hours of complete bliss. The memory of it was a cameo cut deep in his heart. And then Doctor Bashford — shepherding them off to the reception, a reception that had turned into a noisy revel that wound up on their doorstep. What a relief had flooded them when the last hilarious acquaintance had departed. They were together again, because they were alone. They had sat down on the window seat then, in the unlighted room, and all the mysteriousness of the dark void of an Arizona night reached out before them. A quiet star appeared above the dim outline of the far-off mountains, like a small candle on a huge altar. The flame of its radiance was as blinkingly bright as a diamond, as bravely constant as true love. A yearning had risen up in him, a vast choking desire to put into speech something that he could not find words for. His whole being had seemed bursting with an emotion too big for his capacities of expression. And Marilyn, as though thinking his very thoughts, had tried to express their feelings by some lines of an old song. He'd never forget the sweetness of her voice as she quoted:

"I love thee, I love but thee,
With a love that shall not die
Till the sun grows cold,
And the stars are old
And the leaves of the Judgement Book unfold!"

He was going to recapture that joy now. She was dead but she was holding him to that conviction she had once expressed. "I love the, I love but thee, with a love that shall not die." She had not vouchsafed a demonstration of her existence by the perfume for an idle reason. Marilyn was not like that. He had needed her, oh God, how he had needed her! She could not remain deaf to that urgent necessity that had almost led him to shuffle off this meaningless, solitary life. She had met his extreme need. But it had been merely a ray of light, and the ensuing darkness seemed all the more insufferable because of it. He had tried to dream of her. And he did dream. Chaotic, frightening phantasmagorias, of which he could recall nothing when he awoke except that Marilyn's blackened, convulsed death mask had floated in and out of them. And that was not Marilyn. It was a travesty that Death's macabre hand had placed over her countenance. His need to see her, to assure her that he had not forgotten, that he was loyal to her, grew until it was an imponderable burden.

And now he had found a way. A dubious way, a highly risky way; but possible costs meant nothing to him.

He locked the doors of the house and went into Marilyn's room. It adjoined his. He had unpacked her possessions and everything was just as it had been before her death. He went back to the living room, seated himself on the sofa and watched the day's dying reflected in the changing color of the Catalinas. The mountains shrouded up in gloom and the slow twilight merged into night. Sequins of silver dotted the skies. Slowly he rose and entered Marilyn's room.

From her wardrobe he drew a white gown . . . her wedding dress. Lovingly he fingered the white crisp taffeta material of the bodice then draped it over a chair. He put out the lights. A wan shaft of moonlight filtered through the window. He placed the chair with the dress in the beam of moonlight. In a dark corner of the room he placed an armchair, sat down and fixed his eyes upon the moon-silvered gown opposite him.

The noises of life outside were shut away. Inside the house was a pregnant stillness. Gayle sat staring steadily, purposefully at the line of the bodice on the gown. His reading had made clear to him that hypnotic trance is really the result of the mind acting upon itself. Suggestion

[50]

did it. The suggestion could come from someone outside or from one's own self. Once in the hypnotic trance his own mind could guide him.

The suggestion he was using was his desire, fierce and burning, to see his dead wife. His eyes fixed on the bodice of the dress, he let his longing to see Marilyn sway up and surge over him in waves of yearning. It was tormenting and yet strangely satisfying. He let all the hungry needs of his heart flood through his being. No need now to mask his face with an impersonal calm. There was no one here to see. He let the barren desires, the driving need of his soul go forth in voiceless yet insistent calls of "Marilyn, Marilyn, dear. I need you. I need you." His thoughts jumbled as old phrases of endearment flooded through his mind. He heard a voice mumbling them. It must be his own. But he did not care. There was no one to hear them. Incoherently his desires merged into pleading, the passionate, resistless torrent of separated love.

And slowly a sense of unreality crept over him. It was like the gradual slipping into a syncope. He seemed to be inside of a body that was strangely large and no longer bound to him. His body was leaning forward rigidly, his whole being one focused point of intentness — for he was no longer alone.

A haze seemed to exude from the moonlight about the chair. It swayed and settled and slowly began to take form. An outline grew distinct before his staring eyes. A face, a form. And with thrilling suddenness Marilyn smiled at him, seated in her chair in the moonlight.

She was flawlessly radiant. Every dear feature unchanged. Even the errant wisp of hair that stole free from above her left ear. She caught it and tucked it in place. For a vague second he thought he could breathe the scent of mignonette. But her fingers lifted and pointed at him. The same ineffable grace of gesture. She spoke: "Gay, dear,

'I love thee, I love but thee,
With a love that shall not die' "

[51]

He answered slowly, continuing the quotation:

> " 'Till the sun grows cold,
> And the stars are old."

She took up the words in an infinitely gentle voice:

> " 'And the leaves of the Judgement
> Book unfold.' "

She smiled at him and he went eagerly to her and sitting at her feet pillowed his head on her lap. She said nothing, and, growing impatient at her silence, he looked up. "Nothing to say?"

"I love you, Gay."

"How much?"

> " 'Till the angels doubt
> And the stars burn out,
> I am yours, Sweetheart, forever.' "

That contented him and his head went back on her lap. Her fingers drifted softly through his hair, about his ears, lulling him, filling him with a deep, dreamy drowsiness. There was no more sensation.

And then he became aware of dull, thudding noises. They rumbled through his head. His chest was tight, and he had a vague sense of falling. He tried to scream and he thrust his arms out frantically for a hold.

The steel gray light of early dawn was outside the window. His right arm lay numbly along the arm of a chair and his left hand clutched the limp folds of Marilyn's dress to his face. He gazed long and stupidly at the garment and slowly the world of reality again formed before him. Stiffly his fingers let go of the dress and he stood up.

He felt inexpressibly cramped and horribly weak. The mirror showed him a face he scarcely knew — the color of dried bone, rigid, taut with lines of strain and fatigue. He felt completely drained of life and vitality. And then, of a sudden, the overwhelming fact hit him: *He had seen Marilyn. He had talked with her, touched her.*

His gaze roved about. The luminous mystery of the night and its silvered radiance were gone. The crumpled dress looked sadly futile and empty. He stumbled to a chair and his head came down in his hands. It was all a delusion and a snare. He knew that in the cold light of dawn. She had not been here — actually. The door between the seen and the unseen was a one-way door through which you could enter but not return. It had not been Marilyn but the power of his own mind to delude itself into the belief of her presence and speech. Marilyn had not returned. There was no return from that land of eternal silence. He had merely succeeded in tearing himself from reality for a while, in living for a brief moment in the world of happy memories that peopled his mind.

And yet, even that was something. To his love-obsessed need it was a great deal. He had paid for it. His body ached. There was a weak shivering in his arms and legs; an over-wrought nerve twitched aggravatingly in his eyelid. Awkwardly he stumbled from the room and to his bed.

It was all wrong — what he was doing — but it brought a temporary reprieve. He would do it again — and again — regardless of the risks involved.

Chapter 6

DOCTOR Bashford finished writing the prescription, tore it slowly from the pad and extended it to the Padre. "As directed, sir," he said. His eyes roved around the room, its low shelves of books, the single clothes closet, the grim crucifix over the bed. Near the window was an L-shaped table heaped with orderly packets of letters.

The doctor stood up hesitantly and then abruptly sat down. "There's something I'd like to talk to you about, Padre." He put his hands on his knees, turned the elbows outward and leaned forward. The Padre's quiet face invited confidence. "Your neighbor — Doctor Wade — tell me, how is he behaving?" The Padre's tufted white eyebrows went up in surprise.

"I assure you this isn't idle curiosity," persisted Doctor Bashford. "I've got obligations toward him. His dad, Jeff, was my best friend."

"He keeps to himself," said the Padre.

"Completely?"

"I've seen him leave the house only once since last week. It was in the afternoon. He did not speak."

"How did he look?"

"Abstracted. Thin. Decidedly not well."

Doctor Bashford shook his grizzled head. "He's off on the wrong foot," he muttered to himself; then lifted his eyes quickly to the Padre's face. "Don't mistake me. Gayle's all right, as straight as a string, but he's harder to handle than a colt with a burr under its saddle blanket. Right now he's fighting the bit."

"He's had a cruel blow," said the Padre.

"Yes, I know that. Marilyn was made for him. Her death knocked the underpinning out of his world. He's lost his balance. He never did do anything half-way — it was all out or nothing." He pulled out a cigar and clamped his teeth on it. "I'm sort of in the place of his dad and I have tried all I can to help. From his questioning of other doctors and the kind of books he has been borrowing, it's plain that he's messing around with auto-hypnosis. That's a dangerous thing. Somebody's got to break it up." He looked searchingly at the Padre. "I've worn out my knuckles on his door. He never answers the phone." He threw up his hands in discouragement.

The Padre gave him no help. His eyes just looked at him, unwaveringly.

Doctor Bashford looked reflectively at his cigar a moment, then turned his eyes on the Padre. "I hate to ask this of you, but you're his closest neighbor and you're in the best possible position. Are you willing to help?"

"Decidedly willing," came the calm reply. "But how?"

Doctor Bashford's ruddy face cleared at this ready acceptance and he gave him his plan in one sentence. "Become his patient."

The Padre shook his head.

"He will handle your case as well as I can," urged Doctor Bashford.

"That does not enter into the matter," said the Padre simply. "You are trying to force an issue. It's not wise in a crisis of this kind."

"Desperate diseases need desperate remedies, sir," came Doctor Bashford's swift reply. "I tell you there is serious danger for Gayle in his present course of conduct. I'm not old-fashioned enough to believe that he needs a soul-doctor," — he drew out the word as though it were something one finds under a rotted board — "but he does need someone to talk to and an interest to absorb his mind. He's losing all hold on reality. If Gayle takes over a patient, he stays with him till Sitting Bull stands up. That's the kind of man Gayle is. His dad was the same way. Loyalty — that's what has got him into this mess, loyalty to a dead woman; and it's loyalty that will get him out of it, loyalty to some sick person."

The Padre's reply came in an even, measured tone. "I'll gladly do all I can for Gayle — *if he comes to me.*" He directed a long gaze at the doctor as though promising much more than merely becoming Gayle's patient. Then his eyes seemed to forget Doctor Bashford and although they still looked at him they did not focus on him. "If the opportunity comes — from without — I'll go ahead," he declared.

Doctor Bashford thought a minute. He was not pleased at this cold declaration and all its "ifs." There was too much imperiousness about it. The old man talked like an autocrat. What did he think he was? — A messenger from the Almighty with special faculties of healing? He took his lip between thumb and index finger and pulled at it. "What do you mean — 'from without?' "

The Padre's gaze was still rather abstracted. "Not of my own contriving," he answered. Then he suddenly seemed to shake off his disinterested air. "I am keenly concerned about Gayle, doctor," he said. "You see I had the pleasure of talking with Marilyn on one occasion — a memorable occasion. What she told me then has some bearing on this present trouble. Believe me, this is not a matter for meddling. Forgive the word. Friends sometimes push God off the earth in their overzeal.

Doctor Bashford stood up, his manner suddenly very stiff. Hadn't he just been told to mind his own business? He picked up his hat. "I bid you good day, sir."

"Good day, doctor," came the imperturbable reply.

Doctor Bashford fumbled with his bag, expecting an apology. None being forthcoming, he stamped out of the house and made his way next door. He jabbed his finger violently against the bell button but there was no sound from indoors. "Disconnected!" growled the doctor. He thumped the panel of the door. There was no answering stir from within. "He's crazier than popcorn on a hot stove," snorted the doctor and stalked down to his car. That mule-headed Gayle didn't want help and that owl-eyed Padre was waiting for the Almighty to cut in on the game. What did he think life was? A faro game and God playing banker?

The car roared away trailing billows of yellow-brown dust.

* * *

Gayle settled deeply in his chair. The house was locked, and night lay deep over the desert. Like an addict to a drug, his craving for these solitary seances grew. He was fully aware of their harmfulness, the mental and bodily strain they put him under, but they were necessary for him.

The daytime was an unwelcome interval, but necessary, for he could sleep and regain needed strength. And he could sleep now. Deep, bottomless periods of obliteration. He had welcomed them, up till yesterday. Last night his sleep had been tortured all through with the face of Marilyn as he had seen it once before, blackened, knotted in the frantic fight for breath. Would that recur? Would he ever erase that monstrosity from the devious crannies of memory? He did not know. But of one thing he was sure. For a time he could bring back Marilyn as he had known her.

His eyes focused on the dress in the chair and his mind merged in concentration about it. A sharp knocking echoed through the house. Irritably, his mind came back to reality. He waited. The knocking came again and again, repeated and more insistent. He made no movement. The caller would tire and go away. But the knocking only grew louder. Thoroughly exasperated, Gayle stood up, went to the living room and snapped on a light. He opened the door.

"Doctor — "

"Yes?"

It was Manolo, hair-touseled and excited. "The Padre hurt himself. You will come?"

"Call Doctor Bashford. He is in charge."

[57]

"They call him. He is away — a sick one at San Xavier. The Padre is in pain — pobrecito! — You come?"

Automatically Gayle went for his bag.

The door of the Padre's house was opened quickly to him by a lady. "I'm so glad you came, doctor," she said. Her voice was calm though there was worry in her face. "He fell and struck his knee. It is arthritic, and the pain —"

"Must be intolerable," Gayle cut in. He followed her into the Padre's room. The old man was lying on top of the bed; his countenance was ash white. His pajama leg had been slit open and a cold compress rested over the knee.

Gayle removed the compress. The knee was red and rounded with swelling. Very gently he fingered the joint for a possible fracture. The Padre's face was working with twitches of pain, his eyes blinking, but the lips stayed silent.

"He was trying to get into bed — " explained the lady.

"Yes, yes," said Gayle preparing a syringe with a half grain of morphine. "We'll soon have you eased of that pain, sir."

The old man's eyes steadied on Gayle's face. His voice was apologetic. "Sorry you had to come. Jessie was alarmed. I told her not to disturb you. It could have waited till morning."

Gayle stiffened a trifle, then, as he saw the agony in the old man's face, he relaxed. "That wasn't right. A doctor is for the people — just like a priest."

The old man's eyes held his. "Like a priest," he said.

Gayle administered the narcotic and as he watched it take effect and wipe away the lines of pain from the old man's face he was struck with the thought of how much medicine had accomplished for alleviating physical pain and suffering. Why had there not been something it could do for Marilyn, something that would have worked like this, easily, swiftly, surely, eliminating the pain and fear and congestion from her blood-darkened face? In time there might be. Medicine was a fight for the future.

He folded a pillow and placed it beneath the injured knee. "That will be the most comfortable position for him. Keep the cold compresses on." He closed his bag and left the room. The lady went to the door with him. "That's quite a load of pain he's carrying," he said to her. "When did he fall?"

"About half an hour ago."

Gayle shifted his bag to his other hand. Pain was a doctor's foe, to be met whenever the challenge was cast.

"I didn't want to send for you, doctor," she explained. "He expressly forbade it. But I knew he was suffering a great deal and Doctor Bashford was not available."

"Did he say why you shouldn't call me?"

"No."

"If he should need me at any time during the night, call. At once. Don't consult him. I'll be over in the morning and arrange for an X-ray, just to be on the safe side."

He went out into the night and her softly whispered "Thank you" went with him.

*　　*　　*

Gayle mixed a drink and sat down by the window. The sky was peopled with steady stars. He looked at them without seeing them. Who was that gray-haired lady? Marilyn had spoken of her. He remembered now that Marilyn had called her "gracious" — "the gracious lady." She was just that. Marilyn had had that curious faculty of giving you the key to a person's character in one adjective.

What was the reason for the Padre's refusal to call him? Distrust, delicate consideration? Could it have been the latter, and in spite of his pain? Pain makes one so selfish. But the Padre was evidently built on a larger scale; he could control pain, be above it, think of others in spite of pain. Of course, it was a physical pain, and that was nothing like the dull empty ache of an abiding loss. Yet it was pain. What reservoir of strength did the old man draw from? For the first time since Marilyn's death Gayle found his

[59]

curiosity aroused. He finished his drink and went to bed. He set the alarm clock. There was a job on hand for the morning.

*　　*　　*

Over the phone, Doctor Bashford's voice was as scratchy as a cactus. "Gayle speaking, Hi."

"I've been up all night," rasped the old man, "taking calls you should be handling. Where have you been? I've called you every day for weeks."

"Sorry. A patient of yours, the Padre next door, had an accident last night. He fell and hit that arthritic knee. They couldn't reach you, so they called me in. I administered half a grain of morphine. Told him I'd see him this morning — O.K.?"

Doctor Bashford sat up suddenly in bed. "The Padre?" he yelled. "Well, I'll be — . Yes — yes, yes. Of course it's O.K., you dolt. And listen," — his voice suddenly lost its rasp — "can't you do an overworked old man a favor and take over the case of that old Padre? I'm drowned with work."

"I thought the patient decides on that."

"Oh, he's a congenial old duffer. I'll convince him if you're willing to take over."

"Don't know that I am."

"Well, when will you know?"

"I'll call you back later. Go on back to sleep."

The receiver clicked and Doctor Bashford stared at the phone, then he scrubbed his fingers ecstatically through his thatch of gray hair. He pointed a stubby finger at an imaginary presence. "Padre, you have a new doctor." And with that pronouncement he turned, shot both hands under his pillow, humped his back into the air adjusting the blankets and buried his face in the pillow.

*　　*　　*

Gayle stopped before the Padre's gate. A rabbit sat by the roadside, its ungainly upright ears a transparent orange color in the morning light. It bounded away leaving its offspring, a fluffy little thing, scurrying pathetically about

for cover. Funny about rabbits. They seemed the only crea-
tures that did not protect their young. He did not like
them. The law of mutual protection ran all through nature —
man and beast. Life would be a sorry spectacle without it.
He pushed open the gate and went up to the door. The
lady admitted him.

The Padre was considerably improved. Gayle expressed his
satisfaction. "But you will have to stay in bed some time,
sir."

The old man nodded his acquiescence.

"I was speaking on the phone with Doctor Bashford about
you this morning," said Gayle. "He is rather rushed with
work these days."

The Padre looked up. In the young doctor's face he saw
the desire, and the impossibility to speak about it. Medical
ethics held him fast. "I would be very grateful if you would
take care of me, doctor," he said simply. "Do you want to?"

"Yes; I do." He picked up his hat. "I'll arrange matters
with Doctor Bashford." He paused at the foot of the bed.
"By the way, you must have had a great deal of pain last
night before I administered the sedative. You stood it sur-
prisingly well."

"I had something to hold on to."

"I rather thought you did." He twirled his hat. "It's
readily apparent, isn't it, in extreme pain or loss? I mean
whether there's something to hold on to."

"Decidedly."

Gayle turned away. Whatever it was the Padre had, he was
not scattering it to the four winds. Evidently he valued it
very highly and would not part with it lightly. Well, it might
be something worth while. He would go slowly.

On his next visit the gray-haired lady met him at the
door. Her blue eyes smiled a gracious welcome. "Paul has
told me that you are to attend him, doctor. I'm pleased
and grateful."

It was charmingly sincere the way she said it and Gayle
bowed with gratification.

She extended a hand. "I am Jessica, the Padre's sister."

"Oh." Gayle's hand met the soft firmness of her clasp.

"I kept house for him ever since his illness."

She led him to his patient and then quietly left them alone.

Gayle put his bag on the desk. "I didn't know that the gracious lady was your sister, Padre."

A pleased look came into the old man's eyes. Gracious lady. The phrase called up memories, soul-searing memories, and yet memories that were now ineffably sweet. He found Gayle's gaze intent on him and he smiled. "I was far away for a moment. Thinking."

Gayle's eyes questioned him.

"It's amazing," said the Padre, "what composite traits are in a person. Evil and good, rocklike determination and affable graciousness."

He was talking of some occurrence in his past life, something that had to do with his sister. The Padre's gaze came full upon him and for one uncomfortable moment Gayle felt as though he were being X-rayed and cataloged. What was the meaning of that prolonged gaze? Did the old man see him as one of these complex beings? He wasn't. He was a simple person, distracted just now with the permanence of a great loss.

His gaze slipped to the red address book in the Padre's hands. He nodded his head at it. "Thinking of writing some letters today?"

The old man closed the book and slid his thumbs in a slow caressing movement over the worn leather binding. He gestured with it toward the desk. Gayle looked. There was a stack of letters on it.

"Is that the morning's mail?"

The Padre nodded.

"You have a lot of friends."

"I don't know any of them. They are just people with problems."

"What kind of problems?"

"The whole gamut of them."

"Do you have an answer for them?"

"Yes."

"For every one? — Always?"

The old man nodded. "It's in here," he said and held up the little red book.

Gayle gazed at him blankly for a moment. Was the old man a religious crackpot? He had impressed him as eminently sane, sure of himself, and that unshakable placidity had drawn him like nothing else in his experience. "To my knowledge, there is no cure-all for human woes," he stated bluntly.

The Padre made no reply.

"We have had a considerably bigger book than that, Padre," continued Gayle, "for centuries, and it was supposed to be the solution of all world and individual problems. And we have just as many of both at present. Right now, look at the world — Hitler rampaging over the nations of Europe, England blitzed, the Japanese running mad over China, while we wonder and worry and put our boys in soldier suits and drill them with wooden guns. And individually — well, a doctor sees enough of individual problems."

"A book is a dead thing," replied the Padre dispassionately. "It needs an interpreter. It lives again in each interpretation of it. A few hundred years ago a man took out of the Bible the heart, the core, the all-important principle and — lived it. His experiences and findings he put down in a book of his own. That book came into my hands when I was broken completely, utterly." The old man's eyes mirrored the pain and anguish of some past trial. "There was nothing left to me in life. That book gave me everything — perspective, peace, joy. The salient points I translated and jotted down." He tapped the little red book with an index finger. "They are here. They work."

The sincerity of his assurance impressed Gayle. "Well," he said, "I'm not a religious man. You probably have something that has been of help to you. Your ideas probably would not help me."

[63]

"They will."

The calm assurance of the man irritated Gayle. "You mean such a truth is ready to hand and no one has capitalized on it?"

"There is no truth but it becomes error if it is lessened or exaggerated. Like food — too much or too little of it, instead of promoting life, engenders death."

"Truth! And how are we to know what is the truth?"

"Not by closing your eyes to it," said the Padre. Gayle's head came up sharply. "There is an answer to every problem. But you have to face reality, facts. The ostrich sees no danger, therefore there is no danger. Don't stick your head in the sand."

"What do I do to get the answer?"

The Padre gave a faint sigh. "We Americans! Always doing!" His blue eyes had a whimsical gleam but Gayle looked back at him with no humor in his gaze. "In the strength of an individual or nation," continued the Padre, "you will usually find his or its weakness. Our outstanding trait is initiative. It has run through our industrial and economic life and made of us a great nation. It is our national trademark. An American is a go-getter."

"What's wrong with it?"

"Just this. You can't apply it always to the problem of a soul. It isn't just a question of another man to be beaten to the punch, or a supply question, or a labor bottleneck. There's another factor in every soul problem and that factor doesn't declare Himself just when and as we want."

Gayle shrugged his shoulders and stood up. "You are stepping out of the natural in order to get the meaning and the answer to a purely natural problem. It's not needed."

The Padre's voice became very grave. "You discover the real meaning of the natural world by stepping outside of it into the supernatural."

"I haven't had to do that yet," retorted Gayle.

"Neither have you got the answer to your problem yet," came the gentle rejoinder.

A sullen look came into Gayle's gray eyes. "No," he admitted in a low voice, "I haven't." He sat down again. "How would you go about it?"

The Padre's fingers slowly interlaced and he looked at them very carefully. "I would just let go," he said. His eyes came up and met Gayle's blank stare. "Do nothing. Wait. Hang on. Wait. Nothing happens by chance. There is design. You have to discover the design. Time will show it."

"And what do I do in the meantime, while I'm waiting? While this problem is an ever-present pain? While I'm torn with the hourly loss — the emptiness of life — the uselessness of things?"

There was an infinite pity and a profound understanding in the eyes of the Padre. "You take your place with the other thousands who are on the bottom of the dark wheel of suffering. You grow slowly into the fulness of a man. Strength doesn't come merely from doing, from achievement. We have to go back in our suffering to our pioneer forebears to learn that. Strength is just as much in the ability to endure. The wheel revolves, by an immutable law. You will climb out of this darkness of loss. Day goes down into night, but night is always swallowed up by the new day. There is something of that cosmic law in the life of every one of us. And in the meantime — you don't quit. You have a job in life. Go out and fulfill it, patiently waiting while you work."

Gayle looked at the Padre. The words were sincere and they were the words of an old man. Was it experience talking or just some drivel from his theology books?

"I have gone through this, Gayle," he said reading the question in his eyes. "No one can compare the extent or degree of suffering and loss between individuals because there is always the human equation to consider — the individual reaction to suffering, illness, ingratitude, malice, death and hopeless loss. In all humility I say I have had a full cup of it."

Gayle came over and took his hand. "Thank you, Padre," he said. "You can't imagine how I've puzzled over that strange appearance of the mignonette." He released his

[65]

hand. "I've gone to all lengths to — to — well, to see Marilyn again."

The white eyebrows lifted slightly. The old man's words came slowly. "You don't know why she gave you this sign, Gayle. It does not necessarily mean that she is trying to get in contact with you again." He looked at his hands. "Indications are against that idea."

"But she had some reason, some purpose. And how am I to find out what she wants?"

The Padre's eyes came up slowly. In them Gayle read his answer.

"I guess you're right," said Gayle. — "Wait and see."

He took his hat and left the house.

Chapter 7

DOCTOR Bashford came up from his chair with alacrity. "Well, Gayle, Gayle, my boy, are you a sight for sore eyes!" He shook his hand clear up to the elbow. "I thought you'd never come out of your oysterhood."

Gayle sat down and lit a cigarette. "I've been taking care of the Padre for you," he said.

"The Padre? How is he? What are you doing for him?"

"I've kept him on the sodium salicylates but intend to try some vitamin D therapy."

"That's right. Nice old duffer to talk to, isn't he?"

"He is. We had several long sessions."

Gayle puffed quietly at his cigarette and Doctor Bashford began telling himself what a wonderful little fixer he was. The boy was coming out of it. Gayle regarded the ash on his cigarette. "I think I'll take up work again, Hi," he announced and looked up in time to catch the satisfied smirk on his friend's face. "You look like a burro with a briar. Does it mean that much to you?"

"Every bit of it, Gayle," replied the other. "These past two months I've been like a man with his right arm gone."

"I'm sorry, Hi. But —" He spread his hands.

"I know, I know, lad. And this is what you need. Taking care of others' bellyaches helps you to forget your own troubles." He kicked at his wastebasket. "The *locum-tenens* gave me notice this week. So you're just in time. Lots of stuff for you. And there's been a woman calling for you on the phone for the last three days. She won't give her name."

"Woman?" Gayle looked puzzled. "I can't imagine who that would be."

"Well, get into Marge's office and have her line you up with work. Rattle your hocks, cowboy!"

He grinned happily as Gayle stood up and walked from the room.

*   *   *

Gayle was soon back in the routine work of the clinic. He had always been thorough-going, efficient, sure in his work but now he found himself handling his patients with a curious gentle sympathy. He could understand their sufferings and ills better, for he carried with him his own ever-present suffering.

His evenings were devoted to reading. Philosophical and metaphysical works, treatises about the soul, about immortality. When darkness had settled deep over the land he would leave the house and walk in the foothills. Not on the roads but into the wild stretches with greasewood and cactus about him and the silent stars above. There was so much to think about.

Ever again and again his mind would come back to one subject, would twist and turn it over, like some curious mystic key that held the solution of his problems if only he could read it right.

The cryptic appearance of the mignonette. There had been peace, contentment while it lasted. Just as though Marilyn herself had been present. It had changed his mood completely from utter despair to serene joy. Evidently she had wanted to eliminate the melancholia that was driving him to suicide. That meant she wanted him to live. But she knew that he could not live without her. Then what?

Would her spirit inform some other body? Was it possible that Marilyn was walking the earth in another body and that he was to seek her out? Fantastic. Metempsychosis — the transmigration of souls. It had been dealt with long ago and discarded. But was it so wild and fantastic as it sounded? Marilyn could not live without him either, he was sure of

[68]

that, and what other way would there be for her love to exist after death?

The urge to do something about the matter rose up so frequently within him and his utter inability to fulfill it left him with feelings of futile sadness. Then he would revert to the Padre's advice and let himself go limp. Waiting — trusting. How long, how long? Something of his youth died in those solitary walks, and in its place a steady, patient strength began to be born.

Several months slipped by and one day he found a letter on his desk. It had a Tucson postmark and smelled of a rather emphatic perfume. He slit it open, all unknowing that that act marked the end of his long period of waiting. A check was neatly folded inside. It was made out to him for the sum of eighty-five dollars and was signed "Sheila Starr." The message was brief. She had phoned several times but could not reach him. Things were looking up. She was a regular entertainer at the Desert Moon. — Would he come and see her?

The redheaded girl at the Desert Moon. He let the letter slip to his desk. What seeming coincidences life is made up of! He had met her only two times, yet both days had been such important ones in his life's calendar. The day Marilyn died; the day he had touched the bottom of despair. Sheila Starr . . . somehow she was bound up with the events that had altered his life. The memory of her vivid hair, so remarkably like Marilyn's, filled him with a quiet pleasure. He would take advantage of this invitation. He would see her again.

That evening he threaded his way among the tables at the Desert Moon to a place up front. There was a pair of khaki-clad selectees at an adjacent table. Young, fresh-faced boys. They were telling their girls that they might be shipped to the Philippines and they did not like it. Alaska would be better. The Philippine assignment drew such an assortment of "shots" that everyone got sick from them. Gayle's eyes noted the wholesome look about the boys and the evident straining after a good time. They were slightly homesick and more than a little worried. The headlines of the papers were growing ominous for them these days.

The orchestra blared a fanfare and the M.C. introduced Sheila. She came out and sang. Gayle's eyes followed her intently. The close-fitting green gown accentuated the grace of her movements. Marilyn moved that way, not as voluptuously, but with the same delicious grace. The wealth of red hair called up poignant memories.

Sheila's gaze suddenly detected him and her face lighted up. She finished her song and made her way directly to his table.

"Well, hello, stranger," she greeted him gaily.

"Hello, Red," he replied, standing up. He looked into her eyes and a faint ripple of disappointment went through him. They were the same. They were not the eyes of Marilyn. Blue eyes, but no depth, no soul. He could not read them. He could not explain just wherein the difference lay.

"I received your letter," he said as he drew up a chair for her. "I'm here to tender a receipt."

"As formal as all that?" she smiled. "I thought we were friends. At least you have been." Her face grew serious. "I guess I've been the cause of the long silence." Her look was pleading. "I didn't know about — about your wife, that last time you were here." There was frank sympathy in her eyes. "I'm sorry."

Gayle's heart gave a queer little jump. Her sympathy was genuine and it touched him. It was the first sympathy, since Marilyn's death, that had reached him.

"It's all right, Red."

"Sheila, to my friends."

"Sheila, then. The last time I was here I had just come from my wife's grave. The bottom had fallen out of my world."

The simple words carried the whole story to her and she understood now what a need he must have been in for sympathy and understanding. Inwardly she cursed the selfishness that had kept her so preoccupied that night with her own troubles. A golden opportunity had slipped through her fingers. "I wish I had known," she murmured, her look appealingly contrite. "Maybe I could have helped."

"Thanks, Sheila," he said quietly. "But I don't think you could have — not the way I was feeling then."

He ordered some drinks and she told him of all the good fortune that had come her way. "The new dress seemed to start it, Gayle. I had a regular run of requests for songs. It kept going along every night and they were coming through with real moola. Which was all right by me but then the regular entertainers began griping that I was stealing the show. Tony didn't want to lose me, though, so he got me fixed up with a union card and top billing."

"That's good, Sheila. I'm glad you're set."

Her eyes grew warm with the sincerity of his words and for a fleeting moment Gayle stared at them. Then the expression fled. She stood up. "The orchestra's readying another number for me. Will you come again, Gayle?"

"Oh yes, I'll come," he agreed.

She smiled happily as he left her and the smile was still on her face as her deep, smoldering voice sang "Sleepy Lagoon." She was visioning herself with a tall dark-haired man at her side.

* * *

Gayle kept faithfully to his routine of work, but now, twice a week, he exchanged his solitary evening stroll for a trip to the Desert Moon. Each time it seemed that Sheila's eyes gave more evidence of that softness, that openness that had shone so sweet from Marilyn's eyes. He watched for it, loved it when it was there, and then grew suddenly sad when it disappeared.

With womanly patience Sheila studied him, chatted, was sympathetic when he grew silent, was gay when his mood was light. He never looked at another woman. Shrewdly, Sheila began to grasp the situation. It was the similarity to his wife that at first had drawn him to her. It drew him

[71]

more now. He was still in love with Marilyn, or thought he was. Sheila would build on that, until he saw so much of Marilyn in her that he could not help himself. It was the only way to win out against a dead woman.

Sheila had come up the hard way, paying for everything with work and worse. She knew Gayle was worth any price, any effort and she set about her work with patient thoroughness. She sought out people who had known Marilyn. It was cleverly done. From seemingly chance conversations she gleaned a mannerism of the dead woman, a type of hair dress; from another source she obtained a photo and learned her style and likings in clothes. And the results of her findings were judiciously handled. They were not dumped upon Gayle in one crude, devastating heap. One small detail at a time was insinuated into her talk, her gestures, her dress. So that Gayle fell gradually and surely under the spell. His visits to the Desert Moon grew in frequency until they were a nightly event. He did not drink much nor dance. It contented him to see Sheila, to talk to her. He never stayed later than eleven o'clock. He was rigid to his routine. But gradually the sense of aimlessness was falling away from him. He grew almost gay and the cold suffering began to fade from his gray eyes.

Sheila was well satisfied with the success of her plan. Gayle had definitely changed. His interest in her had advanced beyond the mere friendship stage. And then for several weeks she seemed to be stalemated. She could not get him any further under the present circumstances. They had to be alone for that. But Gayle never invited her to go anywhere with him and he left too early to take her home at night. In the meanwhile her feelings about him were getting out of control. It was not doing her any good seeing him every night and having to confine herself to a shy touch of the hand. She fretted and made a dozen plans and discarded them.

And then unexpectedly the big opportunity came. Gayle arrived one evening and as Sheila came up to his table she saw the ghost of a sardonic smile on his face. "What is it, Gayle?" she asked. "Has something good happened to you?"

He looked at her. She was interested in him, eager to share his happiness. "I've just been told that I'm looking like a cross between a weeping willow and a walrus. Doctor Bashford cannot stand it any more. He ordered me not to appear at the clinic till Monday."

"Three whole days' vacation!" exulted Sheila.

"A man of leisure is looking at you."

"Gayle, will you stay on then tonight and take me home?"

"Why sure. Where do you live?"

"Over on Westmoreland."

"I'll be ready."

It was past midnight when Gayle drove Sheila home. The night was crystalline clear and brisk, the sky one vast swarm of stars. After the close atmosphere of the night club the air of the outdoors was singularly sweet and good. Sheila was arranging a silk scarf about her throat. "Have to protect the cash register," she explained.

"Better put that wrap on, too," he cautioned. "You can pick up a cold mighty easy in this cool air." He slowed the car and helped her tuck the wrap about her, his hands lingering over the task.

Behind Westmoreland rose "A" Mountain. A pyramid of dark mysteriousness it faced toward the east. The large white A, made up of whitewashed rocks embedded in the mountainside, shone ghostlike in the moonlight.

Gayle had inaugurated his three day vacation with a few extra drinks and was in a talkative mood. He carried on a monologue about "A" Mountain, its white A, how he had helped paint it when a freshman at the University. Something of his old self-assurance was in his speech. He was confident, capable again, the world was his oyster, there was nothing he could not do if he set his mind and hands to it.

Sheila finally interrupted him. "There's a road up the mountain, isn't there, Gayle?"

"Road? Sure. Want to go up?"

"Yes."

"O.K. You get a good view of Tucson from up there."

As the car wound its way up the slopes, Gayle's flow of talk gradually dried up. Sheila did not break in on his silence. They came to a halt beneath the A. It was huge, looked at so close.

"Pull the car off the road, Gayle," she directed, "and let's look at the city."

They left the car and sat down on a boulder. The lights of the city stretched out below them. "You know the main spots, don't you, Sheila? That's the Pioneer Hotel, the Santa Rita; those twin towers are San Augustin Cathedral — looks ghostly in this light doesn't it?"

She put her hand on his arm and leaned across him. "That carpet of red lights — off there in the south — that's the air base isn't it."

"That's right. Davis-Monthan field."

He was suddenly aware of her nearness, a fragrant feminine aroma exuding from her clothes, the wisp of her hair that feathered his cheek.

A train chug-chugged peacefully in the Southern Pacific yards. Sheila's hand slid quietly down and nestled in his. Through the air came the soft, purring pulsations of a formation of bombers, wedges of red flame drops, cleaving the dark void above them, droning their way onwards until they were above the flickering crimson carpet that marked the landing field. The planes then broke from the V formation and strung out in single file, wheeling in a long arc as they came in for the landing. Huge white lights were turned on in each plane and they floated down through the dark — like lazy, unblinking fireflies. They hung in the air, then slowly settled and disappeared in the maw of red that marked the field.

"Like mallards settling," muttered Gayle.

"Like homing pigeons," murmured Sheila.

Her words stirred thoughts within him. Their difference of viewpoint. The sight of the settling planes called up to him the hunt, to her it symbolized the home. That was the feminine mind, so different in its ways from man's, yet so complementary. Marilyn had not been profound in her thoughts, yet there had been a sureness, a fineness in her grasp of and approach to a problem. He realized that his thinking was not rounded, was not full without her deft additions. How much he needed that bright intelligence he did not realize till now.

"I guess you've got to lose a thing to find out its worth," he muttered aloud.

Sheila was silent for a moment at this totally irrelevant remark and then with swift intuition she bridged the gap of his thoughts. "There's always hope to get it back, Gayle."

"No; this can't be regained."

There was finality in his words and she felt carefully for the phrasing of her reply. "I suppose there aren't two things exactly the same on earth. When you lose one, I mean permanent, the only thing to do is to replace it with the nearest thing like it." She hesitated a moment and then spoke out of her young yet wise experience. "You can't fight life, Gayle, you just have to make the best of it."

He turned on her in swift denial. "Who told you that?"

"No one. I found it out — the hard way."

"I don't agree with it. It's wrong; it's defeatist. There's an answer for every question, but you won't find it out if you don't fight. As soon as you quit seeking you may as well be dead."

"But you said — about your loss — that you couldn't regain it. Are you going to fight death? Is there an answer to death?"

He was silent a moment and when he spoke there was a hard stubborn ring to the sound of his voice. "Maybe death isn't what we think it is. Maybe death is not a finish. Maybe it's only a beginning."

She looked at him a moment. There was no use wasting words on such mental confusion and obstinate refusal to face reality. Wisely, she understood that. It was not answers that he needed, but affection. After a while her head inclined slowly and ever so lightly came to rest upon his shoulder. For some time he seemed oblivious of everything but his thoughts, and then, becoming aware of her he turned his head and she looked up at him. Her lips were partly opened with desire, her eyes soft with pleading. Slowly he bent his head toward her and her eyes closed as she lifted her lips.

A spasm of pain contorted her face. Her eyes flew open. Gayle's hands had suddenly become steel hooks sunk into her shoulders. His eyes were wide, startled, unbelieving — staring into the darkness above her.

"Gayle, Gayle — what is it?"

He stared, unheeding her; his face like a sleep walker's. She jerked her head about. There was nothing behind her. She twisted in his grasp, trying to get to her feet. "Let go! You're hurting me. Let go!"

Of a sudden, a tide of revulsion swept across his blank face; she could read it as plainly as though it were printed there. He jumped to his feet, dragging her upright with him. A bird, startled by the sudden movement, fluttered upward from a near-by bush, beating its wings in fright.

"Come on, quick; get out of here!"

He seized her by the elbow and almost dragged her to the car. Stunned and afraid, she crept into a corner of the seat. He flung open the door on his side of the car and then suddenly turned. Slowly he went back to the boulder where they had been sitting and stood for a moment. He bent over and Sheila saw him pull a handful of leaves from a grease-wood bush and put it to his face. He turned and came back, tumbled into his seat and sent the car careening down the mountain road. Sheila's heart leapt into her throat.

"Gayle — *Gayle*," she cried, "you're going to kill us!"

"Huh?" His eyes came to hers and her stark terror seemed to register with him. "What is it?"

"You're driving too fast."

"Oh!" He cut down the car's speed to a more normal rate. Sheila watched him, her whole being a jumble of indignation, amazement, fear. He seemed utterly oblivious of her. Once he muttered something but she could not make out the words. Indignation boiled up in her. No woman could be expected to have herself handled like a pariah at the moment she had yielded her lips to a man. Was he mad? She had studied him minutely, painstakingly as only a woman in love can. Her shrewd brain told her he was not mad. Something had happened. But what in the world was it? She choked down her cries of reproach, the stinging sarcasms that raced through her mind. Giving voice to them would kill everything between them. Gayle was too much the gentleman to do such a thing without cause. He had intended to kiss her, had wanted to — she had seen the acquiescence in his eyes. That dead wife — had the memory of her risen up at that moment to spoil everything? It could have been. Perhaps he had not kissed anyone since her death. That might explain. It had burst on him as a bolt of treachery to Marilyn and had revolted all the depths of his loyal soul.

She waited, crouched down in her corner of the seat, breathing slowly, deeply until her voice would be calm. She watched his face, dark, absorbed. His hands and feet automatically handling the car.

"Gayle," she finally ventured, "what is it?" She waited and let her voice become low and pleading. "Have I done something wrong?"

He turned a look at her face, a disturbed, abstracted, puzzled look and then he looked back at the road. After a while he spoke. "No, Sheila . . . no."

He stretched out his right hand as though to touch her and she edged over to him and took it, placed it against her cheek. He withdrew it. But she had felt the tremor running through his fingers. He was afraid. Of her!

Wisely she said nothing. In time he would tell her what it was all about. There had been joy in her heart going up the mountain and now, coming down, the deep night of the lowlands seemed to reach out and fill her with its forboding

[77]

dark. Fear and a sense of loss hung heavy over her. The car drew up before her dwelling. A clump of tamarack trees threw a sharp black shadow over the car. Gayle snapped off the headlights. They were in utter gloom. She took hold of the door handle.

"Sheila!" She stopped as he slid across the seat closer to her. "Are you wearing any perfume?"

Her hand stealthily released the catch, and, with one swift movement, the door was opened and she was on the pavement.

Gayle made no movement to follow her. She shut the door quickly. "No," she said with a rising note in her voice.

"I didn't think so," muttered Gayle to himself. — "You — you — didn't notice any — perfume — back there?"

"No!"

Gayle's face was a white blur in the darkness.

The gears clashed and the car blundered away into the night. He had forgotten to put on his lights. Sheila wanted to call out to him, to warn him. But tears came instead; then shuddering sobs. She was afraid now. Very much afraid.

Chapter 8

THE rest of that eventful night Gayle spent walking the graveled path in his garden. It was a tireless, caged pacing with the immense quietude of the skies above him and the impersonal silence of the desert all about him. There was a chill shrewdness in the air but he did not notice it. He had let himself drift as the Padre had advised, had held himself in waiting and something had at last happened. But it had solved nothing. It had only thrown him into a more hopeless conflict of questioning. He began to doubt his own sense testimony. There was an anger deep within him at what he now considered his own gullibility. Believing that stuff that was meant only for hysterical old women or religious fanatics. It was hallucination, it must be hallucination. He had to get it cleared up.

The bloodless white light of early dawn was filling the sky above the Catalina Mountains when he entered the house. He found the card Doctor Bashford had given him. "Mikel S. Tisorek, M.D." He would take a few hours' rest and then see this psychiatrist and lay the whole matter before him. It was a rather humiliating decision for Gayle to make. A doctor should not be a man swayed by chimeras of the imagination. But the matter was out of control. He needed a clear scientific explanation. There was nothing like the cold unemotionalism of science to iron out a problem. Like a shock of ice water to bring a man back to reality.

* * *

He set his alarm clock and pulled off his clothes.

Gayle's car stopped before a pleasant dwelling in the Colonia Solana subdivision. A brief rest, some breakfast and a shower had cleared his mind. He was ready to go into the matter fully.

A woman opened the door. "Doctor Wade is my name. I just made an appointment with Doctor Tisorek by phone."

"Yes, doctor. Come right in."

She led him into a cheerful living room. A small man came forward to greet him. He was in dark trousers and open-throated white shirt, and had a very inquisitive sort of face. On an upturned nose reposed a pair of thick-lensed spectacles. It gave his eyes a fish-like stare.

"Doctor Tisorek?" said Gayle.

"Yes?" The bulbous eyes were frankly inspecting him from behind the glasses.

"I am Doctor Bashford's partner at the clinic. He has spoken highly of your work."

"Thank you, doctor." He pushed a chair toward him. "You said on the phone that you had a difficult matter about which you wished to consult me?"

"Well, I realize that you are here for your health and not practicing, but I am stuck, personally, with an exceptional problem."

The glasses studied him a moment. "Off the record, you will pardon me, but you don't seem exactly in need of psychiatric attention. Perhaps a little nervous, tightly drawn?"

"Certainly glad to hear that," said Gayle seriously. "I had actually begun to wonder. But when you've heard my story you can judge better."

Briefly he outlined the story of Marilyn's death and the appearance of the perfume. He withheld nothing — his melancholia, attempted suicide, the period of self-hypnosis. "I had been back at work for some months and keeping to the daily routine of the clinic. Last night, it happened again. I was up on 'A' mountain with a girl, an attractive girl. It was kind of romantic up there. You know how it is . . . the dark, the aloneness . . . well, I took her in my arms to kiss her. The perfume appeared — suddenly — as quick as that." He snapped his fingers. "The fragrance was all about her head. It was a kind of light flowery fragrance. It was mignonette. In a flash I was filled with revulsion. Not for the girl, not for myself — just . . . just revulsion. I didn't kiss the girl. I came home right away. But I asked her — she did not smell the perfume!"

The little man's eyes glistened behind the glasses. "Yes?" he prompted.

"That's all." Gayle's voice became flat, toneless. "I want you to tell me — am I suffering from hallucinations?"

Doctor Tisorek placed the palm of his right hand on the side of his head then on the back as though feeling for something. "You know what hallucination is, doctor," he replied. "Sensation without an object. Certainly the appearance of the perfume the first time seems to rule out hallucination. You had that man, that Padre, enter the room and he experienced the same thing. It's most unlikely, most unlikely, that two people would have the same experience in the absence of any organic matter. But I must have some more details. First, is there any of this perfume in your house?"

"Yes; but under lock and key. The key is in my pocket and I am alone in the house. The Padre asked me the same question. I looked and the bottle was still in the trunk."

Doctor Tisorek nodded his head of cropped curly black hair then stood up. "Wait a moment. I'll be back."

When he returned he had a handkerchief in his hand. "Will you take a smell of this, doctor, and tell me if you can identify the odor?"

Gayle sniffed tentatively then looked up at the intent face of Doctor Tisorek. "I'm not exactly an expert on perfumes, doctor, but it's some kind of a lilac scent, isn't it?"

The little man nodded, his bulbous eyes still two circles of intentness behind his glasses. "That's pretty close. Take another full breath of it."

[81]

Gayle inhaled deeply. "It's as close as I can get, doctor. Lilac."

Doctor Tisorek folded the handkerchief. "That's good enough." He sat down. "You have had two extraordinary experiences. Because of them you are beginning to doubt the veracity of your sense perceptions. Perhaps there is even a remote fear about sanity?"

Gayle's face reddened. "That's the plain truth of the matter!"

"Well, dismiss it. Your mind is sound. You reason logically. There's no incoherence." He crossed his legs and leaned back in his chair. "The mind is a collective agency for all that happens to us and for all that comes to our awareness. Some people call this the soul. Your mind has had an emotional shock — the death of your wife. Such a shock, deep and sudden, can so sharply upset the mind that it will react on the body. Mind and body are a unit, interrelated, intermeshed. The appearance of the perfume may be either an olfactory hallucination or a conditioned reflex."

"Conditioned reflex? I'm afraid I don't quite understand."

"A reflex, an automatic response from the nerves and senses when the condition that causes it is present. An example makes it clear. A very sensitive, delicate-minded person sees a drunken sot vomiting violently. The coarseness of this happening may so upset the spectator that he becomes sick to the stomach also. Later on, the sight of any drunken person may cause the person to vomit. It's a reflex action, conditioned or brought about by the sight of drunkenness."

"I understand."

"In your case, there would be a conditioned reflex if the first occasion your wife wore mignonette made such an impression on you that the mere smell of any perfume, or the mere thought of her, caused you to imagine the presence of mignonette perfume."

"That's why you asked me to smell that handkerchief a moment ago."

"Yes. Did it call up anything?"

"Nothing."

"Good. The conditioned reflex is eliminated and so is the olfactory hallucination, because the Padre experienced the same sensation."

Gayle looked at him blankly.

"I am speaking only of the first appearance of the perfume. The second one may have been an hallucination. The girl did not experience it, you said. She is a truthful person?"

"Oh yes, yes," Gayle assured him.

"Well, then, we will have to do a little more investigating." He put the palm of his hand at the side of his head a moment. "You have my phone number. If the perfume appears again, call me and just give your name and where you are. I will make arrangements to get to you at once. I will bring apparatus for making some tests." He stood up. "I am deeply interested in all this, doctor, and grateful that you have come to me."

Gayle stood up. "What if the tests show that it is no hallucination?"

"Then we shall know it is a sign."

"A sign?" He took his hat. There seemed to be a great deal of terminology in this branch of medicine.

"In the meantime keep at your work; live a normal life; exercise; some social life."

He did not know what he was asking, thought Gayle. Aloud he thanked the doctor. "At least I know that I'm not a candidate for the loony-bin. I'll call you promptly if the perfume puts in an appearance again."

Gayle drove away in an unsatisfied mood. The first appearance of the perfume was a "sign." The second, probably, an hallucination. To his downright and impatient mind there had been a lot of words but nothing of a solution. It was true, Doctor Tisorek had not had an opportunity of studying the phenomenon at first hand. Gayle fixed his thoughts on a possible future appearance of the perfume. That would give Doctor Tisorek a chance for actual tests, and under scientific scrutiny, Gayle felt sure that this strange phenomenon would yield up its secret. He would certainly spare no pains to get Doctor Tisorek on the scene if the perfume came again.

Chapter 9

TWO weeks slipped by and December came to Tucson, bringing clear, sun-filled days and briskly cool nights. Each day Gayle came to the clinic and listened to Doctor Bashford pour forth a torrent of abuse on the Japanese nation, the Japanese Emperor and his forebears.

"You're a salty old horse-thief," he chided Doctor Bashford one day.

"Salty? When it comes to Japs, I'm saltier than Lot's wife."

"Any reason?"

"Reason? My brother Jed is a captain in the New Mexico National Guard. You know where they are?"

"No."

"The Philippines. Jed's going to be in it up to his ears if those monkeys break loose. I like my relatives living."

"Cheer up, Hi. They say the Japs can't shoot. They've all got strabismus."

The older man snorted. "That isn't what I wished they had. Boils on — "

"Never mind, Hi. I don't think there's any need to put a hex on them yet." He tossed him the morning paper. The headline featured the arrival of Kurusu in Washington.

"I read it," retorted Hi pushing the paper off his desk. "It doesn't change the picture. I wouldn't trust any of them further than I could heave a cow by the tail."

Gayle went out on some calls. He really was not much interested in all the world-stirring events taking place. He lived in a world of his own and Doctor Bashford's vehemence he put down to excess steam. The old man always had to have some peeve by means of which to work off his pressure.

Gayle had been waiting impatiently for another appearance of the perfume so he could get Doctor Tisorek to clear up the matter once for all with his tests. But a watched pot never boils. He began to slip into despondency again. Discouragement rode his shoulders and life seemed a futile round of picayune trivialities.

Since that startling night on "A" Mountain he had not gone to the Desert Moon. Strangely enough he never thought of Sheila. The image of her seemed to have been erased from his mind. But if he was oblivious of her, she was not of him.

It was Sunday, ten o'clock in the morning, December seventh. Gayle was lying abed. He felt sluggish and indifferent. The day held nothing for him, but the summons of the phone finally dragged him to disheveled and reluctant attention. Sheila's voice, thin and hesitant, came over the wire. "Gayle?"

"Yes?"

"Good morning. This is Sheila."

"Oh — good morning, Sheila."

"I haven't seen you for so long. Is anything wrong?"

"No, I'm all right." His voice was surly with that bearishness that goes with the first few minutes of waking.

"Would you take me to a movie, Gayle?" Her voice was apologetic, hesitant. "I'm in need of a let-up."

He hesitated. There was no desire in him to see her, but his mind flashed back to their last meeting. He had treated her very badly and she had not uttered a word of complaint. And here she was making the first gesture of forgiveness. At least he owed her an explanation for his conduct. She must be hurt and wondering.

"All right, Sheila. I'll meet you at Armory Park. Where's the movie?"

"At the Fox Tucson Theater. It opens at twelve thirty."

"I'll meet you at twelve. After the show, how about dinner at the San Carlos?"

"Swell."

She hung up the receiver reluctantly. There was not a thing she could do about the matter. She was just that way about him. And he must be still overboard about that dead wife of his.

She had been eating her heart out these past days waiting for him to come and explain. His failure to do so convinced her that her original surmise had been right. Something she had done, maybe the way she had offered him her lips, had shocked him back into remembrance of his loyalty to Marilyn. It was haywire. Fighting off a dead woman, something you could not see, touch or hear. The odds were all against you. And God knows but this might be a lifelong mania with him. If she tied up with him she would be letting herself in for plenty. She sighed. That was how it hit you, though. The real thing was wonderful, the feeling it gave you, but it was harder than rock and crueler than a whip. It didn't count costs. She began to dress.

Gayle met her in the park. She put her arm in his and they began to walk toward Congress Street. There were not many people abroad. An occasional car with some church-goers rolled sedately by. The bells of the Cathedral sent their mellow summons through the deserted streets. Slowly, Gayle began to tell her how he had loved Marilyn, the words she had spoken to him on their wedding day. He looked down at the pavement underfoot. "I'm telling you this, Sheila, because I know my behavior on 'A' Mountain that night must have seemed crazy to you. I know that I must have hurt you. It surprises me that you want to see me again." He did not look up. If he had he would have found the reason in her eyes, and more than that — forgiveness. "When I took you in my arms I was going to kiss you — and all of a sudden I was overwhelmed, swamped with a feeling of revulsion." He looked at her helplessly. "It wasn't revulsion for you, it was, well — I can't describe it."

Sheila nodded. "I can understand, Gayle. You probably felt deep down in you somewhere that you were betraying

Marilyn. But she is dead. It's over, Gayle. That's finished. There's a new number got the curtain call now."

Her arm tightened about his and her eyes looked up pleadingly. His gaze fell away from her ardent look and they walked on in stony silence. A cowboy minced by on his high-heeled boots, his ruddy young face eager with the expectancy of a full pay envelope and a day in town. A Papago squaw stood stolidly on a street corner awaiting a bus.

Gayle's continued silence offended Sheila. "It's over, Gayle. Do you doubt it?"

"No," he said. "She's dead. I know that. But not for me."

Sheila's eyes widened.

"Tell me," continued Gayle, "didn't you notice anything when I was about to kiss you — no feeling — anything?"

"My own feelings?"

"No, not that."

"There was nothing else."

"Well then — I can't explain."

They came to Tucson's main thoroughfare, Congress Street. Gayle purchased loge seats and they entered the theater. Sheila sat dumbly at his side. She felt so bad that she could not cry. This was what it meant to be in love. To hit a stone wall and go all dead with despair. To know you are beaten, yet hopelessly to beat your head against the wall. About her were dozens of happy young couples. Young selectees with radiant-faced girls, soldiers in mufti, for regulations were then lax and furlough gave them a chance to deck out for the laughing girls at their side. The lights were still up, yet some heads were snuggling close to each other. Everyone seemed to find someone to love — she alone had to fall in love with a sphinx. Oh God, what had she done to deserve this?

And then the lights began to dim, and, with a fanfare of music, the newsreel came on. She did not see it. As the dark closed about her, the tight knot in her throat seemed to dissolve and tears of anger and frustration ran down her cheeks. She made no move to wipe them away.

[88]

The newsreel was finished but the main feature did not start. For some unaccountable reason the house lights began coming up, and Sheila turned her head and dug hastily in her bag for a handkerchief.

A man in overalls walked out on the stage, carrying a microphone. He set it down and walked off. People began to whisper. A puppet appeared from the wings of the stage, a bald-headed, gray-suited puppet that walked jerkily to the microphone. He clasped his hands on the rod supporting the "mike," "Ladies and gentlemen. An important announcement! All soldiers are to report to their barracks. All leaves and furloughs are canceled. All soldiers not in uniform should put on their uniforms — " He forgot the rest and fumbled in his pocket; then he read from a slip of paper. — "Put on their uniforms and report to the nearest army barracks. This is urgent. The Japanese are attacking Pearl Harbor!"

There was a stunned stillness. Then the puppet began to mouth his message again. And suddenly men in uniform were standing up. Some kissed their girls and stumbled awkwardly out of their seats into the aisles. Sheila saw the red troubled faces of them. One girl looked fearfully after a departing man and, abruptly picking up her bag, ran after him and clung to him. Sheila could see the tears in the girl's eyes, and suddenly she was savagely glad. They were getting their lumps. She had been cheated. She couldn't have love. They had it, but they had with it the terror that they might lose it.

People were standing in bewildered groups. "Pearl Harbor? Where's that?" — "Honolulu, you dope." Bits of sentences flew all about her. And then Gayle's hand was laid on her arm.

"I'm leaving, Sheila."

"I want to leave, too."

As they pushed their way down the aisle, a child was petulantly protesting that he did not want to go home. "I ain't seen Mickey Mouse — "

They stood on the sidewalk outside the theater. The sun was benignantly bright and warm overhead. All about them were clustered groups of people. An army car came slowly down Congress Street honking its horn. Some soldiers jumped aboard.

"I'm going to leave you, Sheila," said Gayle. "I've got to see Doctor Bashford."

She looked at him, trying to read his intentions. There was a dull determinedness in his face and an affronted look in his eyes.

"It's all right, Gayle. I'll go home and get close to the radio."

He strode off without another word and as she watched him go, her heart cried out. Much better to have him love her and leave her than to see him so utterly oblivious. She walked past groups of chattering people; some faces were blanched with fear. She felt alien to them. There was no apprehension in her. It was hard to be moved by a national calamity when one's heart had been pulled up by the roots.

Gayle drove to the El Rio Country Club. Doctor Bashford was a rabid golfer and never missed a Sunday. Gayle was sure he would find him there. He parked his car and went into the locker room. A large radio was blaring news of the Pearl Harbor attack. Several men stood around the radio, cigars and glasses in their hands. Gayle saw the manager standing beneath a huge trophy, a mounted striped marlin. He went up and greeted him and asked for Doctor Bashford. "He's out on the course," came the reply. "Should be in in a minute. Bud just went out to tell the fellows about the attack. What do you think of those Jap side-winders?" He did not wait for a reply but began to describe them in steady, variegated, and profane language.

A sherry-faced portly lawyer, a veteran of the First World War, was stamping up and down between rows of lockers, kicking stools, spitting and yelling for artillery, guns, cavalry to blow them, blast them. His cursing grew mephitic.

Gayle found a chair near a window at the far end of the room. He could see the Catalina Mountains through the window, his Catalinas — solemn, stately, strong. He could hear the excited comments of the listeners about the radio, and the pattern of destruction began to take shape before his eyes. The door crashed open and a flood of Sunday golfers poured in, making straight for the radio. Gayle saw Doctor Bashford among them. He had on a dirty white cap, baggy khaki pants, a disreputable shirt. There was a thin line of tobacco juice at the corner of his mouth.

The shouted questions of the newcomers, the jumbled answers of the others drowned out the voice of the radio announcer. Some pulled off their hats. An amazed oath broke out here and there. Gayle looked at them — a rather ragged looking group in their golfing togs, yet they were bankers, doctors, dentists, professors, businessmen and merchants. They represented all the vital interests of the community of Tucson. Some cultured, some crude, all of them up-and-doing men — a typical group of Americans.

Gradually the noise subsided and the men settled down around the radio. One prominent citizen stood apart, tears of chagrin and disbelief in his eyes. Another suddenly stood up and his voice was shrill with anger. "I wrote and wrote to Washington — I pleaded and pleaded about those shipments of ore and oil to the Japs. For months. Now they'll believe me, now they'll believe — the blind, ivory-skulled jackasses!"

A chunky rancher came over to a locker near Gayle and began changing his clothes. Gayle heard him muttering to himself. "Well, it's here. Let's get going."

Gayle caught Doctor Bashford's eye and signaled him. "Joshua!" ejaculated the old man as he came toward Gayle. "What do you think of it, Gayle? What do you think of it? Jed's out there — in the Philippines —" He brushed the back of his hand across his lips.

"I'm walking out on you again, Hi," said Gayle. "As of now."

Hi looked at him. "They'll need you, Gayle," he said simply, "and all of us, I guess. There's going to be a lot of busted heads before this is finished."

"I'm going as a fighting man, Hi — not as a doctor."

Hi's lower lip came down and he gazed stupidly at the grim, dark look on Gayle's face. Slowly his hand crept forward. Gayle clasped it.

"There will be enough doctors, Hi."

The older man shook his head. "I don't know about that, Gayle, but I understand the way you feel. Your dad was an Arizonan clear through."

"They sunk the Arizona," said Gayle.

He left the club and drove out to his ranch. They had the news. He stayed overnight but early next morning he and two of the ranch hands got into the car. They drove one hundred miles to Phoenix, the capital. A long line of men stood before the post office. They took places at the end of it. When the scar-faced recruiting sergeant for the Marines asked Gayle his occupation his reply was ready: "Rancher," he said.

Chapter 10

WITHIN the next few days the radio, from the instrument of casual entertainment in the homes of Tucson became the focal point, the heart-throb of the city. It was turned on all day and late into the night, and from its pulsating announcements new pieces of the horrible picture began to fall into place. The virtual annihilation of our air force in the Philippines; the landings on Luzon; the wrecking of Cavite, the only base for our Asiatic fleet. And all the while rumor ran rife about the extent and permanence of the shipping and plane losses in the sneak attack on Pearl Harbor. A cold and fearsome hand seemed laid on the heart of the city. People went about their tasks but their thoughts and talk were all along one line now. The queues in front of the recruiting offices grew steadily longer. The President spoke and labeled December seventh for history — "a day that shall live in infamy."

And all this while the Arizona sun beat down clear, and warm, and serenely on Tucson. But at night the quiet of the desert world was troubled. Trains began to move. Long lines of them, endless processions of them. The locomotives chuffed hoarsely through the night and strings of crowded cars hammered and clacked along in their wake. It was like the veins of a stricken body rushing the saving blood to an afflicted member. And from Davis-Monthan Field monster planes, sluggish under their loads, roared off the runways and turned their blunt noses toward the West Coast.

By day the trains streamed back with groups of children and sick, with numbers of the old and fearsome from the

West Coast. Air-raid wardens began to organize. Red Cross classes to form. Barrels of sand and buckets were placed in homes and on roofs.

Gayle had passed his physical and was to leave for boot camp in a few days. He had arranged most of his affairs at the ranch and the clinic. There was just one other matter.

He found the Padre in his usual afternoon location, the portico in front of the house. There was a newspaper on his lap. He tapped it with a long thin finger and quoted: " 'I read the newspapers to see how God runs the world.' "

Gayle took a chair. "Just now it looks like it's running on its own — and it's upside down." He sat frowning a moment. "I'm going away, Padre, and it looks like Doctor Bashford will have to take care of you again."

The Padre looked at him inquiringly.

"I've enlisted."

The old man was silent a moment. "You have your commission already?"

"No; I'm going as a private — a marine."

There was a dubious twist to the Padre's lips. "You should be in the medical corps."

"They will have enough doctors," said Gayle shortly.

"Not when this war is fully under way."

Gayle was silent a moment, fumbling about in his mind for words that would explain what lay at the heart of his decision. At last he spoke. "These past weeks have been like a new life as far as my medical work is concerned. For the first time I've really understood what a sick person goes through. I could feel their suffering, their loss, their need. Pills and operations answer only a part of their need. I see pretty clearly now that a real doctor has to give himself, identify himself with the patient's need, he's got to give more than technical knowledge — do you get what I'm trying to say, Padre?"

"Yes. You mean that to scientific skill you must add personal sympathy and love."

"That's it. You are only an automaton without that. The

needs of other people do touch me now, and yet seem remote. It's because I have got nothing to give them. I'm just a spectator. If I can't do the job right I won't do it at all."

"I see." The Padre's fingers slowly interlaced. "But there's your son. You have an obligation to him too, Gayle."

"I know," retorted Gayle quickly. "That's what I want to see you about. There are more risks in being a fighting man than being a medical officer. I'm not looking for legitimate suicide. It's the way the whole thing hit me when the news broke. This is my country and nobody is going to knife it in the back and get away with it." He was silent for a while, looking into his thoughts. "It's not good for me to be idle. I know that now. There must be something for my hands to do or all life loses its meaning. I can't do the work for which I was trained. It's false to me if I can't give it my whole self. I'd do harm not good to those who come to me. All that's left for me is to do what I can." He turned to the Padre. "I don't want Bucky brought up in the home of strangers. He's three years old now. I plan to have him live in my home with his nurse, Nora. But I want a governess. or some sort of person like that, to stand in the place of a mother to him, to make the house a home. What do you think?"

"Yes; it's the right thing."

Gayle placed his fist into his left hand. "I'll run an ad in the newspaper for a woman to take this job. Will you have your sister make the selection?"

"Jessie?"

"Yes. I'm very busy just now. I've got a great deal of confidence in Jessie."

"Very well. I'll tell her to select one or two of the applicants and send them to you. You make the final choice. Bucky's your child."

"Thanks, Padre." Gayle stood up. "I want to see you again before I go. There have been some developments about — about that other matter. But I'm too busy right now."

"Any time. — About the ad for the governess. Manolo can take it to town."

"Send him over in half an hour. It will be ready then. And thanks again, Padre."

*   *   *

The afternoon of the following day the Padre sat in his wheelchair, gazing with quiet satisfaction at Jessie in an opposite chair, her fingers busy with some sewing. The smooth beauty of her gracious face was good to look at. Much had happened to these two.

She looked up. "Deep thoughts, Paul?"

He smiled a slow guileless smile, opened his lips, and quoted: " 'Who shall find a valiant woman? Far and from the uttermost coasts is the price of her. She is like the merchant's ship, she bringeth her bread from afar.' "

"It couldn't be me you're thinking of?" she teased, her eyes again on her work.

He did not reply. She looked up. He had turned his gaze toward the gate. She swiveled about in her chair.

A girl in a trim dark suit had set her satchel down before Doctor Wade's gate. She consulted a slip of paper, then picked up her bag and pushed open the gate. She walked up to the door and knocked. There was no answer. She tried again. Helplessly she looked about and her eyes spied the Padre and Jessie. She came down the walk, unlatched the gate and came over to their enclosure. She deliberated a moment, then opened the Padre's gate and came hesitantly toward them. Jessie stood up and the girl stopped.

"I'm looking for Doctor Wade," she said in a quiet voice. "Do you know if he is at home?"

She looked a bit forlorn standing there in the bright sun, holding her satchel. Jessie went down to her. "I think he is," she said and placed a hand on her arm. "Won't you sit down a moment?"

The girl's eyes lit up and she accepted the chair with a little murmured "thank you." She sat upright in it, toward the edge, making the Padre think of a little girl on her best behavior.

"I just arrived in Tucson an hour ago," she explained, "and came here on the bus. It's quite a walk from the bus stop."

"Wasn't the doctor expecting you?" asked Jessie.

"I wrote him a letter after Marilyn died, and another one recently. He didn't answer either of them."

The Padre had been scrutinizing the girl's fresh young face, the placid brow beneath the saucy little hat, that curious open expression in the eyes. "I believe, Jessie," he said in a musing tone of voice, "that we are talking to Marilyn's little sister."

The girl cast a quick look at him and colored slightly. "How did you know?"

"You have her eyes," he said simply.

She looked pleased at that. "I'm Ruth."

"Glad to meet you, Ruth." She stood up and put her small hand in his. "This is my sister Jessie."

"The rest of the name is Hutchinson, Ruth," said Jessie laughingly, "and my brother has a Reverend in front of it too. Just call him Padre — everyone does."

Ruth's face flowered into a smile at their friendliness.

"Doctor Wade is busy packing, Ruth," said the Padre. "He's probably got his head down in the bottom of a trunk and did not hear you."

"Packing?" The light went out of her eyes. "Oh."

There was a pause. "What's the trouble, Ruth?" asked the Padre kindly.

"I thought he could help me," she said. "He's the only one I've got left. For the past few years I've been taking care of my mother, you see. She had been so ill that I could not even come for Marilyn's funeral. Marilyn's death finished mother." Her lip trembled a trifle. "Marilyn used to send us money and we got along. After mother's death I didn't know what to do. I wanted to take up nursing — it's a little late to start — but I thought if I came here Doctor Wade could help me to get into some local nursing school. It seemed extravagant, the trip out here; I had so little money. But I was alone and — I wanted to see Marilyn's grave and be near it. We cared so much for each other."

Her eyes were misted with memories. After a time she looked at the Padre. "Where is Doctor Wade going?"

"The Marines."

"Oh!"

The Padre's fingers began to interlace and the index fingers touched tips. "Have you seen Marilyn's boy?" he asked.

"No. They wanted to visit us, but Doctor Wade was afraid to have her leave this climate. And, of course, I could not leave Mother."

"He's a wild young scamp," said the Padre. "The doctor calls him Bucky. He's like a young broncho."

She did not seem interested, and a pathetic little droop took over the corner of her mouth.

A swift glance flashed between Jessie and her brother. He began to speak. "Doctor Wade was here the other morning, Ruth. He intends to keep his house open while he's away. His idea is to see that Bucky has a home. There's a maid to take care of the housework." He picked up a newspaper. "This is our afternoon daily, Ruth. — If you're looking for a place," — he paged noisily through the sheets, and found a spot in the advertising section — "this might interest you."

She read the item, and the languid droop suddenly left her face.

"Governess — for Marilyn's boy — my nephew. Oh, I'd love it!" Her eyes were shiny with expectation.

"You'd like it?"

"Dearly."

"Well, there's a formality before you put in your application. You have to go before a Board of Examiners."

"A Board of Examiners?" Her eyes were apprehensive. "I'm not a very learned person — " She faltered and tiny lines marred the smooth skin between the curved brows. "I hope they will not be too hard."

"Would you mind standing up, Ruth?" said the Padre.

Slightly mystified she rose to her feet. The old man noted again how attractive she looked, with the natty hat perched on her upswept honey-blonde hair, and the wondering look in her light blue eyes.

The Padre did not turn his head as he spoke. "All right, Jessie. What's the verdict?"

Ruth turned to Jessie her eyes pleading for an explanation. Jessie's face broke into a motherly smile. "Don't be alarmed, dear. *I* am the Board of Examiners."

"You mean just you?"

"Yes, dear." She turned a mock severe look at her brother. "At your age — torturing the child — and calling me a Board!"

Ruth sighed in relief. "I'm not afraid. Go ahead and examine me." She was bright and eager now.

"First question," announced Jessie. "After that walk from the bus stop, are you thirsty?"

Ruth's face underwent several quick changes. She finally replied. "Yes — Jessie."

"I'll get you a drink."

"Call Doctor Wade, Jessie," directed the Padre as she was entering the house, "and tell him you have an applicant."

"Of course, Paul." The door closed on Jessie.

"But she didn't examine me," complained Ruth.

"Didn't she?"

Ruth looked at his benevolent blue eyes and suddenly felt a foolish desire to cry. It was so good having people kind and understanding like this.

Jessie brought her a tall glass of orange juice. A piece of ice tinkled in its cool depths.

"Doctor Wade will be expecting you in fifteen minutes, Ruth. I didn't tell him who you were. Surprise is a good sales element."

When she had finished her drink Ruth stood up and took her satchel. "Come inside and dust up a bit," offered Jessie. "And you can leave that satchel here, Ruth, while you attack Doctor Wade."

A few minutes later, Ruth went down the walk. She was light of heart, her face freshly powdered, her little hat bravely crowning her blonde hair. The Padre's eyes followed her and his mind faded back to the memory of another girl who had walked down the same path, not so very many months ago, with the same unstudied grace.

*   *   *

Gayle had made a discovery. The meeting with Sheila on December seventh had brought back the awareness of her very sharply. Though he had said nothing at the time, he had noticed her tears while she sat beside him in the theater. He had puzzled over them and her efforts to conceal them. In spite of the preoccupation of enlisting in the Marines and of settling his affairs, he had found time to give thought to this suddenly new aspect of his personal problem. His thoughts had focused about Sheila. Free of her presence, a strange picture began to come clear in his mind. Over a period of time he had been growing more and more deeply interested in her.

What had drawn him to Sheila? A similarity to Marilyn. The luster of that abundant hair. The likeness had grown the oftener he had seen it. Mannerisms, dress, gestures had become Marilyn's. Those items had not been there at first. How had it happened? And the answer jumped into his mind with intuitive certitude. She had discovered his secret — his loyalty to Marilyn — and she had traded on it! He went over all the little tricks of behavior and speech she had employed, and a very sour taste came into his mouth. A vast disillusionment filled him at the realization that a woman could be so designing as to do this to a man's most sacred ideal. It made him bitter. Women were ruthless beings. Where a man was concerned anyhow. Sheila had decked herself out in the external trappings, the shell of another woman in order to draw his loyalty away from Marilyn and get it for herself. Did she not realize that Marilyn was not just these external things? It was the soul beneath them all that had made her what she was to him.

He realized now what a precipice he had trod, and it made him afraid. He had no love to give any other woman and yet his eagerness for everything reminiscent of Marilyn had led him to see her in this hard-souled creature. He was too impressionable. He must guard himself against any similar entanglements. There must be no further errors on that score. He would avoid women and everything that would suggest Marilyn in them.

All of Marilyn's belongings he packed in her trunk. After all he did not need these inanimate reminders. She was as fresh and living to his mind as though she were present. It was sacrilege to have others imitating her, and it would be agony to go through another ordeal of pain like that which he had just suffered. Everything that had been Marilyn's went into the trunk, all except the little gold cross she had worn. He cut a bit of string from a silk fishing line and attached the cross to it and hung it about his neck. Then he locked the trunk and put the keys in his pocket. He stood up, perspiring, his hands dusty, his hair disheveled.

He looked about him, and felt a curious twinge of pain in his heart. This was farewell. He had nothing but memories, and this house held them all, sweet memories, as ineffably dear as the delicate fragrance of Marilyn's perfume. It was like snapping the last paper streamer that bound his ship to a happy shore. The future was an horizonless ocean and a clash of unfriendly waves.

Feeling vaguely lost, he wandered into the living room. Above the mantelpiece was the landscape Marilyn had purchased. The blue bonnets, the wayward little path — at the sight of it the ghost of a smile came up in his eyes. How she had prized that picture! He had never learned just why it was so dear to her. The blue flowers in the foreground had something to do with it. But, after all, the reason was not significant. All important was the fact that it had filled her with serene pleasure, and her pleasure had made him happy. They had been that way.

He recalled the advice Doctor Bashford had quoted to him when Gayle announced his intention of marrying. " 'If you can laugh together, weep together, see the sunset together — it's safe.' " And it had been just that way with them. Tears, laughter, even silence they shared. Two people and one soul. Only now, did he fully realize what his decision to enlist would mean. The house was vibrant with associations. The window seat and the sunsets; this very room where the perfume had appeared. . . . He was putting himself outside the realm of her memory, away from the multitudinous fragile mysteries of her influence. Outside, in the rush and scurry of a world at war, could there be time for memory?

He lifted the gold cross that hung about his neck and gazed at it. Here in the house there was a wealth of mementos to feed his memories; out there in the battle and blood and foreign places there would be only this little gold symbol — a cross — to stand between him and emptiness.

A great loathing to leave rose up in him. From deep within his consciousness welled up that shadowy foreboding that clouds every heart on the verge of a long journey. The sense of one's futile smallness, the possibilities of evil and disaster, the severance of home ties, the definite relinquishing of a part of oneself, the vague premonition that if one returns everything will be different. And somehow Gayle knew, with an overwhelming certainty, that he would never be the same after this leavetaking.

There was a gentle knock on the outer door. He went hastily across the living-room and opened the door. A girl stood demurely in the doorway, a nice-looking girl, tastefully dressed.

"Yes?" he said.

"Doctor Wade?"

"That's right."

"I've called about the position of governess for your boy."
She held up a newspaper.

"Oh yes, Jessie phoned about you. Come in."

She entered the living room. "Take a seat," he invited
with a vague gesture.

She went over to the sofa and sat down primly in the
center of it. He looked at her a moment and she returned
the gaze with an appraising look. Gayle was suddenly aware
of his dusty hands, disorderly hair. Her eyes rested a moment
on the wide-open V of his shirt. The little gold cross was
very prominent. He shoved it back and buttoned his shirt.

Her gaze drifted about the room; there was a pleased,
impressed look in her eyes as she noted the exquisite things,
the deft arrangement. To Gayle it betrayed a person who
was not used to such things, who was slightly awed and yet
appreciative and eager to possess them.

"I'm going away—the Marines," he explained. "I've left the
management of this affair to my good friend, Miss Hutchinson." He looked at her a moment in stony surprise. Her gaze
had suddenly fixed on him and there seemed to be a little
devil of laughter lurking beneath that lovely staid expression
of hers. Where had he seen just that —? He shook his head.

"You will pardon me, but you seem rather young for
taking on this kind of a position, Miss — what did you say
your name was?"

She turned her eyes full on him. "Cameron — Miss
Cameron."

"Cameron!" he ejaculated. "Did you say Cameron?"

"C–a–m–e–r–o–n." She spelled it out with prolonged
distinctness.

"That's the right spelling, too," he said dazedly. "It was
my wife's name — her maiden name."

"I know that."

"Funny you two should have the same — what was that?
What did you say?"

"I said, I know that your wife's name was Cameron."

"How did you know?"

"Because her father was my father," smiled the girl. "Marilyn was my sister."

Gayle sat down very suddenly. He looked at her stupidly. She stood up. "I'm Ruth," she said.

His eyes went slowly and steadily over her as his brain fought with this unexpected happening. She did not resemble Marilyn, except in build. They were about the same height. The hair was totally different, the eyes a thinner shade of blue. Then he recalled that lurking smile — now he knew! That was a characteristic of Marilyn. And abruptly he remembered Sheila. This whole thing would be a snare and a pitfall. Probably after a while he would be seeing Marilyn in a hundred turns of expression and speech and walk. He did not want this manikin about. If he came back, he would have this reminder of the physical aspects of his dead wife to confront him every hour of the day. He did not want that. The memory of Marilyn was enough for him. Having Ruth around would be just a slow build-up for another shock of disillusionment and pain. And he had had enough of both.

His staring silence perplexed Ruth. "I wrote you, doctor, but you did not answer," she began.

"No. I — I've been upset since Marilyn's death."

"My mother died soon after Marilyn passed away."

Gayle mumbled something. She took it for an expression of condolence. "I came out here to ask your help," she explained. "I thought of going in for nursing and intended to ask your assistance. But the Padre told me to try this." She held the newspaper hesitantly forward.

Gayle stood up. "The governess job is out. You would not fill the bill. But I'll help you with the other idea. There's a nursing school here and I'll see that you are enrolled. I'll foot the bills."

She looked at him pleadingly. "I'm grateful, doctor," she said, "but — but wouldn't I do for the governess? I know I'm young but I've always been taking care of the house for mother. I like children. I'm sure I'd get along with

Marilyn's boy. We . . . we used to talk over the way a boy should be brought up and I'd try to train your son as she would have. Being hers, he'd be very dear to me."

It was hard to refuse her. There was something of Marilyn's sweetness in her way of speech, there was Marilyn's pleading in the frank sincerity of her eyes. He had to be rough to break the spell she was laying on him. He gave a sharp negative shake of his head. "No — and that's final."

He saw her shrink a little as though he had dealt her a blow. Swiftly he turned his back and stalked to the table.

He kept his back to her. There was no sound of any movement. The room was of a sudden surcharged with the conflict of warring emotions. Gayle, tense, hard in his rejection of her. Ruth, shocked, wordless with the blunt finality of his distrust and opposition. His face was toward the picture, but he did not see it. He was a rock of defiant determination. The sanctuary of his love would be kept clean from even the possibility of encroachment. It had been violated once. It would not happen again. And through it all his innate kindliness rose up pleading with him for the girl, but the deeper loyalty held him fast to his purpose.

Through the tumult of his mind the bright, restful peacefulness of the picture gradually found its way like an angel presence, quieting, softening the confusion, the intolerance within him. He stared at it, and a silence deepened about and within him and brought a feeling of a benign and loving presence.

"Winding paths lead through the happiest lands." The words welled up in his mind out of the happy memories of the past. For a moment he was back again to his marriage day and Marilyn was at his side, imparting to him her mood of musing peacefulness and contentment.

And then it came to him. Faintly, hauntingly sweet, ineffably fragrant. As elusive as a wisp of vapor, as soft as the velvet touch of red petaled lips. He crouched forward, clutching the table with both hands. With the suddenness of passion his whole being was absorbed in a gust of sensation, of consummated realization. Over and about him swirled the mignonette, dizzying, drenching him with its heady fragrance. His brain rocked and reeled. Again! It was here again! — the innermost soul of him was glad surprise, completion, an indefinable delight and yet mingled with it, woven through it was a curiously thin, faint thread of uneasiness, a small, cold, clear line of dissatisfaction. It was as swift as thought, as passing as breath. For the briefest of moments he hung quivering at the table's edge and then through his stunned mind lanced one word — one name — one thing to cling to in this maelstrom of madness — Tisorek! He had to get Doctor Tisorek at once!

He spun about. Ruth stepped back in alarm at the congested, contorted visage he turned on her. "Get out," he ordered. "Get out of here!"

She could not move.

He took hold of her and pushed her stumblingly out of the door. He slammed the door shut and sprang to the phone. The line was busy and the fingers of his unoccupied hand drummed frenziedly on the table top, his whole being a fever of impatience. There was a strange current of discomfort cutting through his unrest. His tongue kept passing over his lips as though trying to dislodge a bitter taste from his mouth. Abruptly his call went through and he spoke urgently into the phone.

A little while later Doctor Tisorek's car came to a flashing halt before the gate. He came in quickly, a large suitcase in each hand.

"My God, doctor," burst out Gayle, "I'm going nuts."

Doctor Tisorek's fish-eyed spectacles stared at him. "Sit down. I'll soon tell you if you are."

Gayle slumped into a chair. "It's — "

"Never mind. Never mind. Just sit. I'll do the investigating."

Gayle watched him set to work. He started sniffing around like a dog in a strange house. He saw him stiffen suddenly as he came to the table. "It's here?" he said.

"That's where I noticed it."

"H'm. Localized. Right over the table." He puttered around, sniffed around the table, over it, under it. It would have been ludicrous to Gayle if it had not been so vitally important. The doctor began to unlimber his suitcases, drawing out mysterious jars with heavy metal tops. He set to work.

"What are you doing, doctor?" asked Gayle.

"Taking samples of this air. For chemical analysis."

He finished with that and then started collecting things. Dust from the sofa, the doily from the table. He labeled them and placed them in separate jars. It looked rather inane to Gayle, yet there was a painstaking seriousness about the little man and a scientific eagerness gleaming from behind those thick-lensed glasses.

He finally closed his suitcases and then stepping back to the table swished his hat very vigorously through the air above the table. He turned to Gayle. "Now if I could see the rest of the house." Gayle conducted him from room to room, showed him Marilyn's trunk, opened it and pointed to the bottle of perfume, assured him it had not been disturbed, indicated the marker he had placed on it some time ago to make sure.

They returned to the living room and stood by the table. Gayle looked at him.

"Yes," said Doctor Tisorek, "I smell it. It's still here — and only here. It's very strong." He picked up his satchels. "I'm going to test these things."

"When can I have your conclusions?"

"I'll phone them as soon as I finish these tests."

Gayle's eyes held another question. The brain behind Doctor Tisorek's goblin-like eyes was a very shrewd one. He answered the unspoken question. "No, Doctor Wade, you are not unbalanced. That perfume is actually there. Be sure of that. It's — it's — the most extraordinary thing in my experience!"

He hurried from the house.

Late that night Gayle's vigil at the side of the phone

was rewarded. It rang shrilly and Gayle snatched the receiver from the cradle. "Yes? Doctor Wade speaking."

"This is Doctor Tisorek. The tests are finished. All of them, and checked."

"What's the vedict?"

"Nothing."

"Nothing? What do you mean?"

"There is no trace of any organic matter in the air from above the table. That air was impregnated with perfume. The natural order of things would require minute particles of the matter to appear. Nothing appeared."

"There hasn't been a mistake? I mean — "

"There is no mistake — neither in the tests nor in our sense recordings, yours and mine. The tests show no perfume; our senses recorded the opposite."

"Well then, what is it?"

There was a slight pause. "We have a word for this sort of thing, doctor. It may not be very satisfactory to you, but it really sums up this whole case."

"What is it?"

"It's preternatural."

Gayle hung up. After all that fussing around, the doctor did not know what it was all about. And he used a word to cover his ignorance. "Preternatural!" Gayle spat out the word contemptuously.

Chapter 11

J ESSIE met Ruth at the gate. She took one look
at her and thought of a broken-winged bird. Bewilderment,
hurt, and pride were struggling in Ruth's face. Jessie's arm
slid about her. "What is it, Ruthie?"

"He didn't want me."

"He didn't? That's strange." She walked her slowly up
to the portico. "Come in and tell us about it."

Ruth was one of those girls who detest crying in public,
and Jessie thoughtfully led her to a room. "I'll be back in
a few minutes, dear. I'm fixing a place for you. Supper will
be ready soon."

In the course of the supper Ruth told the Padre and
Jessie about Gayle's abrupt refusal to engage her, but could
not bring herself to tell how roughly he had pushed her out
of the house.

"It seems the Board of Examiners was overruled," said
Jessie with a wry little smile. "But never mind, dear." She
took Ruth's hand and gave it a comforting pat while her
eyes telegraphed a message to the Padre. He nodded acquiescence. "Stay with us, Ruth, till you have all your plans
settled, won't you? We are rather lonely here, just we two."

Ruth did not answer and they could see she did not dare
trust her voice for a reply, she was so touched by their offer,
but her eyes spoke her acceptance and her thanks.

* * *

Gayle strode up the path and stopped before the wheelchair. "Good afternoon, Padre. Getting some afternoon sun?"

"Good afternoon, Gayle."

"I've got some important matters to discuss with you, Padre." There was a brooding, trapped look in his eyes. "Yesterday it happened again."

"No?"

"May I wheel you into your room? I've got to talk this thing over with you."

"Certainly."

As Gayle wheeled the Padre into the portico the door of the house opened and Ruth stepped out. She smiled. "Going in already, Padre?" And then she saw Gayle and her features froze. She stepped hastily aside and walked away from the portico. For a moment Gayle stood irresolute. "Just a minute, Padre."

He went quickly after the girl. "Miss Cameron." She turned. He stopped abruptly. "It — it just now came to me," he blundered out, "about your visit yesterday afternoon. I guess I was rough, kind of. Something — something happened. I'd like to apologize for my behavior."

She looked at him but said nothing. He could read her eyes as plainly as Marilyn's. The child was afraid — of him!

"Look, Ruth," he said soothingly. "There's nothing to be afraid of. . . ."

She refused to smile and her silence kept the burden on him. Gayle shrugged his shoulders. "I'm sorry about the governess' job but there are considerations connected with it and I can't go in to them now. I will pay for all your expenses at the training school for nurses."

Her chin came up with an imperious tilt. "You will when I ask for charity, Doctor Wade. And that will be a long time from now."

She turned and left him. His gaze followed her a moment, the neat skirt, the white blouse, the proud little head. Then going back to the Padre's wheelchair he wheeled the old man indoors.

The Padre settled himself alongside the L-shaped table and Gayle drew up a chair facing him.

"What does preternatural mean?" Gayle asked.

"Preternatural? Beyond the normal. You'll find it in the dictionary."

"And outside of it too. Listen to this."

In crisp sentences Gayle told of his experience on "A" Mountain and of the appearance of the perfume again yesterday afternoon. He finished on a sardonic note. "Preternatural — it's just a word that says nothing."

"There's another word, Gayle, that might explain matters. Science doesn't like to use it — supernatural. 'Preternatural' leaves the door open for a possible natural explanation later on. And science deals only with natural laws."

Gayle made no comment and after a while the Padre continued. "You were wrong to give way to melancholia and the first appearance made that clear to you — is that right?"

Gayle nodded.

"I think your second step — taking up with Sheila — was also in the wrong direction. The perfume on "A" Mountain was accompanied by a sense of revulsion, you said?"

Again Gayle nodded.

"And what was the sensation you experienced yesterday afternoon?"

Gayle's forehead wrinkled. "I can't say. I was too excited at the time. I wanted to get the psychiatrist before it vanished." He thought a while. "There was always a sense of comfort accompanying the appearance of mignonette," he said slowly. "The first was all comfort, the second seemed mostly revulsion. The last one — well, yes, while I was trying to get Doctor Tisorek on the phone there was a vague sense of dissatisfaction. When he phoned later and told me his conclusions there was definite dissatisfaction. But that was because of my disappointment at the way he summed up the case."

"Not if it was present before he gave his decision," pointed out the Padre.

Gayle looked up at him. "What are you trying to do, Padre? Find some motivation under all this?"

"Nothing happens without design," came the assured response.

[111]

Gayle looked skeptical. He did not like oracles.

"You doubt that?" questioned the Padre. "Nature is evidence for it. It is purposeful. Law governs the whole thing, from the stars to the single-celled amoeba. Science is just a striving to discover and formulate the laws of nature."

"Of course," assented Gayle, "and it's all too regular and unified to be the result of accident. But I've often wondered whether it could not have been brought about by some force inherent in nature itself or by the adaptation of elements to their surroundings."

"That's just giving the problem a new name," replied the Padre. "Where does that 'force' come from, what is it that causes the adaptation? It's either an intelligence or chance. And if you have ever played cards or rolled dice you must know that chance doesn't work that way."

"No; law is not accidental or it is not law," agreed Gayle. "It must be a proof that there is a directing intelligence. But that's in nature. Man's a different proposition. He's self-determining."

"From where I sit, it looks mighty strange for all creation to move according to a universal design and for man alone to be left rudderless. Isn't he a part of creation?"

"He's king of creation. The king is a law unto himself."

"Is he? *Noblesse oblige.* A king, to be a king, is bound by the laws of royal behavior. It's our free wills and intellect that makes us lords of creation, Gayle, but free will is not license and our intelligence has limits."

"What does it all mean then?"

"That you can't have order without the submission of one thing to another. He lets us see that. The plant dies that the animal may live, the animal is slaughtered that man may exist. With men and their individual fates we can, occasionally, see the reason behind it but usually only in retrospect. Life would be a dreary story if all the details of the plot were blueprinted for us at birth."

Gayle's eyes looked frankly into the Padre's. "Do you honestly believe there is a design for each individual?"

"Yes."

"But how can that be and yet leave a man free will?"

"We were all made for the same purpose, Gayle. In the last analysis we are just so many tiny streams running back into the ocean of the divinity. We came forth from God, we go back to Him. There is no meaning to anything, if that isn't true."

"Why not?"

"The effect cannot be greater than the cause. If you deny that, there is no basis for thought, you must scrap all your mathematics and logic. The first intelligence, the first will — where did it come from? There must have been an intellect, a will, to produce them. And that intellect and will had to be at least as great as all the intellects and wills that have since come into existence." He paused and looked seriously at Gayle. "That begins to give you an idea of a Divine Being doesn't it?"

"But I still don't see how the individual is free."

"The general purpose is the same, but the design for the individual is different for every man. He sets the end before us, indicates the means, and leaves it up to us. You can take the good, or choose the evil. You can fulfill the design or frustrate the pattern. Everything is good in itself. It had to be. He made it. It is only our abuse of things that makes them evil. It's up to you."

"Why do that? We are just men — we can make mistakes. Why did He expose us to the possibility of completely missing the fulfillment of our existence?"

"I don't know — fully. Perhaps He had enough of mechanical adoration from the inanimate and animal creation. Perhaps He wanted something similar to Himself, an intelligent, self-determining being, that would understand the Good and freely turn to it. He had enough manikins, so He created man."

"It looks like the price of being free," said Gayle slowly. "Funny, that our biggest gift should be our greatest danger. Another one of life's mysteries."

"It is a mystery — a mystery of Divine Goodness," assented the old man. "You can't understand it fully, Gayle. He wouldn't be God if you did."

"No; I suppose not. That would bring Him down to my level, make Him finite, if a finite brain could comprehend Him." His thought probed into this fact. "Would you say then that the incidents, too, of our lives are His designing?"

"Yes. The good He wills, the evil He permits."

"Permits, eh? Well then, what do you imagine would be His purpose in permitting my happiness to be snatched away from me at its very peak? It seems to me that only a cruel, a sadistic mind would give joy to snatch it away."

The Padre gave a sigh. "There are a lot of egotists in the world, Gayle, but they are that way for only one reason — they willed it to be so. He created us *social* beings, and His design for the individual takes that important fact also into account. Right now what is loss for you may be gain for another. Ultimately it will be your gain too, but you can't wait for the future to disclose that fact." He paused a moment and folded his hands. "Did you ever stop to think of the evils that might have befallen Marilyn if she had lived? Crippling disease, insanity, blindness?"

"No," replied Gayle. "There was too much happiness in our lives to give thought to that."

"Yet they were possibilities. Her being taken away from you, when and how she was taken, may have been a kindness."

"I would sooner have her dead than disfigured or suffering," agreed the young man.

"And there is this, too, to consider. You say you were at the peak of your happiness. Well, if there's one thing sure on earth it's this — no human joy stays that way. It grows and declines. Additional time would have seen your love changing, settling down to a quiet sameness, perhaps dwindling, and you vainly striving to bring it back to its former state. Don't complain about what was taken away. Be grateful for what was given."

Gayle shook his head in stubborn dissent. He could not visualize his happiness yielding to the inevitable inroads of time.

"That's hard to take, isn't it, Gayle?"

Gayle nodded. "It still looks all wrong to me . . . to hurt a person for no reason."

"There is reason, plan, behind it all, Gayle," assured the old man. "Believe me. In sorrow we see only the present pain. If we could see the whole pattern it would be different. But that is not the way we are made. We can only learn from events as they occur."

"What is life then? A cryptogram?"

"You could call it that. A seeming confusion of letters. But there is a cipher to the whole thing, and the key to the cipher is faith. It puts the jumbled letters into line, gives them meaning, and you can begin to read the wonders of a personal love that directs and watches over you."

"Do you mean to say, that I am to see in the death of Marilyn the action of a *loving* Will?"

The Padre's eyes grew solemn. "A king can come to you in disguise. He's not less a king because his clothes are ragged, unattractive, maybe repellant. The will of God can come to you in a million ways. It comes to you every moment of your life. Your job is not to pass judgment on the king's attire but to acknowledge the person of the king beneath it."

"Did He have to beat me to my knees in order to have me acknowledge Him? Does this Will wreck a person to show its love?" His voice was bitter with hurt.

There was no answering sharpness in the Padre's reply only a gentle understanding. "There's an old proverb, Gayle, that says, 'God writes straight with crooked lines.' " He waited a moment to emphasize that thought, then calmly continued. "I've always felt, Gayle, that there is something divine in every one of us and that this life is just a proving grounds for it. Suffering brings it out or smothers it."

"I've seen enough of suffering in my medical work," returned Gayle quickly, "and I've learned to hate it. It makes

[115]

men petty, mean, degraded. They turn into animals. There is no manhood in a suffering person."

"You are describing the ones who fought it. Acceptance changes matters." He caught Gayle's glance. "I did not read that in a book, Gayle. I had a spinal operation some years back. As you see, it kept me alive. It was a delicate job, a skillful job, but I still am a close friend with pain."

Gayle's memory went back to the night of the Padre's accident, and his mood quieted as he remembered the uncomplaining sufferance of the Padre. "It's true," he said, "there have been some patients who did make me wonder at their submission and acceptance of suffering. But they were a small number — exceptions. For the most of them suffering was just a degradation."

"Humiliation would be the more correct term, Gayle. He has to 'char before He can limn,' and the fire He uses is suffering. It comes different to every man. Some get it all in one shattering heap, some get it in stiff jolts, interspaced, others get it in minute but continuous dribbles. It's the way we take it that counts. It's the test stone of whether the divine is to emerge or the animal. We are free in that. We can go either way. Up or down."

"I guess that makes some sense. A man is not a competitor until he gets into competition. I know the uniform will not make me a soldier, but battle will."

"That's true. But don't lose sight of this fact, Gayle. You can't always be an active agent. At times you have to adopt a passive attitude. Not like a lump of inanimate mud, but an intelligent expectancy. Wait and see the way the Directive Will wants us to go. As soon as the design of that Will is clear then switch to action. Prudently, cautiously though. Tentatively, even hesitantly till sure, because we make mistakes so easily."

Gayle nodded his understanding. Certain aspects of the Padre's conduct were coming clear to him. "You think there is a connection between what was happening at the times the perfume appeared?"

"It begins to look that way."

Gayle thought a moment. "Yesterday afternoon I had just refused Miss Cameron the job of governess and the mignonette appeared." He looked up slowly, a light growing in his eyes. "If there is a connection, that would mean the perfume's appearance and the vague sense of dissatisfaction indicated disapproval."

"Possibly."

Gayle thought a while. "I'd be willing to chance it," he finally said. "Suppose I hire her?" He was reluctant to give in to the idea. He did not welcome another talk with the girl.

"Try it," counseled the Padre.

"I will." He was silent for a while and when he spoke again there was a musing melancholy in his voice. "I've been rather disillusioned about women. They are not all like Marilyn. I'm not going to make the same mistake twice."

The Padre's mind failed to follow the drift of his thought. "What are you thinking of, Gayle?"

"I'll offer her thirty-five dollars a month," said Gayle, his voice still abstracted. "If she accepts, there will be one hundred dollars deposited to her account monthly. But she will not know about that until — well, until I know I've done the right thing."

Understanding came to the Padre. "I don't think she is a selfish girl, Gayle," he said simply.

Gayle's thoughts flashed to his meeting with Ruth and that eager, possessive look that had showed in her eyes as she gazed about the living room. "You can't know, Padre," he replied bluntly. "A woman can be devious and ruthless. I've found that out. The right kind of woman for this governess job will not mind the matter of pay." The Padre's face still showed doubt and Gayle flung out his hands in an impatient gesture. "Oh, it's all useless words!" His eyes were suddenly fixed straight and sincere on the Padre's. "I'm just a man, Padre, and I'm trying to keep faith with Marilyn."

[117]

It was luminously clear then to the old man. Gayle's self-reproach for the Sheila Starr episode. To him it had become a disloyalty to his dead wife, a defection engendered by his own very human need and fostered by a designing woman. Abnormally sensitive to that fact he dreaded the possibility of another lapse.

"I see," said the Padre his voice full of understanding.

"It's a square deal," continued Gayle. "The budget will be generous, and you may tell Jessie that if Ruth has any particular needs she may advance her the money."

"Very well." The Padre sat back and studied the young man's face, heavy with thought. There was a silence between them for a while and when Gayle spoke there was that curiously detached quality again in his voice. " 'Who knows if life be not death and death be not life?' I read that the other day. It kind of stayed with me. I've been so tangled up with things that seem to have nothing to do with real life yet that are more important than life." His eyes were abruptly bold as his mood crystallized. "Just what do you think of this whole affair, Padre?"

"What I think," came the measured response, "is that there is evident design in it all. I'm putting my mind to it patiently, painstakingly — along with you. What the design is will come clear."

Gayle's voice was tinged with bitterness. "It's a stupid game, torturing a man this way."

"There was a time when I thought just the same way," said the Padre. "When you walk at night through an unlighted street things have no true perspective — "

"That's how it is all right, an unlit street, and all you can do is grope around. But I don't seem to catch hold of anything. It's like walking in a dream world. What's the purpose of the whole thing?"

"Is it essential that you know now?"

"It would be a lot more comfortable."

"But it might defeat the very intent of the design. That very sense of futility, of helplessness may be what is needed."

"For what?"

"For finding yourself."

Gayle's head bowed and after a moment his reply came, slowly, a hard-won concession. "I'm lost all right," he agreed.

"Just now, yes. You are in a maze of doubt and questionings. But, Gayle, you are growing. The fiber of something greater than strength is spreading surely through you." He gave a resigned sort of quiet sigh. "It's like everything else in the business of life, lad, you pay the price and you get the goods."

Gayle stood up. "I hope it's true what you are saying, Padre. No; I feel that a lot of it is true." His hand slipped into his shirt front and disclosed the little gold cross. "I'll tie some of your thoughts to Marilyn's cross. That ought to carry me through whatever lies ahead." He tucked the cross back into his shirt and ran a hand nervously through his hair. "It's still rough riding, though."

"Put out your hand for help. You're not alone."

A warm light glowed in the young man's gray eyes. "Padre, that's the truth, and it's a comfort. That sickening phrase about the brotherhood of man somehow sounds right after a talk with you."

The old man shook his head sharply in negation. "I didn't mean that. Brotherhood of man! I have no patience with the fuzzy thinking of people who prate about the brotherhood of man and have no mention for what it presupposes."

"What's that?"

"Fatherhood."

"Of course."

"What I wanted to say was that no matter how bleak the outlook you can always say 'Our Father.'"

Gayle blinked. "Kind of forgot that, I guess."

"We all do. Till we get hurt. Maybe that's why He allows things to happen to us."

Gayle came over and took the Padre's hand in a firm

clasp. "I'll fix up matters with Ruth now. And thanks, Padre, for the help."

The door closed quickly behind him.

*   *   *

Gayle found Ruth at the side of the house. Jessie was showing her the poinsettias that were blooming so vividly in the bright December sun.

"Miss Cameron?" said Gayle.

She turned abruptly and over her face fled an Oh-that-man-again expression. "Yes?" she ventured.

"I've reconsidered. The job of governess is yours if you still wish it."

Her eyes showed swift pleasure and then doubt.

"No," said Gayle; "it isn't charity. I've reconsidered. You will at least have a trial and will be paid. Not much, but you will have your board and lodging and, say — thirty-five dollars a month?" His eyes were intent upon her, an expectancy in their gray gaze, but Ruth shot a happy glance at Jessie and then quickly faced Gayle. "I accept!"

Her ready acceptance disconcerted him. "The pay is not much," he said half apologetically.

"It's enough," came her sprightly assurance.

"Very well. My car will be here for your use. Perhaps Jessie will plan the budget with you, and if I can have it this evening I'll arrange with my lawyer to foot the bills. There will be the three of you, Bucky, Nora, and yourself. I'm going to bring Bucky and Nora home now. Could you take over, this evening?"

"Yes. I'll bring over the budget estimates this afternoon."

"Thank you." He strode away, feeling rather paltry for having doubted the girl.

"For heaven's sakes, child," exclaimed Jessie. "Thirty-five dollars! You can't buy pins for that."

Ruth smiled at her. "It's all I need. I'll be happy taking care of Marilyn's baby." Her hands came up in an impulsive gesture. "And a house all to myself!"

Jessie gave a half-sigh, half-smile. "Oh youth! — And what about when he comes back?"

"I don't know," replied Ruth, a delicate wrinkle corrugating her brow. "I didn't think of that. He's such an abrupt, unhappy sort of person, Jessie. How *ever* did Marilyn manage to be happy with him? She *was* happy, I know."

"Love, Ruthie, love," came Jessie's airy reply. "You haven't seen the real Gayle." Her voice grew earnest. "He was a very carefree, buoyant youngster not so long ago. Since his wife passed on he has become a man — a very serious one."

"And a rude one, too."

"Why, Ruth!"

"He pushed me out of the house yesterday."

"He did? You didn't tell me."

A faint pink came into Ruth's cheeks. "I didn't intend to, Jessie. It just spilled out."

"But why not?" She waited, but Ruth made no reply. "Under the circumstances many a girl would have been on the stiff side with this reconsidered offer."

"Oh, I didn't want to hurt him, Jessie. He's still grieving about Marilyn."

"You dear child!" breathed Jessie. — "Come on, let's go budgeting."

That evening Ruth was installed in the Wade home. Nora, the billowy-bosomed maid, brought in Bucky, a sturdy, black-haired miniature of his father. The boy had had a very, very busy day and was not particularly interested in anything unless it had a mattress and pillow on it. Gayle stood by, unbelievably stiff, and introduced them. "Bucky, this is your Aunt Ruth. She will take the place of your mother."

The boy looked at her. "Aunt Woof?"

Ruth smiled engagingly. "Do I get a kiss?"

He came readily into her arms and buried his face in her shoulder. His small nose tiredly rubbed the side of her neck. "You smell like flowers," he declared in a limp voice.

She gave a delighted laugh. "And you are a sleepy boy, aren't you, Bucky?"

"You betcha," he mumbled sleepily.

"Let's tuck him in, Nora."

They went off to their rooms at the rear of the house. When Ruth returned, Gayle was nowhere in sight and his door was closed.

The next morning she was up early and, aided by Nora, prepared a bounteous breakfast. It was to be Gayle's farewell breakfast, for he had told them he was leaving today. They waited impatiently, fidgeting back and forth in the kitchen to keep things warm. Finally Nora's patience fizzled out. "He's dead, that's what he is," and she went to Gayle's door and rapped resoundingly on the panels. There was no reply. She pushed open the door. The room was empty and the satchels gone.

A moment later Nora's buxom form surged into the kitchen. Ruth looked up, and read disaster in Nora's face. "He went!" exclaimed the maid and thrust a note at Ruth. "That was on his dresser."

Ruth was deeply upset. Not even a farewell for his son! She opened the missive: "Miss Cameron: I want to tell you that the room adjoining mine is locked. I have the key. *It must stay locked — always.* G. Wade."

She folded the letter and put it in her pocket. "He doesn't want anyone to enter Marilyn's room, Nora."

*   *   *

The somber cloud of war settled more deeply over the country. Frantically the factories were converting to war use. Shipyards began their race with the daily sinkings in the Atlantic. In the Pacific the picture grew even more ominous as the Japanese went swashbuckling from one conquest to another. And all through American homes ran the sharp sword of separation as the manhood of the country was funneled into uniform.

But Ruth's little world was filled with sunshine. There was a steady coming and going between the Padre's home and her house. Jessie was mother and sister to her. Nora was a treasure. And Bucky the joy of her life.

And then one day Ruth called on the Padre.

"Have you the address of Doctor Wade, Padre?" she asked.

"Yes."

"May I have it? A friend of his, a Miss Starr, called today and asked Nora for it."

The Padre gave her the address. "Don't you write to Gayle?" he asked.

"I? Oh, no."

"Why not?"

A fragile ghost of distaste fled across her features.

"Ruth," said the Padre, "Jessie told me about Gayle's behavior. It must have seemed unpardonable to you, but, believe me, 'to know all is to forgive all.' Gayle has had a rocky road these past months."

"I'm not vengeful, Padre, I've forgiven his rudeness. But I can't think of him with — well, what could I write to him? He would just consider it an intrusion. He should write first."

"You are right, of course, Ruth. And yet, I wish you would write to him — regularly. Say, once a week? You see, Ruth, Doctor Wade was very much in love with Marilyn, very much. He still is. In fact, as far as his loyalty is concerned, she has not died."

His eyes fixed her with their frank gaze. "Am I right in thinking that you agreed to take charge of Bucky out of love for your sister?"

Her eyes did not waver from his. "Yes, Padre, that and my . . . my — I haven't a single relative. Part of Bucky is Marilyn."

The old man nodded understandingly. "I rather think the care of your sister's boy entails a double responsibility — caring for and helping her husband."

"But he's a grown man."

"With the soul of a bewildered boy. He hasn't just lost his wife, he's lost Bucky, too."

Her eyes were suddenly thoughtful. "Yes; I saw that the morning he left," she agreed.

"From what I know of Gayle, that fact is a shocking revelation of the turmoil going on in his soul. Loyalty is the breath of him. He's good, clean, and sincere with a devastating thoroughness. Don't you want to help him?"

"What must I do?"

"Try to make him realize that he is a father. Not by preaching. Just write and tell him what Bucky says and does. His love for the boy is still there but it's numbed by the shock of what he has lost. You have to bring it to life again."

"I understand, Padre."

"Confine your letters to that. It shouldn't be hard."

"I'll do it," she agreed, but her eyes looked troubled for her thoughts were of a sudden busied with the outlook for a very dubious future.

"What is it, Ruth?" he asked gently.

"The future, Padre — when he returns."

"Climb that hill when you get to it. Gayle may never come back; he may come back with his problem all ironed out, or — he may come back worse. It may be too much for you to stay on then. You will always be free to leave."

"I'll not leave while I can be of help to Bucky and to him." She said it solemnly, as though it were a sacred promise made to some unseen presence. Then she turned her eyes on the Padre. "Tell me, Padre, why did he treat me so roughly when we first met? He actually pushed me out of the house like an unclean thing. Something happened — upset him. What was it?"

"I can't tell you that, Ruth. I know what it was, but it was told me in confidence." He folded his hands and his eyes took on a faraway look. "Some day he may tell you himself. When he does, you will know that your work here is accomplished, and you may go."

Chapter 12

L IFE in the United States Marines was good for Gayle. The strenuous physical routine of boot camp, the rough, tough, male atmosphere, the *esprit* of that corps shook his mind free as nothing else could. All about him there was that spirit of bluff camaraderie, growing hourly, daily into something deeper, more enduring, the traditional loyalty of the corps, so famed in history and countless action-packed battles. It answered to a personal trait deeply embedded in his own character. The officers were veterans of many campaigns and knew how to toughen men and mold them into reckless fighting machines.

A routine of drills made up the day, and the nights were a sleep of oblivion. He had no time to ponder his troubles, except for a short period each evening. Those brief evening lulls bred in him a hunger for a word from a friend, some news from people he knew. One day a letter came from Sheila.

It was a brave letter. She tried to be newsy and gay, but all through it, ran the subtle under-current of her own feelings and affection. Gayle read it, reread it, studied it, and began to understand. She was in love with him, sincerely and deeply! And the knowledge of that fact changed his view about her past conduct. Her shoddy attempt to usurp Marilyn's place in his affections somehow took on a different aspect. He, who had been driven to such extremes by the depth of his love for his wife, could well understand, and even forgive, the excesses and mistakes to which a kindred spirit had been driven.

He wrote her a reply. There was no reference in it to past events. Just a record of his present-day life and companions.

A few days later Ruth's first missive arrived. He opened it eagerly and then blistered the air with a curse. The letter began: "Dear *Doctor* Wade:" The female idiot! But he read on. It was all about Bucky. It pleased him. He sat down and wrote a brief reply and told her to address him as Gayle. What did she think would happen when they went overseas and a censor opened his letter and saw the *doctor* in front of his name?

Her reply was very apologetic, and he did not answer. But her letters came unfailingly each week. He grew to look forward to them. She wrote interestingly, naïvely disclosing much of herself in her recitals of Bucky's adventures. The picture of the boy began to take sharper outline in his consciousness and with it, love for his son awoke to new and fuller life.

The months sped by. He took no furloughs. He was content now. He was physically hardened, his mind absorbed with this business of war. His comrades were skilled in the use of their weapons. They were ready to fight.

And then one night they entrained. This was not another maneuver. The scuttlebutt said it was the real thing. They were heading for the West Coast.

*   *   *

It was August sixth, a moonless night on a sluggish sea. The troop laden ship left a luminous wake, eerie, corpselike in the waters. Gayle stole away from the crowd of marines and their horseplay. Tomorrow they would move in. They knew their destination now. Guadalcanal. This might be his last chance for a letter and he wanted to say something to Bucky. He found a deserted corner and hunched down over his letter.

*   *   *

Through August and September the radio had been carrying the tense news of the American invasion of the Solomons, with Guadalcanal holding the limelight. People dusted off geography books, and the newspapers carried outline maps. Anxious fingers traced the steady forward push of our forces through difficult terrain, and, gradually, a long sigh of relief was drawn as the people back home saw the vaunted jungle fighters of Japan beaten at their own game.

There had been no news from Gayle in two full months. Everyone had begun to wonder and to worry. And then one day Ruth appeared before the Padre, a very serious look in her eyes, a bedraggled sort of letter in her hands. "He's at Guadalcanal, Padre," she said and handed him the letter. He opened it and read.

"Dear Ruth:

We are going in tomorrow. By the time you get this letter you will know where we have hit them. It is very dark tonight and I am all keyed up. What the morning will bring none of us knows. For some of us it's going to be sudden death, that is sure. A fellow gets a new slant on life when he is going to lose it. Lots of things you would do differently if you had to do them over. I want to thank you for all the letters and the news about Bucky. There's nothing I'd like more right now than to be with him for just an hour. You are doing a good job with him. Keep it up. If I get knocked off I want you to stay with the boy and finish the job you have started so well. Make him square to his word and loyal to his friends.

We will do our best tomorrow. Tell the Padre we could use a few prayers if there are any lying around loose.

Sincerely,
Gayle Wade."

The Padre looked up. Ruth's eyes were filled with worry. The war had touched another life. "This letter is very old, Padre. I'm afraid something has happened. What must we do?"

"He tells you in the last line."

"Oh, I have been praying for him," burst out the girl. "Every day!"

"That's all that's necessary. Now trust."

*   *   *

The tide of battle swept up past Guadalcanal into the northern Solomons. America was proud; its face cleared. And while the country felt its courage mount amazingly at the success of the first onslaught with the enemy, it thought little of the graves on the distant island, the mute crosses that marked the price of victory. And then into the harbors of the West Coast came silently-gliding ships, hospital ships with cargoes of broken bodies and blasted minds. And on one of them was Gayle Wade.

Chapter 13

WEEKS of tedious silence, of prayerful, fearful waiting finally ended for Ruth. A notice came to Doctor Bashford's office from the Government. "Gayle Wade, Marine PFC., wounded in action."

He hurriedly called Ruth and the Padre by phone, gave them the news and then started wires going. Gayle was at the Naval Hospital in San Diego. Doctor Bashford was off at once to the coast in an airplane. He came back with news that allayed Ruth's anxiety. A Jap knife thrust had severed all the tendons above Gayle's left elbow. It was a bad cut and might leave him with a stiff arm. But he was alive and safe.

To the Padre, the blunt doctor told the rest of the story. "Padre, the boy's spirits are lower than a snake's belly. It has been all hell and hot water for him. He was in that fight on the ridge at Guadalcanal and at Tenaru and I think he's a little shell-shocked or something. They gave him a medal, the Purple Heart, and he's due home as soon as he can get a furlough. Tell that sister-in-law — the Cameron girl — to handle him with kid gloves. He looks like he's ready to fight a buzzsaw and give it first bite."

The Padre nodded thoughtfully.

For several days he waited patiently, but no word came from Gayle. One morning Ruth came hastening up the walk, her face flushed, the morning paper outspread in her hands. "He's coming home, Padre. See, it's in the paper."

Jessie's head popped out of the door. "Gayle?"

"Yes," said Ruth. "There are several of them . . . injured Marines. What will we do?"

They talked it over. Jessie and Nora would prepare the lunch and Ruth and Bucky would meet him at the depot. The Padre and Jessie would join in the meal and make it a welcome-home party. There were just two days left before his arrival. Jessie ran indoors for the cook book.

"Ruth," said the Padre, "do you remember our talk some time ago — about Gayle, if and when he returned?"

"Yes."

"Well, it's here. And it's not going to be easy."

She looked at him inquiringly. "Is he hurt worse than we thought? Doctor Bashford said it was just — "

"He didn't tell you all. His physical hurt is not so great, but it seems he is upset a great deal — mentally."

Her eyes widened.

"Oh, no," protested the Padre. "He's not insane or anything like that. "It's just — well, I handled a lot of the boys after World War I and I think I know what it is. War is a sickness and everyone in it is infected with its virus — fear and hate. Gayle will have a dose of that, I'm sure. Don't think he's going to sit down to our welcome-home party and slough off all the nightmare life of the battle-field. A man that has gone through battle is drained of physical, neural, and mental energy. The physical energy is soon restored. The others take long periods of rest and time."

She nodded her alert little head. "Is there something I can do?"

"Patience, more patience, and understanding," he counseled. "There's a dark caldron of bitter sights and stenches stewing around in his subconscious mind. Grim death and unmentionable memories. He doesn't want to talk about them. He wants to forget. And he needs help. Will you remember that?"

"Yes, I will, Padre."

"It is a job," he warned.

"I'm not afraid of it, Padre. I may ask for help if I'm in need?"

"Without restriction."

There was quite a crowd at the station as the Golden State Limited clattered in. A large group of people moiled about an empty wheelchair. Ruth caught snatches of their talk. "It was Benson's boy — Jim . . . caught a hunk of shrapnel in the spine . . . legs paralyzed . . . Veterans' Hospital. . . . That's his mother . . . some soldier . . . her old man got the same dose in World War I."

Ruth clasped Bucky's hand more tightly as she caught sight of that mother. There was such restrained grief in that kindly face, such a tragedy of patient endurance. It frightened her to see what war could do to people so far from its battle scenes, how far and into what distant homes and unsuspecting souls its shadow could fall.

They were opening a window in the train and the crowd surged forward. Attendants eased the stretcher carefully through the window. For a moment Ruth had a glimpse of an eager, smiling, young face on the tilted stretcher. Paralyzed for life! Oh the courage of these boys!

And then she saw Gayle. She hardly recognized him in his uniform. He was descending from the steps of the car, his face rather pale. His gaze swept the crowd about the wheelchair, then turned to a near-by porter. He picked up a small satchel and strode toward the exit.

Ruth suddenly awoke. Picking up Bucky, she ran forward and put herself in Gayle's path. His eyes were bent on the ground.

"Hello, soldier!" she welcomed him.

He looked up, startled.

"Here's a boy to greet you."

"Bucky!" His eyes lighted up, and the satchel slid to the ground. She noticed then that his left sleeve was tucked in his pocket. He pushed in close to her and took Bucky in his right arm with a huge hug.

"You little rascal," he breathed happily. "You're as big as a house."

Bucky imprinted a wet kiss under his right eye. "Daddy,

I love you," he stated laboriously, "and —" he looked at Ruth. "Aw, I forgot the rest, Aunt Ruth."

"That's all I need to hear," laughed Gayle. Bucky reached for his cap. "Okay, okay," said his father placing the cap on his head. "Fits you like an umbrella, you little leatherneck."

Ruth picked up the satchel. "I have the car here, Doctor Wade."

He stopped in his tracks. "After all those letters — *Doctor* Wade? Cut it out. From now on just plain Gayle, P. F. E. — Private For Ever — honorably discharged." He mouthed the last words unpleasantly.

"I thought it was a furlough," she said.

"A permanent one." He did not seem happy about it.

They got into the car and Ruth maneuvered it smoothly through the traffic. Bucky chattered away at a great rate and Gayle's face had a quiet pleasure on it as he listened to the youngster. After a while Ruth timidly put the tips of her fingers on the empty sleeve. He looked at her, surprised at the concern in her face.

"Is it — is it still there?"

"The arm? Of course." He threw open his coat. "I've got to keep it in a sling for a while yet."

She gave an audible sigh of relief. "I was afraid for one moment."

"No," he said. "I didn't lose it. I lost — other things."

Her eyes looked full into his and a shock went through her. There was such an out-of-this-world look in them. Futility, disappointment, a look of haunted misery.

She turned away but the vision of his face stayed right in front of her. The pallor of his complexion, the large grayish patches beneath his eyes.

Bucky crawled onto Gayle's lap and kept babbling all the way home. Neither Gayle nor Ruth exchanged any more words.

The festive meal was not a success. Gayle seemed sincerely glad to have the Padre and Jessie there. After one long searching look at him the Padre became very reticent.

In the midst of the meal a bomber went sweeping over the house top, filling the building with its roaring rush of sound. Gayle half rose, grasping the edge of the table, his face drained of color, his lips taut lines through which his teeth gleamed like a cornered animal. Everyone stared at his sudden fear.

The Padre's voice was casual, reassuring. "The air traffic out this way is strictly American, Gayle."

Jessie's hand found Gayle's sleeve and drew him back to his seat. "No use looking for a foxhole," she smiled. "This is the home front. Our trouble is rationing . . . in spite of which . . . how about some more coffee?"

Ruth saw how his hand trembled holding the cup.

Everyone felt constrained to do his best to offset the tension and only succeeded in increasing it. Jessie's tactful efforts alone kept the affair from being a complete failure. Ruth was heartily glad when it was all over.

Gayle saw their guests home and Ruth bundled Bucky off to bed. Nora and she did the dishes and tidied up the kitchen. She wanted to tell Gayle that he should sleep late. Breakfast would be ready when he woke. She went to the living room.

He was hunched forward in a chair, looking at something cupped in his hands. Evidently he had started to undress and had suddenly interrupted it. He had on trousers and undershirt. The partly open door of his room showed the sprawled out contents of his satchel and a murderous looking bolo on top of it.

She stood away from him. "Aren't you well, Gayle?" she ventured.

He looked up, "Oh, hello, Ruth," and then his eyes went back to the object in his hands. His shoulders gleamed white and sinewy in the room's bright light, and the small gold cross, pendant from a string about his neck, glittered as it caught the light.

"Is there anything you would like to have before going to bed? A warm drink or something?" she asked.

[133]

"See that?" He held up his right hand and she drew closer.

"It's a medal, isn't it?" she said.

He clenched his hand about it. "The Purple Heart!" He gave a bitter laugh and Ruth suddenly realized that he was not talking to her. "A million machine gun bullets, flame throwers and stinking jungles . . . disease, shells, bombs, bayonets — they didn't kill me. Hundreds of guys with everything to live for . . . they got knocked off. Grand guys. They shared everything with me, like brothers. I'd have died for any one of them — gladly. All I get is a scratch." He punched the palm of his right hand against his upper arm. The end of a raw scar showed from beneath his under arm. His gaze centered on it with a concentrated bitterness.

Ruth, startled by the vehemence of his tirade, moved uncomfortably from one foot to another. She felt vaguely that there was something he needed to talk out with someone, but she had no way of knowing what was turmoiling in his mind. In the Marines he had found escape from his problem. In the hard round of campaigning he had found forgetfulness of a sort, and his innate sense of loyalty had discovered comrades who had reciprocated his affection. It had been a paradise after the nightmare of questioning and doubts and loss in which he had been living. His war-shocked nerves, the melancholia that had blackened his days in the hospital and on the ship, gushed up in him, a drowning acrid tide. "They washed me out — because of a bum arm — they kicked me out — and gave me — a medal!"

He flung the medal violently across the room. It hit the sofa and bounced to the floor. "I don't want medals. Every look at it will remind me of Bud who shouldn't have died, and I'll think of myself who should have. I don't want a medal. I want — oh God, I don't know what I want." His head dropped down into his hands.

Ruth picked up the medal. She turned it over. It was inscribed with his name. Her whole soul was sick with shock and apprehension. She did not know what to say. She feared to say the wrong thing. Hesitantly she ventured a thought of consolation. "You have other friends, Gayle — your friends here at home. They will make it up to you, won't they? I mean for the ones you have lost. There is Doctor Bashford, and the Padre, and Jessie, and . . . and . . . I will try to help too."

"I know — I know," he mumbled, "but this is different."

She could not understand. No one could, unless he had been through it, what those friendships formed in the bright hard flame of danger and death meant. The intense loyalty of his nature had caught fire with the gay, fearless brothers in arms, and abruptly their lives had been snuffed out. Once before he had given himself wholly — to the love of a woman — and in a sudden gust she had been snatched away. Again with Bud. Each time a part of him had died. What was life? Just a tantalizing taste of happiness and then irrevocable withdrawal? Was it all cruelty and impermanence?

His eyes came up and stared blankly at Ruth. He saw the medal in her hand, the reverent way she held it. "What are you looking at that thing like that for?" he asked.

"It . . . it means a great deal to me, Gayle — and to every American."

"You can have it." He fingered the cross hanging from his neck. "This means more to me — Marilyn always wore it."

"I know. I gave it to her."

He paid her no heed. "I wore it every day since she died. It's always been good luck for me. That day on the ridge, when I tangled with that Jap, I didn't have it on. The string had broken. I got wounded. I sent a corpsman back and he found it in my foxhole. I wear it always." His eyes were suddenly filled with brooding memories.

She held up the medal patiently. "You paid for this, Gayle — dearly. Your country is proud and grateful — for Bucky's sake — "

She stopped. He was paying no heed to her. The dark patches beneath his eyes looked alarmingly large as fear rode up in his eyes. He looked like a man about to have a seizure. "I . . . I've got to take my medicine. Can I have some warm milk, Ruth?"

She looked at him a moment in alarm and then hastened to the kitchen. When she returned he held two capsules in his hand. They were filled with a yellow powder. "I . . . I don't sleep well," he explained and gulped down the medicine and milk.

"Hadn't you better go to bed now?" she ventured hesitantly.

"In a minute, in a minute. As soon as this stuff takes hold."

She sat down on the couch opposite him. He began to mumble to himself. What was the sense of it all? The plan, the design? "We learn from events as they occur." What had he learned from all of this? Only one thing — that he was not fated to die. He was not afraid to die; he had nothing to live for, and that was the reason why death would not touch him. To himself he said that he must be quiet and calm. He must not rush into friendships. Life could hurt him. What he had to do was to wait, to go into a thing coolly, knowing that it might be taken away from him the very next minute. He had to brace himself up to that fact, for that was life.

His head nodded. Ruth came over and touched his arm. "You had better go to bed; you're nodding." He stood up obediently. "Sleep late, Gayle. You need plenty of rest."

"No — no rest. If I rest, I think. Work — that's the way out — keep working." He made his way clumsily toward his room.

The next morning he put in an application at the Consolidated Vultee Aircraft Company to test-fire the machine guns for the bombers.

Chapter 14

RUTH'S life of blissful contentment suddenly
changed to one of bewilderment and care. She had had
but two brief encounters with Gayle before he had left for
war. There had been nothing on either occasion to influence her in his favor; rather the opposite, but she had
thought him fundamentally a sincere, gentlemanly person.
Now she doubted if he were even that. He provoked and
irritated her.

Most of the time he was surly and abstracted in thought.
A series of diathermic treatments restored in great measure
the use of his disabled arm and after two weeks he was able
to take up work at the Consolidated. Each morning he rose
at seven, took a shower, and sat down to breakfast. Ruth
rose earlier to have it ready for him. He looked like a million
other war-workers clad in jumpers, with identification badge
plainly displayed. Some of the color had come back into his
face, but those grayish patches persisted beneath his eyes,
giving him a strange lost-dog look.

Most of the time Gayle looked and talked like any normal,
plodding worker, but beneath the surface of that exterior
there was another individual crouching. A mud-blotched
Marine, taut for the attack of a wily foe; a fighting man
coiled to strike, with blood lust and shattering sights filling
his brain, with frustration and fear and bewildered questioning still bubbling around in his mind. The phantasm of war
skulked through the crannies of his brain, torturing him,
and eventually breaking forth in abrupt replies, in uncon-
sidered rudenesses.

Occasionally he would say something about the guns he had test-fired, or he would make a comment on the fighting in the Pacific. He did not care about the European war. "That's the Atlantic Coast's war," he would say. "The Japs are the Pacific Coast's war."

His language was full of Marine slang, and vigorous epithets came easily to his lips. It distressed Ruth to hear him so unrestrained in front of her. At times she imagined that he used such language deliberately, and that outraged her. But she stubbornly kept her peace. Deep down she sensed that he was trying to hold on to something that he cherished. He had been happy among those reckless fighting men, his loyalty to them still endured and now he was excluded from them. But he was still a Marine — if it was only in their lusty language.

And then one day Bucky, playing with some toy soldiers on the floor, let out a round, man-sized curse. Ruth dropped her work.

"Bucky!" she exclaimed. "Where did you learn to say that word?"

"Daddy says it," came the trusting reply.

"Don't you ever, ever use that word again." Bucky looked at her and grinned affably. "Young man, I mean what I say. Understand?"

Bucky's face suddenly stiffened. He knew that tone of voice, and his hands slid reminiscently over the seat of his small trousers. "Yes, Aunt Ruth."

Ruth kept her indignation stoked all day. That evening she met Gayle as he entered the house. He looked weary and the shadowy patches beneath his eyes were more prominent than ever.

"Gayle."

He mumbled a "Hello, Ruth" and turned toward his room.

"Gayle!"

He turned back. "Yes?"

"I've put up with a great deal these past weeks. I mean

[138]

your language. You can't realize how distasteful it is to listen to the rough things you say. And today Bucky used a vile word. He heard you use it."

Gayle fumbled with his cap. "I didn't know." He looked ashamed and slightly bewildered. "I'd better speak to him."

"I've done that already. He won't repeat the mistake, unless you provide him with further opportunities."

"I'll watch myself. You didn't hit him?"

"No."

"I don't believe in that sort of thing."

"I do . . . when all else fails."

Gayle opened his lips and suddenly snapped them shut. "I'm still his father."

"But I'm raising him."

"I can always get someone else."

"Two weeks' notice should be sufficient. You have it as of now."

She stalked from the room, her head, with its crown of honey-colored hair, held high.

Later he came to the kitchen. He had bathed and was neat in fresh white shirt and slacks. "I didn't mean what I said, Ruth," he apologized contritely. "You go right ahead with Bucky as you want. And I'll K.P. my language. You can remind me if I slip."

She smiled then. This was how she had visualized him. He shook his head pathetically. "I'm still kind of foggy sometimes. Everything happened so swiftly these past months. I keep remembering faces and words. The officers and my buddies, how they looked and laughed and spoke. The memories of them keep riding through my brain and . . . and I guess I'm not always aware of what's going on around me. Sometimes I speak without knowing what I'm saying."

Her heart went out to him with a surge of sympathy. He was just a grown-up Bucky who needed mothering.

"I know, Gayle. Your head is still filled with the war. Why don't you rest and give your mind a chance to forget all that you have gone through?"

"There will be time enough for that when the war's over." His face took on a stubborn look. "I've got a job to do. My whole squad died on the Ridge. I can't sit around. I owe them this."

He was silent during supper and afterwards sat on the sofa in the living-room, watching the old rose coloring flood the ancient Catalina Mountains. Then he began to croon a song in a low eerie tone. Ruth busy clearing up the dining room could hear him. That song would drive her mad. He was everlastingly humming or singing it. "Blues in the Night." His voice, lugubriously low, came to her: "now the rain's a-fallin', hear the train a-callin', whoo-ee. Hear dat lonesome whistle, blowin' 'cross the trestle, whoo-ee. . . ." She clattered the dishes into the kitchen, went to the bathroom, put two small plugs of cotton in her ears, and then went back to her work. But the cotton wads were no help. The song was running in her head now. She went into the kitchen and told Nora to turn on the radio — loud.

A few minutes later Gayle left the house and walked over to their neighbors. Ruth heaved a sigh of relief.

The Padre was watching the lights on the Catalinas. Gayle came up and sat down on the floor, his back against one of the pillars.

"The mastery of the Master," said the Padre gesturing toward the mountains. "It's a baeutiful God that can make such beautiful things."

"Yes," said Gayle. He had not come to discuss the landscape. "I'm working at the Consolidated, Padre."

"Jessie told me."

"When I was discharged they told me to get into some war work where my experience would be useful."

"There's a shortage of doctors in Tucson."

"I know." He waited a while. "I can't go back to medical work yet."

"For the same reason as before?"

Gayle nodded assent.

"You can't give it what you feel it demands?"

"That's the trouble," came Gayle's reply, "and there's another reason added to it now. My nerves are too rocky." A shadow came into his eyes. "When I got into the scrap my hackles were up. Pearl Harbor made me want to sling lead. But there was a selfish motive twisted in with it. I see that now. I was thinking of myself. I wanted to shake free of my problems. It worked too. While I was with the fellows and fighting, my mind was too crowded to think."

"And now?"

"I'm back at the same old crossroads. My head is all a jumble. Only worse. It's not only the old problem. I'm still out there on Guadalcanal fighting Japs — every night . . . and part of the day, too."

"That's natural. Battle fatigue, they call it in this war. Your subconscious mind is filled with the horrors of battle. All those violent emotions and savage encounters are stored up in your mind. You have to let normal sights and sounds and emotions saturate your mind now and drown out those abnormal phantasms. That means — rest."

"No; I can't see it that way just now. I've got a debt to pay. Becker, Ray, Squinty . . . all of them were knocked off . . . right alongside of me." His jaw squared as the muscles knotted over it. "That's the worst thing about war. Having your buddies killed. Guys you played poker with the day before, fellows you trained with, argued and fought with. But good guys — straight as a string, they'd go to bat for you, come hell or high water. Underneath the same fundamental ideas about life and the way to live it. . . . And then they're gone."

"That's life Gayle . . . a meeting and a parting. In war the tempo is accelerated."

"I guess you're right, but it doesn't make the facts any easier to take!" He pointed to the little red book on the Padre's lap. "You've got something there, Padre. When I was up against the real thing I found it out. All you can do is let go . . . resign yourself. It made me calm and not afraid."

[141]

The two men sat in silence, the strange loveliness of the distant mountains filling their minds with peace. And then Gayle began to talk quietly, reminiscently, half to himself. "There were times, in the evenings, when I could think dispassionately of all the strange things that had happened to me. Perhaps because I was dog-tired physically, perhaps because I was away from all the people and places connected with it . . . but I could look at things objectively, like a stranger. And I believe I've got the score now. I figure it this way. The mignonette appeared the first time to keep me from a coward's death. The second time to prevent me from wrecking myself by a loveless marriage. The third time . . ." he frowned. "I'm not sure yet about that." He put his clenched right fist into his left hand. "I know what all this means now Padre. Marilyn loves me still . . . she's watching over me, even after death." His fingers slid into his shirt front. "I never talk of these matters to others. They'd think me nuts or some sort of mystic screwball."

The light had faded from the Catalinas and the mountains were suddenly jagged flat pieces of black cardboard against the sky. He stood up. "Got to get to bed, Padre. I'm test-firing a new gun tomorrow and all the brass hats will be there."

"You're sure this is the right thing for you, Gayle?".

Gayle paused. The Padre's face showed some concern. "You rather jumped into this job," cautioned the old man.

"Yes, I did," he admitted. "But that was the way I felt then. I still feel that way about it."

He walked off, an overcast look on his face.

*　　*　　*

Late that night Bucky called fretfully for Ruth. He had been dreaming, and woke up frightened. Ruth hurried to his bed.

"What is it Bucky?"

He told her he had had a bad dream and now he was thirsty. She got him a drink and stayed with him till he fell asleep. Returning the glass to the kitchen, she glimpsed a light in the living room. Cautiously she opened the door. Gayle, clad in his pajamas, his hair touseled, sat on the sofa, a half-burnt cigarette between his fingers.

"What is it, Gayle?" she inquired from the doorway. "Sick?"

He looked up a moment. His eyes were dull. "No. Can't sleep."

"I'll warm a glass of milk for you."

"Don't bother. I didn't disturb you, did I?"

"No. Bucky woke me. He had been dreaming. He's gone to sleep again. Won't you try a glass of warm milk? It might help you sleep."

"All right."

She brought him the milk. He thanked her.

"Maybe if you took your medicine, Gayle, the sedative, it would help."

"I've been taking too much of it. Besides I've got to have a clear head tomorrow. I'm test-firing a snorter of a new gun tomorrow. I'll be leaving early. Don't bother about breakfast. I'll catch a cup of coffee downtown."

He went back to his room. The milk stood untouched on the table.

Chapter 15

Nora, looking like something dropped from Mars, came into the kitchen. Her skirts were tucked up and sections of an extravagant petticoat were showing; on her head was a wild-looking bandana for a dust cap; in her hand was a duster held like a truncheon. She was armed, cap-a-pie, for the regular weekly house cleaning.

Ruth was seated at the kitchen table, a cook book and a heterogenous mass of ingredients outspread before her. It was to be a cake. Ruth's eagerness to help out with the work of the house, her kindly, understanding ways had accomplished that minor miracle of endearing herself to the maid. There were few secrets between Nora and Ruth. When things became too trying Nora would comfort her. "What is it now, Miss Ruth?" she would inquire. "The doctor got a spell of the war blues again?"

"Blues?" Ruth would reply. "It's the deep indigoes, Nora." Then Nora would console her with the assurance that it would pass off, and, in proof thereof, would recount anecdotes of the days when Gayle was carefree and gay.

This morning Nora was a bit on the important side. "Miss Ruth, in the course of my cleaning in the bathroom of the doctor, I came across this."

"Yes?" murmured Ruth abstractedly. Her left hand traced a line in the cook book and her right hand extended palm up toward Nora, the fingers wiggling a command. Nora put the object in Ruth's hand and stood waiting for a comment. Ruth's thumb slid idly back and forth over the small gold object and suddenly a message was flashed to her preoccupied mind. Her head jerked away from the book and looked at the little gold cross in her hand. "Oh, good heavens!" she exclaimed in one quick gasp. "Marilyn's cross!" She jumped to her feet, upsetting a cup of sugar. "Gayle forgot it in his rush this morning. I'll phone him. No; I'll take it to him."

"What for?"

"He's superstitious about this cross, Nora."

"Time he was cured then," commented Nora placidly; and then, as Ruth still seemed undecided, "Don't be silly, Miss Ruth. It's a long trip out to the Consolidated, and they won't let you in without one of them picture badges. And I'm thinking if you convince them to pull the doctor away from his work to see you, he's not going to like it."

"I suppose you're right, Nora," she admitted reluctantly. "And there is so much work to be done today. I'll put it round my neck so I won't forget about it."

She slung the cross around her neck and went back to her work. Half a dozen times she started for the telephone and then turned back. She felt vaguely uneasy. And then as she began to mix the dough she hummed a song. "Evenin' breeze'll start the trees to cryin' . . . and noon'll hide its light — when you get the blues . . . in the night —" She threw the spoon into the batter. That hateful song! What was the matter with her? She grew irritable. Was she worrying about Gayle? Had his stupid notion about Marilyn's keepsake invaded her mind too?

She would call him up and get the thing off her mind. Just as she approached the phone, it began to ring. She snatched up the receiver. A heavy voice spoke her name. "Miss Cameron?"

"Yes."

"This is Doctor Bashford. Gayle's been hurt. I've got him here at the hospital."

"Hurt?" Ruth slid weakly into a chair. "Is it bad?"

"Bad enough. So far I've found several fractured ribs and a badly broken hand. His back seems injured too. Listen. . . ."

"Yes."

"He's kind of whoozy and keeps yelping for a cross or thing-a-majig for his neck. Know anything about it? It's a job to keep him quiet."

"Yes. I've got it here."

"Good. Bring it out right away, will you? He's in room 25. Got that? 2-5. There's a special nurse. She'll let you in."

Ruth stood up and took the cross from about her neck. For a moment she looked at it with a mixture of fear and wonder. Then she ran from the house.

Jessie saw her hurrying from the house and hastened to the fence. "What is it, Ruth?" she called.

"Gayle. He's been hurt. He's at the hospital."

"Want me along?"

"Yes, yes, Jessie."

As she drove Ruth told her about the premonition that had disturbed her all morning. "It's all my fault," she said. "I should have taken Marilyn's keepsake to him as soon as Nora found it."

"Nonsense," chided Jessie. "The accident probably happened before that."

At the hospital Jessie took command. "You run up to Gayle's room. I'll locate Doctor Bashford and get the details."

Ruth knocked at Room 25. A nurse opened the door.

"I'm Miss Cameron," explained Ruth.

"Oh, yes. Come in."

Gayle was propped up in bed, his eyes wide, an unfocused look about them, and he was talking in a steady, incoherent stream. "Shock," the nurse explained.

Ruth knelt at the side of the bed. "Gayle," she said.

He babbled on. It was a curious jumble: Marilyn; and gun mounts; a battle curse; the color of her hair. Ruth kept staring helplessly at him, and suddenly, in a very natural gesture, he put forth his right hand and ran it in a caressing motion over the side of her face and hair. It was the first time he had ever touched her, and a pleasant current thrilled through her. She held out the cross. "Gayle . . . the cross. Marilyn's cross."

[146]

For a fleeting second there was intelligence in his eyes as they passed over the object she held, and his unbandaged hand made a feeble effort at a gesture toward his neck. She put the cross carefully around his neck. "Everything's all right now, Gayle," she said. But his talk was rambling again.

The nurse tapped Ruth on the shoulder. "They will be in directly for some more X-rays." She nodded toward the portable X-ray machine standing in a corner of the room. "There's nothing else you can do for him now."

In the hallway Ruth encountered Jessie and Doctor Bashford. "Doesn't look too bad, Miss Cameron," he said. "Three ribs broken, left-hand and thumb fractured in two places. The back injury must be very painful but it is only muscular."

Ruth's eyes suddenly lost some of their fear. "Are you sure?"

"That's all the X-rays show."

"What happened?"

"Test-firing that new gun. The first burst tore the gun loose from its mounting and drove him clear through a wooden partition in back of him. He held on to the gun, luckily, or it would have sprayed lead right and left. There was a whole squadron of brass hats lining the sides for inspection."

"He's completely out of his head, doctor. I couldn't get a sensible word from him."

"Well, what do you expect? Couple of tons recoil from that gun . . . it must have been like getting kicked by a herd of wild horses. I'm going to strap up those ribs and give him a sedative. We should be able to move him out of here in a few days."

Fortunately there were no complications and after five days Gayle was able to be moved. Doctor Bashford arranged with Ruth to have a hospital bed installed in Gayle's room. "His back is going to be as creaky as an old door," the doctor told Ruth. "This bed makes it easy for you to raise and lower him."

After the ambulance brought Gayle home, Doctor Bashford drew Ruth into the living room. "I don't like putting the care of him on you, Miss Cameron, but the hospital is jammed. All he needs now is rest. See that he stays in that bed. The shock of the accident has stirred up all his battle memories. If he starts yelling at night, give him one of these." He handed her a box of tablets. "I'll drop in every day and check up on him."

He went to Gayle's room. "You wooden-headed Injin, sit in that bed and stay there till I let you up. I've just been giving directions on how to handle you." He drew closer to the bed. "That nurse . . . not bad, boy, not bad." He gave Gayle a prodigiously slow wink and left.

Ruth came in and began to tidy up the bed.

"Don't fuss around, Ruth."

She stopped at once. "I'm sorry."

"I'll holler if there's anything I want."

Ruth nodded and started for the door. "Thanks for bringing the — for Marilyn's cross."

She turned back swiftly. "Were you aware then?"

"Yes, I remember it." His eyes, filled with brooding, looked at his bandaged left hand. "Don't ever let me forget to wear that thing."

"Yes, Gayle."

She went out and brought in his laundry and began putting it in his bureau.

"Not there," he suddenly ordered. "The socks and hankies go in the other drawer."

She looked up. "I rearranged the things in the bureau while you were at the hospital, Gayle."

"Well, rearrange it back again. I want my things where I can find them."

"Very well." She began to take the things out. "Tell me where to put them."

"Never mind. Put that stuff back. I'll fix it when I can get up."

She tumbled the things into the drawers and left the room.

Two trying weeks ensued. Ruth had not known a person could be so contrary. She was eager to do all she could for Gayle, but he was as glum and unresponsive as an oyster. He was unaware of her, indifferent to her ministrations or critical of her attendance. But she felt sure it had nothing to do with her personally. He was in a world apart, sealed up in gloomy caverns of thought, and she could do nothing to bring him out of it. When he affronted her with his blunt sentences and brief requests she could forgive it. It was not the real Gayle then. It was some embittered creature superimposed by his grief for his wife or by the harrowing memories of battle experiences.

He resented his helplessness bitterly. One day when she had finished changing the linen on his bed and was putting things to rights in the room he suddenly burst out. "Why don't you get about your work? You're here to take care of Bucky . . . not me."

"I'm not neglecting Bucky," she said patiently, putting back a stray wisp of hair from her face. "I'm sorry if I disturb you, but Doctor Bashford insists on these things. It is impossible to hire a special nurse."

She hurried from the room. There was a curious pain in her throat. She was hurt and offended. Wasn't there one kind thing he could say? She sat down dispiritedly and fumbled for a handkerchief.

"Ruth!"

She stood up quickly, dabbed at her eyes and hastened to his room. He wanted to sit up. Very carefully she brought the upper half of the bed upright, adjusted the pillows, brought him a book. Over his bed hung the knife he had brought back from Guadalcanal. It was a murderous, wicked-looking thing and all out of keeping with the rest of the room. But she did not dare mention the matter to him.

"Anything else, Gayle?"

"No. That's all. Thanks, Ruth."

She turned to leave.

"Ruth!"

"Yes?"

"I . . . I'm sorry I'm this way. I mean the way I act." His face was dark with a sort of shame. "I say things I don't mean to say. They just kind of jump out. And afterwards I could kick myself."

Her eyes softened. "It's all right, Gayle," she replied.

"I keep trying," he explained, "but I can't do what I want . . . I . . . I get feeling low and black, and then any noise or talk makes me snarl like a cat." His good hand fumbled through his hair. "I was never this way before."

"I understand, Gayle."

"Take that cussing. We didn't do much of it among ourselves. But in battle you yell everything that comes to your lips. And then afterwards the words stay with you. It's like they got written into you with fire and blood, and you can't erase them."

"They will go away in time."

"It was better when I was working. If I could get up and around! If I could hammer my way out of this nightmare I'm in, these moods!"

"They're pretty bad, aren't they?"

"Sometimes I'm just closed in. It's like a black box. And I feel droopy, sad. It — it makes you feel like you want to cry. What for? What am I sad about? I'm not crippled. I'm alive. The other guys are dead." He looked up at her, suddenly self-conscious. "I'm not telling you this for sympathy. I'm not that kind of cream-puff. But it's hard enough living with myself these days. I can't understand my own mind. It must be pretty tough for whoever's around me."

"I'll try to be patient."

"You are, Ruth. I'm not. Maybe that's my trouble. I want to bust things. I feel smothered some times, smothered with thoughts and I can't crawl out from under them."

She went up to him then and taking his hand stroked it reassuringly. "They will go away, these thoughts, in time. I'm sure of it, Gayle. Keep trying. We'll all help."

[150]

He looked up at her. "Thanks, Ruth. You're right to ride the river with. — You and Hi." Something of the tenseness went out of his face as he spoke and Ruth's smile broke free. Being classified with Doctor Bashford might have been a dubious compliment for some people, but Ruth knew Gayle's estimate of Doctor Bashford, and was profoundly pleased.

She left the room singularly light of heart.

Doctor Bashford arrived and pronounced himself pleased with Gayle's progress. He removed the tape from the ribs. On his way out he paused a moment to look curiously at Ruth's shining face. "Angels without wings," he muttered, and drove off.

Ruth's heart sang for the rest of that afternoon. Then for several successive days Gayle was sullen, and silent. All her efforts to rouse him, to interest him, to lighten his mood seemed unavailing. Not a word crossed his lips. Finally Ruth's patience wore thin.

"Gayle, can't you even speak to me? I'm trying to help you, but I can't do it alone."

His face had been averted but now he suddenly faced her. His eyes were hot, tortured. "I *am* trying. Can't you see?"

There was a slight break in his voice, and his hands were shaking. Into Ruth's mind came a sudden ray of understanding. He was fighting speech, deliberately choking it down, because it would be the offensive language of his shattered nerves, the inconsiderate expression of his darkened thoughts. He knew that now, and knew that he could not control his thoughts, but he was struggling, desperately, to keep from giving them outward expression. He did not want to offend her.

"Yes, you are trying, Gayle," she acknowledged humbly. "Good soldier." She turned at the door. "You must be patient with me, too, Gayle. Sometimes I'm slow to understand."

He made no reply and she closed the door quietly and

went to her own room and sat down heavily on her bed. Caring for him was like wandering around in a dark room. You located the furniture by striking against it. One just had to go groping carefully forward, tensed all the time. Days and weeks of that. It was not a pleasant outlook for the future. Why didn't she pack up and leave? A person could not put up with this sort of thing indefinitely. But she knew she couldn't leave. And then in a vague sort of way she wondered why she couldn't. She was free. She could find work elsewhere. A delicate wrinkle furrowed her brow. She felt so harassed and irritated she could not think.

There was a medley of shrill cries from the porch. She went to the screen door. One of Manolo's swarthy youngsters was ensconced in a shell hole and Bucky was wriggling his way toward him.

"Bang! Bang! You're dead!" shrilled Bucky.

"Bing! Bang! Bing! I am not" retorted the pseudo-Jap.

"You're dead, you're dead," screamed Bucky. "Lay down, you're dead, you stinking — !"

The screen door banged as Ruth rushed out. "Bucky! What did I tell you about using that word?"

Bucky looked up, startled, in the midst of his military maneuvers. Instinctively he started a movement to the rear but Ruth caught him by the hand. "Go home," she ordered the other youngster. "Bucky is not going to play any more today."

Bucky was led reluctantly indoors. With sudden dispatch Ruth had him across her knee and brought her hand down briskly on the seat of his play suit. "Oh, good heavens!" she exclaimed, her face contorted with pain. She plunged her hand inside his trousers and brought forth a piece of flat wood. "What's this?"

"My pistol," said Bucky sorrowfully.

Her hand was stinging with pain. "Sit down there on the sofa. You don't move from the house for one solid hour."

"Aw —"

"Young man!"

Bucky subsided.

Ruth bathed her hand in cold water, till the pain had eased, and then took some sewing and sat at the other end of the sofa. After a fidgety silence Bucky inched over toward her. He tentatively fingered the edge of her house apron, looking into her face all the while for a sign of relenting. Ruth kept on with her sewing.

"Can I go out now?" he ventured.

"No."

He stood up and his head was just above her shoulder. Carefully he edged his chin over onto her shoulder and then spoke right into her ear. "I won't say it again. Honest."

"I hope not. It's a filthy word." She did not turn her head.

"If I won't say it again, then can I go out now and play?"

"No."

After a moment he returned to the attack. Burying his head on her shoulder, he kissed the base of her neck and then began to blow softly down the back of her neck. A smile twitched at the corners of Ruth's mouth but she swiftly suppressed it. Putting her sewing aside, she took Bucky in both hands and set him down beside her. "No wheedling, young man. You are just as stubborn as your father, but I'm just as determined as your mother. You don't go out till the hour is up."

Bucky's lower lip came out in a most astonishing pout.

"Ruth!"

She stood up. Good heavens, had Gayle been listening? His door was slightly ajar. She entered the room.

Gayle lifted a resentful gaze to her face. "Let Bucky go out and play."

Ruth's chin tilted up. "If you have been listening, you must realize the answer is no."

Gayle's face reddened. "He's not going to be punished for a thoughtless slip."

"Tell that to him yourself. I am leaving, right now." She spun on her heel and walked firmly from the room.

Her house apron came off and was flung on the bed. From

[153]

the closet she drew her satchel. Her hand was trembling. She began to pack. Hastily her meager belongings went into the satchel; then gradually more slowly. What was she dallying for? She sat down on the bed. The summons did not come. She was sure that Gayle would relent. She was in the right and he would soon realize it and there would be a "Ruth!" and she would go to his room, accept his apology and everything would be all right again. She waited but no call came. And suddenly she was lonely and afraid. She didn't want to leave. This was home. And she had slammed the door on herself. She could not go back on the words she had said. It would be too humiliating, and moreover, she was right about Bucky, and if Gayle could not realize that, then it was better that she leave now. If he was going to spoil the boy, she would not be a partner to it.

She began to put on the trim dark suit which she had worn when first she came to Gayle's house. Whatever was wrong with her? Why was there such a pain at the thought of leaving? Hadn't life been a mess these past weeks? Do this, do that; no thanks, no recognition. It would be like getting out of a cage to get away from that brooding introvert. She could be happy, duty-free; do what she wanted. Why did she keep straining her ears for Gayle's summons?

She sat down at her mirror. A puzzled face looked back at her. Bucky was very dear to her but she was not thinking of him just now. It was amazing. Her thought was all about Gayle! Leaving him this way. It tore at her.

Her mind began slowly to revolve over incidents, words, feelings. She cared for him, more than for Bucky! He was sick, bewildered, his mind in a chaos of questioning. The mother always cared more for the ailing child, spent on it more attention and love. That was it. Taking Marilyn's place, she was in the position of the mother of the house, and the greater needs of Gayle had touched her more, had called forth from her more of the maternal.

She went to the door and opened it. Gayle did not call. Should she go and submit? And suddenly her face paled.

She closed the door. It was acknowledgment from him she wanted! That was what the entire thing was about. She wanted him to smile, to take notice of her, to submit to her judgment in certain things — to care. Yes, that was it, she wanted that and wanted it terribly. But even without it she could be happy, she had been happy . . . as long as she could do things for him. That was what this strange reluctance to leave meant. She could not brook the idea of not taking care of him, of being separated from him, of not seeing his face.

Feverishly, fretfully she began to pace the room, denying the truth, twisting and turning like an animal caught in a trap. Se didn't know much about such things, but it didn't happen this way. Oh God, no! It was a mistake. She was imagining things.

She put on her coat, adjusted her hat, and picked up her satchel. Determinedly she went up to the door, and then that sick, afraid feeling went all through her. It was like a nausea. And starkly in her mind rose up the picture of Gayle's dark troubled countenance. The satchel slipped from her fingers and her face contorted.

"Good God, I'm in love with him!" Her lips were stiff and the words seemed spoken by someone else.

She sat slumped on the bed, her face blank with the shock of discovery. The bitterness of it! Trying to help him, and then getting enmeshed herself in his topsy-turvy life. Thank God, it might not be too late. She would see the Padre and Jessie right now and say good-by.

She walked out of the room dazedly, thinking how she had been carrying on, blissfully unaware of the thing befalling her. One found things by losing them.

Gayle's voice called out, strongly, imperiously. "Ruth! Say, Ruth!" But she walked right out of the house.

*   *   *

Her face was so pale that the Padre's eyes showed a flash of apprehension. "What's wrong, Ruth? Are you ill? Sit down. I'll call Jessie."

[155]

"No. I'm all right." She sat down. "I've just had a shock, Padre, that's all. I — I'm here to say good-by."

"It's Gayle?"

She nodded. Then she told him the details. They seemed so insignificant now.

"We had a quarrel over Bucky. I hadn't really meant to leave. I thought it would . . . well, wake him up to the fact that I'm in charge of Bucky. It turned out differently. I made a shocking discovery. I mean it shocked me. I hated to leave. It made me sick and afraid to think of leaving. I cared for Gayle . . . too much."

The Padre's eyes were very gentle as he looked at the pale face opposite him. "Are you sure of this?"

Her eyes met his very frankly. "I have been puzzling over myself for the past few weeks. The answer came today. I am sure." Sharp distress showed in her face.

"You're not very happy about it, Ruth?" His voice was filled with compassionate questioning.

"Happy?" Her eyes looked away. "Oh, no, Padre, it — it hurts. I've been loving him all these weeks and he never even sees me."

The Padre could not find words in the face of such open suffering. One seldom can. After a long time his lips parted, but he did not speak to her. It was a soliloquy, an unconscious musing aloud. "The pity of it! She undertook the care of Bucky and, later, of Gayle, out of a sense of obligation to Marilyn, and now she is tangled up in a love that —"

"Is hopeless," she finished. She turned back to him. "I know that his loyalty to his dead wife is an obsession. Marilyn was a saint. And she loved him completely. I can understand his deathless devotion to her. There is no room there for for me."

"A selfish saint?" objected the old man. "That's a contradiction in terms."

She ignored his protest. "Oh, if I had only left when I intended to . . . right after he returned from Guadalcanal. But he was so miserable, so . . . so haunted, that I wanted to help. I wanted to bring back laughter and joy to his eyes. And now I'm chained. I can't tear myself away."

"Then you aren't going to leave?"

She looked humbly at him. "I want to, but I realize now that I can't. Just to be near him will be good."

Bucky came up the walk. "Aunt Ruth," he began without preamble. She looked at the boy, a miniature of Gayle. Small, sturdy, his dark hair confusedly framing the intent young face. There was love here and in the loneliness of her loss it was sweet.

She pointed a finger at the Padre. "What do you say?"

Bucky's eyes followed the admonitory finger, and speedily grasped the implication. "Oh — good afternoon, Padre. — Aunt Ruth, Daddy says to come home. I didn't go out."

The Padre's eyes opened wide at this declaration. Ruth looked up at him with a tired droop to her lips. "At least this part will be easy. Come along, Bucky."

Ruth went directly to Gayle's room. There was that shamed, uncomfortable look on his face again. "I'm sorry, Ruth. I got out of line again. You take care of Bucky. I'll not interfere. That's final." She did not say anything, and his gaze noticed her suit. "You won't go away, will you?"

"Not as long as you need me."

"Thanks, Ruth." There was an humble sincerity in his words that touched her, and then suddenly his hand caught up the bed spread in a convulsive clutch. "Why don't you hit me with a bat or something when I sound off like that?" he blurted out.

"That's a little drastic," she said with a weak smile.

"It might wake me up," he mumbled.

An awkward silence hung over the room for a few moments, then Gayle pushed himself into a more upright position. "Doctor Bashford says I can try getting up for a little while tomorrow. Maybe I'll sleep better after I get moving around. If I sleep better I'll behave better." His brow clouded. "I dream such damnable dreams. And they stay with me all day. That's the worst of it."

She looked at him with a new awareness. There was a sweet eagerness to cup his face in her hands, to look in his troubled eyes and assure him that her love would take away all his fears and unrest. But she just stood mutely at his bedside. Only her eyes told the truth, and Gayle was not looking at her.

That night Ruth lay awake through the silent hours pondering this new reality that had come into her life. There was a sweetness in it, a terrible, suffusing ecstasy that would rise up in a wave, filling her whole body with a delicious sense of well-being. There was, too, an empty hopelessness which left her with that tight bitter constriction of the throat when one wants to cry and the solvent tears will not come. Taut, tired, she stared wide-eyed into the darkness, and no gleam of hope filtered through. Several times Gayle's voice carried to her, incoherent, mumbling in his broken dreams.

Chapter 16

THE next morning Gayle was seated on the porch when Doctor Bashford arrived.

"Well, well, the boy's up again!" greeted the older man, "How does it feel?"

"Not bad. I had a tough time last night. — If I could only sleep!"

"What do you expect? That's part of the price. We all had the heebie-jeebies after the last war. You're not normal if you don't have them after going through that mad hell." He stood up. "I'm prescribing a Tequila Monster for you every morning at breakfast."

He went out to the kitchen and told Ruth how to concoct that famous Arizona drink of tequila and grapefruit juice.

The rest of the day was a tense, brooding stretch of monotony. Gayle made it that. He came indoors and sat on the sofa, staring off wordlessly at the mountains. Occasionally he would begin to hum the refrain from "Blues in the Night." The nerves of Ruth and Nora were stretched to the breaking point. If he would only do something or say something!

But he was shut up, closed against them. There was an armor of hard, sullen defiance about him that rejected all their advances, their ministrations, all their attempts at conversation. And gradually it beat down their efforts, subdued them, made them all captive to its brooding silence.

The atmosphere of his mood hung over the house and all in it like a sulky displeasure, an impending disaster. Even Bucky felt it. His boyish efforts to interest Gayle in his games were repulsed, his inconsequent prattling was coldly disregarded, and so he turned entirely to Ruth and Nora for companionship.

Breakfast was the time that Gayle would be at his worst. His face was ravaged by restlessness and his eyes circled with the fatigue of the night. He could not sleep. Ruth solicitously inquired about the mattress, the blankets, the windows, but he pushed her inquiries roughly aside. "It's not the bed," he blurted out. "It's my head." He struck his forehead with the palm of his hand. "It's full of stuff that churns all night long. Those damnable dreams —" He stood up abruptly and left the table.

Nora made up his room each morning and reported that Gayle was smoking too much. "There's a mountain of cigarette butts in the ash tray. That's why he doesn't sleep at night, Miss Ruth. If he keeps it up he'll get galloping consumption."

Ruth brought the fact very casually to his attention and discovered that he would waken from some nightmarish dream and could not get back to sleep. He would light a cigarette. He couldn't read and he had to do something. Then he would walk the floor and the smoking and the walking would go on for hours, until sheer exhaustion claimed him, and he would lie down to sleep.

After Ruth had passed on this information to Nora, the ash tray became their barometer of how difficult the day was to be. When it was heaped high they braced themselves for a stretch of smoldering surliness, of sulphurous silence; when it was empty or carried only several stubs they sighed with relief and knew they would have merely a moody aloofness to contend with for that day. But it tried the souls of both of them. They moved in a little world of apprehension, for the tenseness kept building up, tightening their faces, filling their consciousness with that vague dread that precedes some catastrophe. It could not go on indefinitely this way, and, even though it might mean tragedy, they began to pray that something would happen, anything, so long as it would break that band of lowering, mutinous gloom that held them in its slowly tightening dark coils.

And then one day Ruth chanced to go into Gayle's room with his linen. She glanced about her, vaguely aware that something was different, something was not in its accustomed place. Her eyes lifted to the wall and with a cold little shock she saw what it was. The knife! It was gone.

She hastened out to the kitchen. "Where's Gayle?" she asked.

"Out in the back," replied Nora, gesturing with a ladle. "I heard the screen door bang a minute ago."

Ruth hurried out. There was a *ramada,* an arbor with a red-tiled roofing over it, in the rear of the house, and he was sitting motionlessly there in the deep shade, his back to her. Ruth slowed her pace to an ordinary walk as she came up to him.

"Gayle?"

He turned his head. "Oh, hello Ruth."

She drew a deep breath and looked about her. "It's nice out here today."

He turned his head away from her. "Yes." There was a pause, then, "What did you want?"

She drew closer to him. "I was just in your room. Someone took that souvenir off the wall. I was wondering if —"

"The knife? I've got it here." He held it up, looking along its heavy murderous edge with a mordant absorbed gaze. She followed his eyes and a clammy little ghost of fear quivered through her. "It needs cleaning," he said.

She noticed then the rags and can of polishing fluid in his lap. Her sensation of relief was so sudden that she felt weak. "I'll get some papers," she said. "You'll mess up your clothes and the table."

She hurried back to the kitchen.

"What's he doing?" asked Nora.

"Polishing that butcher knife." There was a tremulous breathlessness in her voice.

Nora looked at the girl, her eyes shrewd with understand-

[161]

ing. "It's getting to be like that, isn't it, Miss Ruth?" Ruth's eyes came up to hers. "You don't know what he is up to, and you're waiting for the worst."

"I'm jumpy, Nora."

"So am I!" She snapped a pinch of salt into the soup with exaggerated violence. "When you see what war does to people you know that General Sherman had the right word for it. There never was a finer gentleman in all this world than Doctor Gayle. Now look at him!" She threw two more pinches of seasoning into the soup. "Half nuts, and driving the rest of us the same. I think I'll be leaving."

"No! You wouldn't, Nora?"

"Wouldn't I?"

"But this is our share of the war. Don't you see, Nora? He faced all the fright and horror of battle to save us, now we have to save him, to make him well."

"I doubt if we can. He's just building up to something. I'm ascared to be around when it happens."

"I know, Nora. I feel as you do, but we can't be less brave than he was, can we?"

The maid looked at her for some time, the pleading in her eyes, the fragile determination of her. She sighed. "You'd have made a good soldier, I guess, Miss Ruth. Well, I'll be staying on, but the way he's been acting, something's liable to pop any minute."

Ruth put an arm about her. "We'll be able to handle it, you and I."

"I guess we can," assented the stodgy maid, but her voice was rather grim, for her thoughts of handling matters were revolving about the laying out of a corpse in a casket.

That same evening Nora was cleaning up the kitchen and turned on the radio. It was some lurid serial dealing with an indestructible hero. The sound effects made up most of the program. Terrific clattering of machine guns and cannon fire kept exploding from the radio. Suddenly Gayle burst into the kitchen, his face quivering. "Turn that off!" he demanded. Nora obediently snapped off the offending radio. "There's enough noise in this house as it is." Gayle's lips quivered as he spoke. He spun about and left the kitchen.

Nora shrugged her shoulders. "The blue fit again," she said.

Ruth nodded. "Indigo."

They both sighed and made for their rooms in the rear of the house.

*   *   *

It was deep night when Ruth awoke. The babbling from Gayle's room came loud and clear to her. She got up and looked at Bucky. He was sleeping peacefully. The babbling was louder and more incoherent than usual. Nora tapped at the door and Ruth admitted her. "Better take a look, Miss Ruth. Sounds a little wilder than usual. I'll take care of Bucky if he wakes."

Ruth put on a robe. Before Gayle's room she waited a moment and then tapped lightly. The voice kept on. She pushed open the door gently. It was dark and the voice suddenly stopped. She stepped further into the room and peered toward the bed.

A rush of hoarse curses made her whirl about. Gayle materialized from behind the door. The door still stood open but Ruth could not move a step. Her lips opened to scream but no sound came. His pajama coat was torn from top to bottom, his eyes enormously big and unseeing. From his lips fell a steady drone of broken words and bestial cries. And suddenly he moved. She saw it then. The bolo in his right hand.

Terror locked her in ice. Gayle's left arm flung around her. She was crushed up close against him. His right arm drew back, the knife point low, for a ripping upthrust.

Ruth's mind filled with death. In one fluid movement her left hand shot upwards, tangled with a string, and then had encircled his neck. Her lips pressed against his. His mouth was partly open, the lips rigid with a curse. She closed her eyes, every fiber in her body tight, anticipating the shattering plunge of the knife.

It did not come. His lips suddenly went soft beneath her caress. She opened her eyes. The wild emptiness was fading from his gaze. She withdrew her lips and kissed him again. He seemed to poise, taut, as though waiting for someone to speak, for something to happen.

There came a dull thud. The knife had slipped from his hand and the point had sunk into the floor. She disengaged her left arm slowly from about his neck. Something was cutting the palm of her hand. She opened it. Marilyn's cross had dug deep into the flesh of her palm. Slowly her fingers opened and the cross swung into place on Gayle's breast.

"Miss Ruth, Miss Ruth!" came Nora's troubled voice from the doorway. "What is it?"

"Hurry, Nora, hurry." Her voice gave a queer little break.

The reassuring bulk of the maid was swiftly at her side. "Miss Ruth . . . what did he do? You're shaking. Are you hurt?"

"No; not hurt. A nightmare. He had a nightmare."

They got him to the edge of his bed. "Watch him, Nora. . . . I'll get the medicine."

Nora gazed wide-eyed as Ruth pulled the knife from the floor and carried it from the room. Gayle sat on the edge of the bed. Tremors ran through him in spasms. There was sweat all over his face and throat.

They managed to get a tablet and some warm milk into him. Wordlessly they watched until his face slackened its tight, staring look. His head gave a sudden nod and his body lurched forward. They caught him and eased him back on to the bed. Nora went to the phone then and called Doctor Bashford, but Ruth crouched at the bedside, watching and praying.

*   *   *

Gayle opened one eye sleepily. It felt as if there was a weight on the lid. Someone was at the door. "Huh?" he inquired drowsily.

[164]

The door opened wider and Bucky made his way to the bed. "Aunt Ruth says will you eat in bed or will you get up? Good morning, daddy."

"'Morning, Bucky." He rolled over indolently and looked at the watch on the table. "Ten o'clock! And I feel as tired as all get-out. That's funny. Tell her I'll get up, Bucky." He closed his eyes. A pair of moist lips found his cheek. Gayle's eyes flew open and he regarded Bucky with a strange look for a moment. He returned the kiss in an absent-minded sort of way. "Run along now, Bucky, I'm awake."

Gayle sat up, and Bucky squirmed off the bed and manfully made his way out of the room.

Gayle's fingers felt reminiscently at his cheek and then slid over to his lips. Last night . . . had he been dreaming? There was quite a merry-go-round in his memory.

He bathed and dressed and went into the dining room. Everyone had evidently eaten. He sat down and Nora came in. She cast a quick look of scrutiny at him. "Good morning, doctor."

"Good morning, Nora." He had intercepted the look. "Where's Ruth this morning?"

"Over at the neighbors. She and Miss Jessie made some cowboy things for Bucky."

"Cowboy things?" She placed some food before him. "What's the idea of the cowboy things?"

She looked at him in contemptuous wonder. "Where have you been living the past two weeks?" she asked. "It's rodeo." She flicked a gesture toward the morning paper. "Don't you ever read it?"

"My gosh, I forgot," he said sheepishly. "I didn't sleep very well last night. I'm still a little fuzzy."

The outer door opened and closed.

"Nora?" called Ruth.

"Yes?"

"Is Mr. Wade up?"

"He's in here eating."

Ruth came in the dining room her arms holding a number of gay-colored bits of clothing. There was a quick inter-change of glances between her and Nora, and then the maid disappeared into the kitchen. Ruth's eyes went swiftly over Gayle's countenance. "Good morning, Gayle. Bucky's going western today. Wait till you see him in these togs."

"You're going to the rodeo?"

"Yes. Jessie will take us in her car."

"Mind if I go?"

"Not at all."

"Let's go in my car. I've got more gas coupons than Jessie."

"That will be fine. I'll go over and tell her."

Gayle detained her with a gesture. "Send Nora. I want to talk to you a minute."

"Very well." She dispatched Nora with the message.

Gayle pushed away from the table and lit a cigarette. "My head is kind of muddled this morning, but last night something happened to me." He searched her face. There were bluish shadows beneath her eyes, but her expression told him nothing. "Did I dream?"

"Did you? What was it about?"

He ran his hand through his hair and over the back of his neck. He slumped forward with his forearms on his knees and his eyes focused on the floor. "I was fighting the battle of the Ridge again. That must have been a dream. It was the scrap where I got this." He lifted his left arm and the short sleeve of his sport shirt slid away disclosing the broad, blue, crescent scar beneath the biceps.

"Oh," said Ruth her face filled with distress. She came over and inspected the livid mark. Her fingers went forward and gently touched it. Suddenly aware of his curious eyes, her fingers dropped away. "It must have been an ugly gash," she commented and went over to a chair and sat down.

"I was fighting the Jap who did this," continued Gayle, "putting the finishing touches on him. . . . That was a dream . . . and then — and then you were there, kissing me." He looked up, his eyes puzzled. "Was that a dream?"

His gaze was desperately intent on her, but Ruth gave

him no help. There was no betraying blush, no word of explanation. She was withdrawn, an outsider listening to a narrative. He must have dreamed the entire thing. He fumbled back into the maze of last night's memories and suddenly an insignificant detail stood out with amazing clearness and importance. He jumped to his feet. "Stay here a minute," he ordered and strode from the room. She heard his bedroom door slam. In a moment he was back. "There's a triangular hole in the floor. The knife fell there. It wasn't a dream!"

"No. All of it wasn't a dream." Ruth lowered her head.

"Why did you kiss me? What was I doing? Did I frighten you?"

"Yes, terribly. You took hold of me. You thought I was the man — the one. . . . Oh, you had the knife and were going to use it."

"My God!" breathed Gayle, and he sank slowly into a chair.

"I knew I must awaken you and feared to startle you. Somebody once told me that if you waken a person suddenly from a nightmare it can do great harm. I don't know if it's true. There wasn't much time to think. I just did it. Maybe I thought, too, that a sign of love would drive out the hate that was filling your mind." Her eyes came up to his. "You mustn't put any other construction on it than that. I had to do something at once. You were going to thrust with that knife."

"I might have killed you," he said slowly. "Do you realize that, Ruth?" His voice was tremulous with emotion and his eyes carried sudden comprehension for her heroism.

His questions were leading her where she did not want to go. "That dream, Gayle . . . does it come often? What is it all about?"

His eyes were fastened on her with strange intentness and she had to repeat the question before he replied. He spoke then in a strange monotone, his eyes fastened on her face, like a small boy reciting a lesson he had got by heart. "That

Jap cut my arm and I put four slugs from my .45 in his gut. He went down. My pistol was empty. I still had my knife. I grabbed him and stabbed. It wedged between the ribs. The blood splotched into my face like ketchup. I had to jerk the knife out. Then I stuck him, again and again." He shook his head and his voice became plaintive. "I didn't have to do that. He was finished. It wasn't square . . . I didn't have to do that."

His eyes broke away from her and his voice took a more normal tone. "I've dreamed that fight a thousand times. It was beginning to fade and the accident at the Consolidated started it up again."

"Don't you think you should leave that work, Gayle?" put in Ruth quietly. "Firing guns is not the way to get rid of these battle memories. Your mind can't heal, till you do. It's your duty to your country to fit into the social scheme again. Doctors are so badly needed just now."

There was a rather long silence. Bucky walked in on them, very self-conscious of his western attire.

"Well, look at Billy the Kid!" exclaimed Ruth as Bucky ran into her arms. She looked at Gayle and said in a low voice. "You owe it to Bucky too, Gayle."

"You're right, Ruth. And in addition I rather think I owe it to you. It hasn't been easy with me these past weeks, has it?" He read the truth in her quickly lowered eyes. "But you didn't complain." His voice was suddenly low, worshipful. "You're a grand little girl, Ruth."

It was the first really kind thing he had ever said to her and she felt wondrously weak. "Here Bucky, let me fix that." She tucked a flyaway shirttail into his trousers.

"I'll phone in my resignation tomorrow," promised Gayle. He stood up and began to walk restlessly about, but there was something of his former vigor and decision in his step. His thoughts marshaled themselves in quick, sure coherence. For the first time in many weeks he was feeling like himself. He stopped beside her chair. "Think you can stand me lounging around for a few more weeks? I intend to really rest, I mean the right way . . . forgetting things, clear out my mind, so I can get back to work at the clinic."

"Wouldn't the ranch be better? Bucky could go along."

"No. Home is the best place."

He watched as she tugged and tied and smoothed Bucky's gear into order, admiring the play of interest over her mobile features as the boy questioned, complained, and preened himself.

Nora came in to tell them that Jessie would be over in a few minutes.

"I'll get my hat," said Ruth jumping to her feet.

"Are you intending to wear that dress?" asked Gayle.

She stopped and cast a quick look at it. It was not particularly gay. She colored. "I'll change it if you don't like it."

"You've got to go western, Ruth, don't you know that? They have a portable jail — the hoosegow — if you're not in western togs they put you in the hoosegow until you pay a fine."

"Oh!" Her face filled with disappointment. "I don't have —"

"Marilyn had an outfit." With studied deliberation Gayle drew a key from his pocket. "There's a trunkful of her things around. I'll haul it to your room."

Ruth had a difficult minute. Sudden joy and bewildered delight danced in her eyes. A flood of grateful words rushed to her lips clamoring for expression. It took effort to choke it all down. "You . . . you will not mind, Gayle? I . . ."

He unlocked the door of the room adjoining his. "There is no one more fit to wear her things than you, Ruth."

*   *   *

People in the rodeo crowds turned to look at the saturmine-faced, broad shouldered westerner, with the graceful woman in a bewitching "cow-girl" outfit at his side. Her crown of honey blond hair made a queenly fillet for the proud little head that just topped Gayle's shoulder.

"Those togs are just perfect on you, Ruth," he told her.

That day was pure bliss for Ruth.

Chapter 17

A SPIRIT of joyousness had come to three members of the Wade household. Nora sang as she worked; Bucky occupied himself contentedly with his toys; Gayle's step was light and quick. Ruth alone seemed unaffected by the general buoyancy. With Nora and Bucky she was content and happy, but as soon as Gayle put in an appearance her manner became restrained, her speech more subdued.

Gayle was faithfully following out his program of lounging around, but it was invariably performed in the immediate vicinity of Ruth. If she was at work in the kitchen he would be leaning against the door jamb or straddling a chair; if she was engaged in cleaning he would sprawl out on the sofa and try to out-talk the vacuum cleaner; if she took some sewing out on the porch he would lounge in the glider. And his eyes were everlastingly upon her.

All of which would have been very sweet to Ruth under normal circumstances, but, things being as they were, it was merely a continuous strain on her self-control. His propinquity made it so much harder to keep a check on her feelings.

The afternoons brought temporary relief. Gayle would saunter off to the Padre's portico. She could see them from the porch, and often wondered what were the topics of these afternoon conversations. Invariably he would return, looking very thoughtful, and would go directly to his room and close the door. By supper time he would be in circulation again and very much underfoot for the rest of the evening.

After the episode of the nightmare, Gayle had come to

some very surprising conclusions, but he spoke about them to no one. In a slow, gradual way, he was evaluating them, testing their authenticity, pondering and — waiting. He felt a curious hesitancy about coming to a decision for he knew now how easily one could err by precipitation and how inadequate one's own abilities were.

His afternoon visits to the Padre were made up of very frank discussions. The very first question he proposed made the Padre aware that the old problem was stirring in the young man's mind and that his dark experiences of war were beginning to fade.

"Padre," he began, "am I free to marry?"

"You know the answer to that, Gayle. Death dissolves the marriage bond."

"Yes, yes; of course, I know. But I don't think that applies to me. I mean, because of what has happened to me . . . Marilyn's disbelief in that 'til death do us part,' and the way she has taken to remind me of it."

"Well, you may feel that way about it, Gayle. But you must know that, objectively, you are not bound. You are free to marry whenever you wish."

"I don't feel I'm free."

"Your loyalty still holds you?"

"Yes."

The Padre's voice was patient, understanding. " 'It is not good for man to be alone,' " he quoted.

Gayle's eyes came up quickly. "What about yourself?"

The Padre smiled. "That's called '*Retorqueo argumentum*,' turning my statement back on me. Well, Gayle, a life of single-blessedness is not the natural order of things, but one can give up a natural privilege for a higher, a supernatural one. The priest is the father of many children . . . spiritual children . . . and it's such a full time job that to do it perfectly rather excludes natural fatherhood."

"I can understand that. But it looks kind of rugged to me. Do you find it a satisfactory sort of existence?"

"Very much so."

[171]

"This single-blessedness . . . What's the set-up in the life of a priest?" For a few minutes the Padre's eyes were filled with a suspicious thoughtfulness, but he resolutely detached his mind from his thoughts and began to outline in detail the required studies, the work, the routine, the hardships, the reward, the ideals. "It's very similar in many respects," he concluded, "to the life of a doctor. I mean, of course, a doctor who finds in his profession not merely a gainful occupation but one of the highest and most helpful callings a man can follow."

Gayle lapsed into thought. "I often wondered why this man was rich, that one poor, this fellow happy, that one always hitting the hard edge of misfortune. There must be different ways for us because we are all different; and the One who made us knows that." He looked up. "Happiness didn't teach me anything, Padre; love didn't either. It was loss that hit me between the eyes — "

"That's the story of every man," said the Padre quietly, "and if you were to tell what you know to someone who is as yet uncrossed by suffering he would be respectfully sympathetic, but it wouldn't mean a thing to him personally."

"You've got to be hit before you learn that the law is for you," said Gayle, "and you will get hit because it's the law of life. Loss and suffering — we've got to face it and learn how to take it. I believe I do know the general answer now, and I guess the rest will be added as I go along." He was silent a while, and, when he spoke again, the meditative mood was gone, and there was decision in his voice. "I'm going back to the clinic soon. I am beginning to feel more like myself again. But when I go into the work this time, I intend to know what I'm going to do and I'll stay with it."

"These are important days for you then, Gayle. Don't jump. Keep clear to the main point."

"And that is?"

"The reason underlying all that has happened to you."

"You mean what it is that Marilyn wants?"

The Padre nodded.

[172]

"It's rather obvious, isn't it?" said Gayle.

"Is it?"

"Why, yes. At least the first two . . . " His voice trailed off into silence. After some time he resumed. "The more I think of it, the more I believe they are interrelated somehow, progressive." He stood up. "Well, I'm not driving my conclusions right into action, Padre. I'm waiting for things to work out. The design is coming clear."

There was a gratified look deep in the Padre's eyes as Gayle sauntered away.

* * *

For several days Gayle went about with a preoccupied air. He still followed Ruth about the house like her shadow, but his eyes were not uninterruptedly fixed on her every movement. Several times she detected a secretive look about him, and she began to wonder what was going on in that dark head.

It was during her sewing hour that Gayle unfolded his proposal. "What are you sewing on now, Ruth?" he asked.

"A dress. Something different." An engaging pink slowly came into her cheeks. "It's going to be slinky."

He smiled. "Let's see. She held it up, giving it a flick here and there to display it fully. It was merely a flimsy bit of gay material. "That's bright enough," nodded Gayle judiciously. His jaw dropped as he saw the cloth's skimpy dimensions. "Is that all there's to it?"

Ruth's self-consciousness merged into a quick trill of laughter. "This is only *one piece* of it, silly. Jessie's doing the other part."

"Oh, that's different. That piece wouldn't make a bathing suit. Will the whole dress be finished by Saturday?" Her needle stopped and she looked up inquiringly.

"We're going out for supper Saturday, just you and I, to the Desert Moon," he said.

So that was what had been in the back of his head these past days. Her eyebrows went up in an entrancing way. "A morale builder?" she asked.

"You could use a little laughing, couldn't you, Ruth . . . and some dancing?"

"Oh, dancing!" Her eyes sparkled. "It has been so long . . . "

"We'll re-learn together."

Ruth put down the trembling exultancy that threatened to invade her voice. "Jessie may come too?" she managed demurely.

The eagerness suddenly vanished from Gayle's face. "Good Lord, Ruth," he complained. "This is the twentieth century! Do we have to have a chaperone?" He drew out the last word disappointedly.

Ruth gave him a prim look. "I thought Jessie was a friend. Do you only remember your friends when you are in trouble?"

"Sorry, Ruth. Of course you're right. Would she like to go?"

"If my morale needs building, how about hers? I am caring for a convalescent; she has a permanent invalid on her hands."

"Very thoughtful, aren't you?" said Gayle with an indulgent smile. "Invite her then, and don't tell her how I had to be reminded. — Say, do you always fix your hair that way, piled up on top of your head?"

She nodded brightly. "Upsweep. It's cool that way and clean."

"Clean?"

Her eyes twinkled. "If you don't wash your neck, it shows."

He laughed but his gaze was intent on the straight white white column of her neck. A girl would have to have the right sort of head, neck, and shoulders to get away with that kind of hair arrangement. He decided that Ruth was one girl that did.

She set down her sewing and checked off items on her fingers. "I'll see Jessie now and find out — one, will the dress be finished by Saturday; two, will she join us."

"Three," mimicked Gayle, "will she dance with me?"

"Four," continued Ruth imperturbably, "you will ask her that question yourself."

* * *

The dress was finished by Saturday and that evening a very expectant trio set forth in Gayle's car for the Desert Moon. There was a table reserved for them, and after cocktails Gayle danced with Ruth and then with Jessie. His face was wreathed in wonderment as he led Jessie back to their table. "Say, you're a surprise, Jessie," he declared drawing out her chair. "You dance like a feather."

Ruth smiled at them. "Jessie does a great many things well, Gayle."

They ordered some Old Fashioned's. A girl with vivid red hair was singing a song.

"What a lovely voice!" commented Jessie.

A burst of applause indicated the completion of the song. The girl made her way to their table. Gayle stood up. "Hello, Sheila!"

"Hello . . . Gayle!" The way she said his name was a caress. There was a soft shiny look in her eyes.

"Some friends of mine," said Gayle, taking her hand. "Jessie, Ruth — Miss Sheila Starr."

Sheila smiled at them and accepted a chair. Her eyes came back to Gayle. — "It's been a long time, Gayle."

He nodded. "December seventh. It was the war did it, Sheila. But I'm out of it now. Discharged."

"I know." She toyed with her glass. "I was wondering if you would ever get in circulation again."

"It wasn't as bad as all that. I'm very much in good health, thanks to excellent food and nursing." He nodded toward Ruth. "My sister-in-law was the cook and nurse responsible."

Sheila's eyes gave Ruth a sustained appraisal. The music struck up, and Gayle looked inquiringly at Jessie. "Shall we?" Jessie rose with alacrity.

Sheila watched them merge into the throng of dancers.

and for one forgetful moment she let the love and longing within her show. And suddenly she was aware of Ruth's silent scrutiny. She gave a hard little laugh. "Guess it sticks out all over me, doesn't it?" she said ruefully.

"I'm truly sorry," came Ruth's soft reply.

Sheila directed a searching look at her. The compassion, the understanding behind her simple words were so deep and true. "Don't tell me that you, too . . . " She gave that brittle little laugh again. Ruth's face colored deeply at the swiftness and sureness with which her jealously guarded secret had been uncovered by this stranger. "Don't mind me," said Sheila with rough sympathy. "Misery loves company — welcome!"

Ruth's embarrassed gaze lowered to the table cloth and some of the cynicism went out of her companion's blue eyes. "You don't look much like the pictures I've seen of your sister," observed Sheila in a more dispassionate tone. "Of course, a little red dye on your hair and a shoulder length bob would change the picture. Probably make you look like her twin. What kind of a gal was she, anyhow?"

Ruth's voice was reminiscent. "Marilyn was everything good. She was too fine, too good for this earth."

"So God took her," drawled Sheila. "The dear saint!"

Ruth's eyes came up defiantly. "She was a saint."

Sheila's laugh was tinged with bitterness. "That's not the word I have for her!" She lit a cigarette and her eyes drifted moodily out toward the dance floor. Suddenly her eyes came back to Ruth. "You know what you're up against in loving Gayle, don't you? Your dead sister! Ordinarily, you and I could settle this matter one way or the other. One of us would have Gayle and the other could go fetch. But you and I are out of this. That sister saint of yours put some kind of string on him that he can't break. She won't let go. She's ruined a good man for anybody else."

"I know how it is," replied Ruth understandingly. "Gayle is there, all the things that draw a woman's love, but when you get close to him there is no soul. Marilyn has charmed it away. She still holds him — the real Gayle. And so you just love on, helplessly, drearily."

Over Sheila's face flowed a look of surprise. How could this quiet girl read her so truly, how could she get so much passion in those simple words? "With me, it's a fire, a slow-eating fire," confided Sheila. "And seeing him, or away from him, it's just the same. I've cursed your sister a thousand times. And yet, being a woman, I suppose I'd do the same thing as she did, if I could — hold him for real keeps." She smashed out her cigarette in a splatter of sparks. The music stopped.

Gayle drew up a chair for Jessie. "How about a dance, Sheila, after a drink?" Sheila's face lit up with swift acquiescence. "I'm warning you," he went on, "you'll have to step some. Jessie is really a dancer." His admiring gaze fixed itself on her. "How do you manage to stay away from the bright lights, Jessie? You love all this, don't you?"

Jessie drew herself up with mock severity. "Duty first," she proclaimed.

"Oh yes . . . the Padre," replied Gayle with a smile. "I can understand your devotion. He looked at Sheila. "The Padre is Jessie's brother, Sheila. You must visit with him some time. He's got the keys to a lot of things we are looking for. You know I used to think this life of single-blessedness was a sheer frustration. He has shown me differently."

"You'd make an attractive monk," said Sheila.

"The kind without socks?"

She refused to meet his effort at lightening the conversation and maintained a sullen silence. The smile faded from Gayle's face.

"You don't need a monastery," he said. "You can carry your singleness, your solitude with you, if you want."

"I suppose. But who wants to?" Sheila's taut words forced his gaze to meet hers.

"There are some who do," came Gayle's quiet response.

"I'll live but once," declared Sheila. "I want all of life

I can get, singly and doubly. When I die I'll be dead an awful long time. Love, lights, laughing — who knows if there is anything after it? Death is the final curtain."

Ruth felt that Sheila's blunt words were a plea for the both of them and her heart went out strongly to the frank-eyed girl.

Gayle's reply was measured, slow. "I wouldn't know about that." He sipped at his drink. "Of course, we try to get all the joy out of life that we can, but life isn't just peaches and cream. It's a pretty rugged business in spots. Suffering, loss, unhappiness . . . and nobody escapes it. There must be a reason for all that. I know that much." He looked up. "Getting serious, aren't we? Let's dance, Sheila."

As they moved off among the swaying couples Jessie noticed that, over Sheila's white shoulder, Gayle's eyes would dart a glance at Ruth. But Ruth did not notice. She was twirling her cocktail glass, gazing unseeingly into its rotating emptiness.

*   *   *

Back in her apartment, Sheila sat before the mirror, brushing out the lustrous maze of her hair. Somehow or other it had finally reached him, the fact that she loved him. If only she had not pulled that stupid trick of imitating his dead wife. That had almost ruined things completely. It still was an awful smeary mark on her slate as far as Gayle was concerned. The gallant fool! He couldn't bring himself to talk of these things. He had brought that lovely sister-in-law along and let her sit there like a bump on a log. Why? Was that his way of telling her, Sheila, that no woman could claim him? Or was it just a subterfuge to enable him to pick up where he had broken off? He was interested in her. How far it went or could go she could not say. It was that dead witch and her obsession that still had a strangle hold on him. She snapped off the light. There was nothing to do now but be herself. Let her love talk. She wanted to sit here and think it over . . . in the dark.

The sight of her golden red hair brought memories that cut and burned.

*　　*　　*

Ruth hastily undressed and got into bed. Gayle had not planned the party for her. She knew that now. He must have seen a great deal of Sheila at one time and she could understand why. There were some similarities, external ones, to Marilyn. Evidently Gayle had extricated himself from that affair before it was too late, but Sheila had been hurt. She was in love with Gayle. Why had he contrived that party tonight? Was he already seeing so much of Marilyn in her that he wanted to make a comparison between her and Sheila? To see which of them was most like Marilyn? Was it possible that he had been disillusioned about Sheila and that he wanted to forestall a repetition by comparing them? One thing was sure. Marilyn was still the object of his devotion. His almost complete neglect of her during the evening, his eyes as they wandered over Sheila's hair showed her most clearly what still held him.

She rolled over and buried her face in the pillow. "O Marilyn!" she moaned and it was half prayer, half complaint.

*　　*　　*

Gayle accompanied Jessie to her door. She turned and looked at him. "Was it a success, Gayle?" His face registered surprise. — "The experiment," added Jessie.

He gave a slow smile. "I didn't think it was that transparent. Yes; I think so. Nothing like putting one's cards on the table — face up."

"That should make for a clear decision."

"It's practically made. I was just testing. Will you tell the Padre I'll be over a little earlier tomorrow afternoon." Jessie nodded. "And Jessie . . . what I said about the Padre tonight I meant. That wasn't part of the experiment."

"Of course, I know. Goodnight, Gayle, and thanks for the dances — flatterer!"

Gayle put the car into the garage and hastened into the house. There were some questions he wanted to ask Ruth. A light was burning in the living room but the house was silent. Ruth had gone to bed.

He went to his room then, but he lay quietly awake. Faces, words, questions flitted through his mind. Marilyn . . . her fingers interlaced with his, watching together the pastel pink light fading from the Catalinas . . . the delicate sound of her voice on the final consonants . . . "till the leaves of the Judgment Book unfold." Sheila . . . the love-light in her wide eyes like a flame . . . "I want all of love . . . singly and doubly." Ruth . . . the low, broad, white brow and proud little head . . . the self-possessed endearing ways . . . her lips on his. The Padre . . . his chiseled features . . . the serene sufficiency of him . . . the personal adequacy . . . alone, eminently sure of himself . . . the pillar of a cloud to wanderers in life's grim desert —

He realized calmly now how much all of them had helped find the key, the answer to his problem; and how one of them *was* that answer. He became drowsy, his eyes closed, and he fell at last into restful slumber. . . .

Chapter 18

G AYLE went to town early the next morning, had a long talk with Doctor Bashford at the clinic, and then paid a visit to his lawyer. There was a satisfied air about him as he left the lawyer's office and walked up Congress Street. He had parked his car on a side street. In front of Penney's Department Store he stopped for the red traffic light — in Tucson pedestrian traffic moves with the light.

A comely, wholesome young woman was at his side.

"Hel-lo, lover," she cooed.

Gayle turned a startled glance at the woman and then felt very foolish. Her arms were outstretched, fingers wiggling enticingly, toward a little boy across the street. The man holding the boy set him down and glanced at the traffic light.

It happened with stark swiftness. The boy, his face shining with the absorption of his joy, toddled away from the curb, his arms outstretched ecstatically toward his mother. A car swung in a right turn from Sixth Avenue. Brakes squealed. A scream pierced Gayle's ears. And then everybody was piling across the street as traffic froze. A prowl car, halfway up the street, sirened its way to the accident.

The mother had the boy in her arms, kissing and fondling the legs that drooped so disjointedly over her arm.

Gayle elbowed his way through the crowd. "I'm a doctor," he said to the policeman.

"O.K., doc," and the officer cleared a path for him.

Gayle's fingers swiftly went over the dangling legs. He turned to the officer. "Both of them fractured. Get us to the hospital at once."

"O.K., doc." The policeman bulled his way to his fellow-officer who, notebook in hand, was interviewing the greenish-faced driver of the accident car. "Bill, I'm running the kid and the doc to the hospital. Be back in a jiff."

"Roll 'em, Tom."

As the policeman assisted the mother and wailing child into the car, a woman at Gayle's elbow let out a gusty sigh. "The poor mother!"

Gayle looked at her, his face stiff with anger. "The poor kid, if you ask me," he retorted.

The woman gave him a frosty stare. "I didn't ask you!"

Gayle slammed the door, and the car, with the siren going full blast, sped through the traffic. The hospital was just ten minutes distant. The child was rushed to the emergency room and Gayle assisted the resident doctor in reducing the fractures. As soon as the essential work had been finished, Gayle hurried out to the anteroom. The child's mother was waiting, her face an unlovely sight with its fear and tears. He patted her shoulder. "It's all right, madam. The fractures are clean, simple. In a few weeks he will be as good as new. There's nothing to worry about."

She lifted a grateful face. "Thank you, thank you for telling me. I was worried." Relief was shining through the eyes all wet with tears.

Gayle patted her shoulder again, awkwardly, and could find no words. All the way home his thoughts kept revolving about the misery of pain that he had seen in the mother's face, and then back to the exclamation of the woman at his elbow — "O the poor mother!" It puzzled him. His own reaction had been a swift stab of pity for the child. It seemed the most natural thing on earth. Yet that woman's words, and then the mother's anguish. There was a vague awareness in him that this was something that he had to get to the bottom of, that he was on the threshold of an important fact.

He came into the house hurriedly, irritated that he could not find the answer to that woman's strange reaction to the accident.

"Where's Ruth?" he asked Nora.

"I saw her go into your room a moment ago."

He pushed open the door. Ruth was kneeling before his bureau, a variegated collection of his belongings on the floor about her.

"Now what?" he asked.

"I wasn't disturbing it, Gayle," she protested. "I was just checking. There are a lot of your things that need mending."

"My things — mending? There are a lot of your things that need buying." She turned a look of slow inquiry on him, and then, as his meaning reached her, she looked self-consciously at her dress. "You do enough without having to sew your own dresses." He handed her a small envelope. "I went to town to pick this up for you."

She drew out the small book and her face filled with amazement. "A savings account!" she exclaimed. "But, Gayle, I — I can't take this."

"You'll have to. It's yours." She looked up at him seeking the meaning of his words. "I guess you must have thought me first cousin to old man Scrooge himself; but, — well, since Marilyn's death I've done a lot of things that looked strange to other people, I guess. A lot of extraordinary things happened to me. I just played my cards the best I could. I tried to do the right thing."

"Yes, yes, Gayle. I understand. But what has that to do with all this money in my name?"

"Before I went overseas I arranged with my lawyer that the balance of your monthly wages would be put to your credit in the bank. What you received was only a fraction of it." He gestured toward the bank book. "That money is yours."

Perhaps she sensed the motives that had prompted this curious arrangement, and so did not probe for the complete explanation. "But Gayle, I don't need this.

"I won't feel right if you refuse it."

"But I have all I need — all the money. My expenses are small."

"So is your wardrobe. It would make me a lot happier if you took this, Ruth. I feel like a dunderhead every time I think of the stupid way I handled matters."

She understood then that there had been doubt about her in this strange arrangement, that he was deeply regretful of it. There would always be reproach in his mind if she did not accept.

"Very well, Gayle. And I'm grateful." She gathered up an armful of clothing.

"Wait a minute, Ruth. There's something else I wanted to talk about."

"Yes?"

He had sauntered over to the window and for a moment his gaze was abstracted. Far down at the end of the garden the palo verde tree was a cloud of diaphanous green. The countless lacelike tendrils of its branches were woven together, like spun silk, into a haze of green chiffon. He thought back to a May day with the tree bending beneath a drift of butter-gold blossoms, and the heart of him wondered if there were but one brief maying time in life and after that a long sere autumn withering away into winter's death. His words came slowly. "I saw an accident this morning."

"In town?"

He turned. "Yes; I was standing on the corner of Congress and Sixth." He narrated the incident. "I hurried over. The mother scooped up the boy. The wheels had broken both legs and they — "

"Oh, the poor mother!" exclaimed Ruth with deep feeling.

Gayle looked at her sharply. The identical words of that woman in the crowd! "Why did you say that?" he demanded.

"What, Gayle?" She had been absorbed in the tragic incident.

" 'Oh the poor mother'? — It was the kid that was hurt. Aren't male children supposed to be sensitive to pain?"

Ruth's face took on an introspective look. "I don't know why I said it, Gayle. It was instinctive. I think any woman would feel that way. The mother did not have the physical hurt, but I'm sure her pain was greater. A good mother is that way, Gayle. The child's need is hers, only hers is greater."

A great light broke over Gayle. Women knew these things by instinct. A man had to have them hammered into him and then blue-printed to make it clear. This was the little piece needed to round out his conclusions.

Impulsively he put his hands on Ruth's shoulders. "Thanks, Ruth, thanks a lot. I've got that clear now." She looked at him in dainty bewilderment. "Go right ahead with that you are doing. I'm going to see the Padre. I'll be back." He gave her a curiously shy, half-repressed sort of look and Ruth could have sworn it was meant to be affectionate.

He banged the door.

Several pairs of socks slipped dejectedly from her hands. "Will he ever be normal again?" she sighed.

* * *

Gayle spread his hands. "Padre, it's all as clear to me now as the palms of my hands. The last appearance of the perfume was also a warning, a warning not to send Ruth away. Marilyn wants Ruth to take care of Bucky. And more, to take care of me . . . to be my wife."

The Padre's face screwed up a trifle. "This could be wishful thinking," he warned.

"It could. But look. When I was about to kiss Sheila, the perfume appeared. It was warning me, and I was filled with a feeling of revulsion. There was nothing like either of those things when Ruth kissed me."

"That would just show disapproval and approval. You are carrying approval to its extreme limit — marriage."

"There's more to it than that, Padre. Listen." He quickly recounted the accident he had witnessed in town and the ensuing events.

"I don't see anything extraordinary in that," said the Padre. "Surely, you have always been aware of the depth of a mother's love for her child."

[185]

"Of course, Padre. I've probably seen a thousand examples of it, but today for the first time it registered sharply with me. It is almost an identification between mother and child. That's what hit me. Mentally she suffers what the child does physically, and added to it is the grief that she cannot actually have the pain instead of the child." He paused. "It's strange, isn't it? These seemingly casual happenings. How often they carry a hidden meaning, an answer for us."

"If we would ponder them we would find the meaning," said the Padre quietly. "Life is an intricate pattern of such seemingly insignificant details."

" 'We learn from events as they occur,' " quoted Gayle softly, and glancing up he caught a satisfied look on the lined old face before him. "I haven't forgotten, you see, Padre. I have given some thought to this event and it has come clear to me — the meaning in back of it. Marilyn wants a *mother* for Bucky. It would be agony for her to see Bucky go through life without someone to soothe and direct and love him, without the word of mother ever on his lips, except as some remote memory."

The Padre's face clouded. "That's a quick decision, Gayle."

"Yes, but I've been thinking a great deal before this ever happened. It was just the one little piece needed to round out the puzzle."

"All of what you say is possible, of course — but do you love Ruth?"

"Yes. It started — well, who knows where interest stops and love begins? But after that — experience — the nightmare — I have been studying her. She's — she's — well, there's a light and joy in her that has brought me back to life."

Over the joy illuminating his face there fell a gradual shadow. "There's only one thing that spoils it all."

"What might that be?"

Gayle's face was profoundly grave and several times he looked hesitantly up at the Padre and then down again at the ground before he ventured a reply. "I'm afraid to go into this."

"Afraid?" echoed the Padre blankly. He studied the intent face before him. "Afraid of what?"

"Love takes away a man's defenses, Padre; it opens you up wide to everything hard and bitter. Life, disillusionment, pain, loss. I've been through it all once."

After a long pause the Padre spoke. "You have learned a great deal, Gayle, and it has been the hard way. But your new knowledge is worthless if it has made you so small that you are afraid to face life. In fact, if the profits of experience have made you so cynical that you withdraw into a shell of protective selfishness, like an armadillo, you have learned nothing. You have only thickened and deepened the selfishness that will keep you a stranger on earth as long as you live."

Gayle's head came up slowly. "You misunderstand, Padre. I'm not thinking of myself," he protested. "Really I'm not."

"Of whom then are you thinking?"

"Of Ruth. I know now that if I awaken in her a love for me it will expose her to all the things that I have suffered. I am afraid to venture that. Things could happen to me and — oh God, can't you understand, Padre? I don't want her to go through the same kind of hell that I had."

"Even if it means that you have to go through another and newer hell — possessing a living earthly love and yet living alone and without it?"

Gayle's voice was low. "Yes, even if it meant that."

It was a long time before the Padre spoke again but when he did there was authority and assurance in his voice. "What you have learned, Gayle, is far greater than the sufferings through which that knowledge came to you. I can understand your hesitation, your fear. But aren't you trying to look into the future? Life will have to come to her too. Who knows but she may already have met it? I rather think her vision of life and its eventualities is as wide as yours. At any rate, I'd let her be the judge of her own fate."

"You think there would be no selfishness in my asking her?" There was eager hope in his eyes.

"It would be selfish not to ask her," responded the Padre quietly. "She may be aware already that great suffering can come to a person because of love. It is possible that she may be willing in spite of that to chance all the disaster that love for another might entail. At any rate, it will be her decision, Gayle."

"Yes, and Ruth would probably be able to face any loss a whole lot more sensibly than I did," said Gayle with a faint thoughtful smile. "I'll ask her then, Padre, to marry me — and you think it's all right?"

The old man's face was creased with a network of wrinkles as laughter awoke deep in his eyes. "I? Ask *her!*"

Gayle jumped to his feet. "Here I go!"

He strode joyously down the path.

*   *   *

Ruth was seated at the dining room table, a newspaper and a collection of ration books spread out before her. There was a frown of concentration on her brow as she consulted the rationing news column in the paper, added up points in the ration books and jotted notes on a slip of paper.

Gayle came in, his face alight with purpose. "Ruth," he said taking up a position at the end of the table.

"Yes, Gayle," she murmured in a faraway voice, without lifting her eyes.

He waited for her to look up, but she continued consulting the newspaper and adding up points. "That son of yours will be barefoot soon," she murmured. "No shoes . . . and no points."

"Ruth."

"And you" — she checked an item — "drink too much coffee. All of Nora's coffee points went down your throat."

There was a sudden crash.

"Oh my goodness!" ejaculated Ruth, jumping like a startled fawn.

Gayle had kicked a chair violently across the room.

"Gayle!" she cried, "what in heaven's name?"

"Do I have to pull the roof down to talk to you?" he demanded.

Ruth picked up the chair solicitously. There were several scratches on it and the front crosspiece was broken. "Look what you've done! You can't replace things any more. You're as irresponsible as Bucky."

He seized the chair. "I'll get the blamed thing fixed." He slammed it down. "I want to talk to you."

Ruth sat down again to her work. "Why couldn't you wait a moment? I'm dizzy with blue stamps and red stamps."

"Ruth, will you marry me?"

"If you knew how difficult it is to keep this — merciful heavens!" Her head jerked upright. "What did you say?"

"Will you marry me?"

"I heard . . . I thought that's what I heard." Her eyes were twin worlds of bewilderment but her heart was thrumming madly. And then in the very midst of that moment of elation a cold little devil rose up in a corner of her brain and jumped her mind back to last night's experience. Gayle had compared her then to the surface Marilyn . . . Sheila. He had found that there was more of the genuine Marilyn in her than in Sheila. That was the meaning of the party. It filled the sweetness of the present moment with a corroding bitterness.

"*Will* you speak?" pleaded Gayle.

Her hands closed convulsively about a sheet of ration points and began crumpling them, shredding them. Aimlessly her gaze was wandering about the room. She finally met his gaze with a nervous smile. "Of all the silly places and times to propose."

Gayle wheeled and started another kick at the chair and suddenly caught himself. He looked at her, his face half-contrite, half rebellious. "I'm sorry. I was always that way. Getting tangled in my own loop. But I'm serious, Ruth. I love you. Will you marry me?"

Her eyes were mistily soft as they passed over his eager, intense face; and they were very sad. She lowered her gaze.

"No, Gayle."

Gayle thrust his hands into his pockets and walked about the room a bit. "I know this has been sudden, Ruth. I mean my asking. And I'm no bargain . . . half shell-shocked and kind of jumpy. But won't you reconsider, think it over? I wasn't always like this and I'm coming out of it now. You've helped me. You noticed that, didn't you?" She nodded. "Later . . . perhaps I may ask again later? Huh, Ruth?"

She did not look up. "Yes, Gayle . . . later."

He picked up the chair. "I'll get this fixed now."

She had to smile at that. It was so like Bucky trying to make amends after a misdemeanor. A moment later the car roared past the window, the chair legs sticking out of the seat behind him.

Then only did Ruth notice the havoc in her hands. Frantically she smoothed out the crumpled ration stamps. Some of them were hopelessly torn. "Another proposal and we shall die of starvation," she said ruefully to herself.

Her mind was in a turmoil. What she had done and what she had wanted to do were poles apart. She felt all twisted up inside. Famine and plenty, fire and ice, that was how she felt. She had to talk it out, get matters clear. She undid her apron and walked over to the Padre's house.

"What happened over your way?" asked the Padre. "A family fight? I just saw Gayle go steaming out with the broken furniture."

"It wasn't quite that bad, Padre. . . ." She fidgeted with her fingers a moment. "Gayle proposed," she burst out. There was a childlike look in her face as though she expected the Padre to be shocked.

"Well, fancy that," said the Padre drily. "It's nothing new, though, Ruth. It has been done before. And the broken chair? How does that enter into the matter. You didn't . . . ?" His inquiring gaze slyly waited for confirmation or denial of his fears. Ruth shook her head in smiling dissent. "No; I didn't think you would."

[190]

"But I refused him."

"No?" There was genuine amazement in the Padre's voice.

Ruth's eyes began to blink. " — There's one of Jessie's on the table," offered the Padre. Ruth fumbled and found the handkerchief. She placed the square of linen across her face and pressed it with fingers of both hands against her eyes. "What is it, Ruth?" questioned the Padre kindly. "I know what Gayle doesn't . . . that you love him."

Her tearful voice was muffled behind the handkerchief. "That's why it hurts so much. It was sweet to hear him propose, and . . . it was hard to refuse."

"Why refuse?"

The handkerchief came away. "He doesn't love *me*, Padre." She blinked some tears from her eyelids. "He loves my sister . . . all the manifestations of her he sees in me. These last weeks he has been just one pair of eyes and ears, watching me, listening to me, trying to catch similarities of speech and gesture. There must be many of them. She and I were very close."

The Padre rubbed the knuckle of his right index finger judiciously along the ridge of his jaw, slowly, repeatedly. "Would it help if I told you that I believe Gayle was sincere when he professed his love for you?"

"No, Padre, it would not help. I, too, believe he is sincere. He really *thinks* he loves me. But it is only what there is in me of Marilyn that he loves. It would be horrible if when the awakening comes he were bound to me by marriage."

The Padre's eyes were suddenly filled with doubt, for she had voiced the very thoughts that had been uppermost in his mind when Gayle had confided his sudden decision a short while ago. "There is a probability, a high probability that what you say is true," he conceded. She could have what she most wanted in life and was casting it aside. It had to be the genuine thing or nothing. His admiring glance was a salute.

Ruth intercepted his glance. "Oh, it's hard, Padre," she admitted. "And loving him as I do, it's killing. Now it will be even worse. A misstep would hurt him too much . . . more than he could stand."

"You could leave," suggested the Padre gently.

"That's the easy way out, Padre, she said quietly, "and I have thought of it." Her eyes were suddenly very humble. "I suggested it recently to him and he got terribly upset. I think he still needs me. And then there is Bucky . . . and . . . Marilyn. I still feel I owe her this."

"Good girl!" breathed the Padre and the way he said it made of it an accolade. "A sacrifice is never made in vain. Hold on to that thought."

"But it's so hard, Padre. There is no outlook. I want to die when I think of not having his love. Oh, why must things be so?"

"Would you rather be without this love?"

"Oh no, no. Even if it's so tangled up with pain and hopelessness it's — it's good."

"Be patient with it then. You'll never find a joy in life that hasn't some dark drop of bitterness in it. It's got to be that way."

"But why, Padre? If God loves us why does He mix things up so? I wouldn't act that way with Bucky."

"That's thinking with your heart not with your head, Ruth. We are not here just for present pleasure. Our destiny is growth — growth toward Him, and He has to accomplish it in us. That is all of life, the big *either* . . . *or* in every human life. Either to submit to His action, and so approximate Him; or to reject and fight what He sends us, and thus become one with the animals and the mud."

"I pray the 'Our Father' every day, Padre," she confided, "and I try to mean it when I say 'Thy will be done.' "

He seemed not to hear her. The bright April sun lay on his face and hands, a warm dry burning. His eyes were abstractedly gazing at a nearby ocotillo. The slim, straight, wands of the plant were scarlet clad with flaming flowers.

And he was thinking, wondering, if flowers too were like men. At night yearning for the day's light to kiss away the shadows and the dew, and in the midst of the daytime's burning heat longing for the dusk to shroud them round with cooling shadows and the cloistral peace of the night. Man — never satisfied with what he had.

He opened his lips. "That flower," he gestured toward the ocotillo. "You know how it came to be? The rain and the sun. They are good for the flower. It's a lovely flower. Once it was merely a slumbering possibility in the heart of the seedling. Submission to outside forces, to sun and rain, brought fulfillment to the seed — the flower."

She looked at him, her eyes confused with the attempt to follow his thought. "I don't think I understand, Padre," she finally said.

"There is a hunger for happiness in your soul. It's in every soul. The Designer who put the flower in the seed, put also the germ of happiness in us. He has to bring it to completion. Sometimes He will buffet us with rain, sometimes shine on us with joy. They are good for us. Submit, and know fulfillment."

His words comforted her. He was so sincere and sure. "It sounds so simple," she said. "Just to give in."

"That's it. But it's not a week-kneed surrender to some impersonal ruthless force," he warned.

Her mind leaped forward with a sure intuition to the truth. "It's like a child submitting to it's father, isn't it?"

"That's the whole thing in a nutshell." His eyes gravely scanned her face a moment. "It isn't new; it is very old, but it has been forgotten. It's solid truth." His mind was still turning over her recent cry of protest, her complaint at the way the events of her life had been mixed up, and he wanted to give her the right answer, the correct viewpoint. He looked up. "Ruth."

"Yes, Padre."

"Do you know the most misjudged man in the world?"

"No."

"The father of a family. His children are the ones who misjudge him." He watched her face, the broad white brow wrinkling delicately with thought. "It's like this," he explained. "They live wholly in the present and to them he's 'out of this world.' He's busy with business, uninterested in their interests, impatient of the latest songs, dances, and styles. Actually he is living every moment for them. But his gaze is fixed on the future, planning, praying, working for their future."

"Yes," assented the girl, "and in the meanwhile the children compare him with other men, and they decide he's crude, because he hasn't got the polish of a movie actor; he's narrow, because he makes them behave; he's not very clever, because he hasn't the money that other men have."

The Padre's gaze had in it a mild amazement. She spoke so truly, and it was hard to imagine Ruth having had such thoughts about her own father.

"How you found that out I don't know, but it's all very true, Ruth. And that's the way most of us act toward our real Father. His gaze is on the eternal horizons and our nose is ground right into the grubby present. From that viewpoint He doesn't look like much of a Father."

"I understand now, Padre," she said. "I never looked any further than my nose."

The Padre's face lit up with amusement. "Not that it isn't a pretty nose," he said with an appraising look.

A light pink suffused Ruth's cheeks and with the naïve self-consciousness of a child her right index finger went down the bridge of her nose as though trying to find the reason for the Padre's compliment. Then her face broke out into a pleased smile and she stood up quickly.

"You know what I read in a book the other day, Padre?"

"I can't imagine," he replied, his eyes still filled with amusement.

" 'Everyone can master a grief but he that hath it,' " she quoted. Her grateful look went straight at him. "It's not true."

"Don't tell me that *I* have disproved that solid statement," he protested.

"You have."

"Really?"

"Truly. You see I know now that He can't love me and hurt me."

"And if your love for Gayle is not reciprocated?"

Her lower lip trembled a bit. "Then I know He will give me something better," came her brave response.

The Padre's eyes were suddenly soft. "He wouldn't be your Father if He didn't. Young lady, you have now all the answers."

"I'll find my way now," Ruth assured him. "I'm so grateful." She hesitated. "May I take Jessie's handkerchief? I want to iron it out. It's all crumpled."

The Padre smiled assent at this departing manifestation of the eternal feminine.

Chapter 19

DAYS ands weeks of sun flooded down on Tucson and, as spring surged onwards, the drab desert floor began to bloom. Colonies of wild poppies opened their thin orange cups and carpeted wide stretches of the adobe draped hills. The magenta blooms of the contorted cholla, the white waxlike flowers of the Saguaro, the tissuepaper roses of the prickly pear spread vivid colors on the drab desert canvas. For Gayle life seemed to open up again, shining new, keenly eager, poignantly beautiful.

At Doctor Bashford's suggestion he handled some routine work each morning at the clinic, and spent his afternoons at home. Life took on meaning for him again. His return home each midday became an event of great significance, for he came bringing a gift for Ruth. From the past of joyous memory he recalled Marilyn's eager expectancy of him each day, and her unfeigned delight in the things he brought her. It was pleasant to find himself reverting to his old customs, visiting the old shopkeepers who had known so well his wife's preferences and supplied them. He brought Ruth a dozen long-stemmed red roses. She thanked him and placed them in a vase on the living-room table. The next day his gift was an exquisite brooch of hammered silver. She thanked him and tucked it away in her dresser. He came carrying a beribboned box of chocolates. Ruth opened it, nibbled at a piece, and thanked him.

Later that evening Gayle passed by Nora's room and, through the open door, spied a strangely familiar looking candy box. He went in and inspected it more closely. It was his gift to Ruth. Displeased, he went in search of the maid. She was alone in the kitchen.

"Nora, did Miss Ruth give you that box of candy I saw on your dresser?"

"Yes, Mr. Gayle. She can't abide that kind of sweets."

"Oh, I see," said Gayle. He was puzzled. Marilyn had had a predilection for that particular type of candy. He dismissed the incident from his mind as being of no importance, and, with dogged persistence, kept bringing Ruth his daily gift.

He made it a practice to chat with her about the people he had met at the clinic that morning. She was restrained, quiet. At the first excuse she would slip away. Over a period of some weeks, Gayle was rather indulgent to her attitude of polite reserve. He was too deep in the realization of this new love that had come to him. There was no doubt in his mind that, as he grew better and more fully himself, she would give the right answer. Hadn't she said that he could ask again? That made things rather evident. Perhaps there were some matters she had to settle in her own mind first. He recalled the day he had hired her. That independent little streak in her.

But her attitude did not change in the slightest and a note of dissatisfaction crept into the harmony of Gayle's mind. She was standing him off. He chafed and fretted and became more insistent in his attentions. A tired, wan look replaced the fresh brightness in Ruth's countenance. Solicitously, he remarked on it. She passed it off with a stock phrase about the dehydrating influence of the Arizona sun.

Nora overheard the remark and later approached Gayle. "Mr. Gayle," she confided, "it's a change she's needing. Take her out for a dip or excursion or something. She's cooped up here all day long."

"What a dolt I am! — Thanks, Nora."

"And don't ask her. Take her."

That evening he casually remarked to Ruth, "Marilyn was keen on horseback riding. How about you, Ruth?"

A vague flash of distaste went over her face. "I never rode a horse in my life."

"City gal, huh?" he said with smiling contemptuousness. "Don't you do anything?" She gave him a look of studied patience. "I mean, are you just a confirmed housekeeper?"

"I can swim."

"You can? That's fine. How about a swim, then?"

"Not just now, Gayle."

He made no further efforts, but a smile of determination settled at the corners of his mouth.

The next morning Gayle came into the kitchen. "I've got the day off, Ruth. Will you put up a lunch for two? I'm taking an all day excursion to Sabino Canyon. Rustle it, please?"

"Very well."

She hastily put up lunch in a basket. It was only nine o'clock but, outside, the sun was blazing in a cloudless sky. Gayle was honking the horn. She took up the basket and went down the garden walk. The palo verde tree had myriads of tiny, hard, green beads bunched along its slim boughs. There would be a million flowers rioting soon on the tree. A butterfly fluttered past and alighted on a flower, its wings quivering in ecstatic tremors. The amber light of the sun, the depthless blue of the sky . . . it was a day to be free. She opened the gate and went up to the car.

"Hop in," ordered Gayle.

She smiled tiredly even while she thought how delicious it would be to have a full day out-of-doors. "I made lunch for *two*," she said, placing the basket carefully in the rear of the car.

"You did? Well, you and I. That's two. Nora's taking care of Bucky for today." She looked at him, her face filled with hesitancy. It would be such a pleasure. His voice took on a pleading note. "Come on, lady." He had the door open and laid hold of her arm, drawing her forcibly into the car.

"But Gayle," she protested weakly, "my clothes."

"Oh, take off the apron. Your house dress is O.K. This is

[198]

a picnic." Laughingly, she submitted and allowed herself to be drawn into the seat beside him. She undid her apron. Her right hand went over the top of her head and smoothed back the hair over her left ear. Gayle banged the door shut. Nora came hastening out with a flat paper parcel. "Your swimming suit, Mr. Gayle."

"Gosh, I almost forgot it. Thanks, Nora."

The car started forward. "Is there a pool at that place?" asked Ruth.

"At Sabino Canyon? You bet. River water, held in by a small dam. A swim will be just right today. The water's fresh and cold. How about it, Ruth?"

"I haven't a suit," she said regretfully.

"Good Lord!" he said disgustedly. "What do you do with all that money in the bank?" She said nothing, and, after a minute of waiting, he tossed the parcel on to her lap. "Nora is responsible for the size and color."

Her fingers hurriedly undid the parcel. She flung out a gleaming-white, satin swimming suit. "What a darling little thing!" she exclaimed, her face filled with a soft glow of pleasure. She turned to him. "You and Nora — it's a conspiracy."

"That seems the only way to get your nose off the grindstone. It's a pretty nose, too. I don't want it ground down to a nub. Now relax. I want to have some fun. Tomorrow I go on full time at the clinic. This will be my last holiday for a long time."

"I forgive you for what you said a moment ago, Gayle," she said generously. He cast a wondering look at her. "About hoarding my wages."

"You do?" He made a formal bow. "Thank you. I accept the apology, Miss Cameron." His voice suddenly rose to a comical wail. "And now let's be human."

She laughed then, and she seemed to emerge from behind that wall of reserve that had bound her.

The Sabino Canyon highway drove straight east, gradually rising as it neared the junction of the Catalinas and the

Rincon mountains. They took the Upper Canyon road, paralleling the river. It was a series of sharp curves with a spillway at each bend creating shaded pools. At one of them Gayle eased the car off the road. Some cottonwoods and mesquites threw an inviting shade over a stone table and a bench. There was an iron grate over some rocks. It made a perfect bower, silent, shadow-filled and cool.

A deep pool, a few steps away, beckoned invitingly. Huge boulders, gray and water worn, pushed their polished backs haphazardly out of the water.

Ruth was a good swimmer, but Gayle was even better.

"I didn't know cowboys could swim," she teased.

"This one can. I was on the team at the University for three years."

They lunched beneath the old cottonwoods. The swim had put an edge on their appetite, and they ate hungrily. Afterwards they sprawled out in the shade.

The sound of the water flowing into the pool was an anodyne for Ruth's tired spirit. She watched it kicking up its white heels as it jumped into the pool, sending out ripples over the calm surface, ripples that were transmuted into quivering lines of light moving over the clear bottom.

Her eyes lifted in indolent contentment to the eastern wall of the canyon, its escarpment stretching straight into the blue. The splintered battlements cut sharply into the sky. A fluff of cloud with sun-embroidered edges lazed above them. Dots of shrubbery stippled the weathered orange color of the flat canyon wall. The sunlight dreamed contentedly over all.

Gayle spoke and his voice was so quiet and low that it did not break the enchantment of the moment. "When I look at all this I know it was worth fighting for."

Ruth stretched forth her hand and touched the scar on his arm. "Do you remember, Gayle, your first night at home?"

"No; not very well."

She told him then about the talk they had had and how

he had flung his medal from him. His forehead wrinkled in serious thought. "I guess I didn't know what I was doing, Ruth." He was silent a moment. "There will be a lot of us that way when this war is over. All I can hope is that every one of them will find a Ruth in their home to tide them over the bad days."

She blushed but could make no light remark to turn aside the compliment. There was too much sincerity in his voice for that. "The medal is in Bucky's room," she finally said.

"It should be in yours," he replied bluntly.

She smiled, and then without answering turned her eyes back to the mountain wall and the clouds lazing above it. After a while her gaze drifted slowly back to Gayle's face. He was propped on an elbow thinking how peaceful, happy, and beautiful she looked. Ruth smiled slowly, comfortably at him.

"You've got such a comfortable way about you, Ruth," appraised Gayle. "How is it you're so hard to please?"

"I'm not hard to please," she murmured in languid denial.

"You are — in the matter of gifts."

His words broke the spell. She sat up. "I don't think so, Gayle. I've been grateful for all the thoughtful — "

"No, I didn't mean that," he interrupted. "What I meant is that it's hard to find out what you like. Your tastes are very different in almost everything from Marilyn's."

He did not see the shadow pass over Ruth's face.

"I've made another try," continued Gayle, "and I hope I've got something this time that you really like." He went to the car and drew out a small parcel from the glove compartment. He put it in Ruth's hands. When she opened it her little gasp of pleasure was so genuine that a quick light came into Gayle's gray eyes. She held it up, a gold chain, the links delicately interwoven.

"It's a joy, Gayle," she said, her eyes shining.

He watched her fondle it in the palm of her small white hand. "There's something that goes at the end of it," he said. She looked up, her eyes expectant. Gayle lifted the fingers of his right hand and with one tug broke the string about his neck. He held out Marilyn's cross to Ruth.

She looked at it a moment as though hypnotized, then slowly turned her head away. "I can't . . . oh, I can't, Gayle!"

He stayed silent so long that she turned back to him. The hurt and bewilderment in his face touched her. "I'll keep this, Gayle. The chain. It's lovely. I'll wear it and treasure it always."

"But, good Lord, this was Marilyn's cross — "

"I know, Gayle, I know. But it means so much to you. Oh — can't you see — I can't take it."

"No; I can't see — " After a while he spoke again. "You'll wear the chain?"

"Yes, Gayle."

"Promise?"

She lifted her eyes to his. "Is that necessary?"

"No; I didn't mean that, Ruth. I know you will."

He was upset and Ruth realized it from his attempt to extract a promise from her. The word of a friend was always sacred with Gayle.

He stayed silent a long time. When he spoke it was a serious, insistent Gayle. "Ruth, I want to be with you, hear you, talk to you, to look at you. If I'm not with you I'm empty, there's nothingness again. Can't you understand? I go away from you, happy, carrying the picture of you, the words you said. After a while it grows dim, the words, and the picture of you, and I've got to come back."

She looked at him long and quietly. The depth and concentration of his sincerity pierced her.

If only he were talking to her and not to Marilyn!

The truth, the limpid simplicity of that love was something to pray God to possess. Her only reply was to turn away from him.

"Ruth, we had fun today, didn't we?" She was silent. "Didn't we?" he urged.

"Yes, Gayle."

"We could do so many things like this together, but you won't let me. For the past few weeks you have been like an iceberg. Why? Is there something wrong? I know I was sudden with my proposal of marriage, but weren't you going to give me a chance?"

A torrent of protestation welled up in Ruth's heart, a rush of endearing words rose to her lips, her love for him rocked her, shook her with its demands for utterance. How her will subdued them, she did not know. A trembling voice was speaking. It must be her own.

"Isn't it just as well that you discovered my shortcomings, my moods, my reticences, while there is still time?"

Gayle looked at the mask that was again covering her features. He gave an angry twist to his shoulders. "You're holding out on me, Ruth."

She made no reply. A rock squirrel scampered fearfully across their vision. A grasshopper dived onto Gayle's lap and scratched his bare thigh with its scaly feet. Gayle's fingers catapulted the insect into the air; it zoomed away to a disastrous landing in the pool. Ruth stole a look at Gayle's frowning face. She could find no words. A hot breeze soughed its way down the canyon. Cicadas were beginning a confused chirring all about them.

They got up in silence, dressed, and drove home. The distant hills, the floor of the desert, the calcined roadway wore the beaten dead look that excessive sun produces. Ruth felt one with them. The ache in her heart was so great that she felt like one quivering exposed nerve. She prayed that she might control the tears till she had reached the sanctuary of her own little room.

*   *   *

The next morning, a dour-faced Gayle drove off to work, and a few minutes later, a distraught-looking Ruth appeared before the Padre. She collapsed dejectedly into a chair. "Padre, I am at the end of my strength. I can't stand any more. I can't."

The kindly old eyes grew more kindly. His hands moved slowly toward her as though they wanted to soothe and comfort; then they dropped back into his lap. His voice was low. "Tell me, Ruth."

"I've stood him off every day, every hour for the past month. I've been cool, indifferent. And all the while I was burning inside. We get nowhere. He is becoming puzzled, irritated. I am just worn out. I can't go on."

"Does he love you?"

"I still think it's Marilyn. Yesterday he wanted to give me her cross, the one he prizes so much. You know what that means. He can't tell the difference between us any more."

"Or simply that he wants you to take her place."

"If I only knew!" The straight little shoulders drooped forward, and there was a pathetic slackness at the corners of her mouth. She lifted a pair of tired blue eyes to his. "Padre, I want to do the right thing but I didn't know it was going to be so hard. I've prayed. Something is wanted of me here. What it is, I don't know. I fear to do the wrong thing. Not so much for my self, but for . . . others."

"Bucky and Gayle?"

"Yes. And yet I can't go on endlessly this way. Is it all right if I try something to determine matters . . . to bring them to a head?" Her eyes were fixed on his in trusting appeal.

"Certainly, Ruth. Waiting for the Divine Will to declare itself does not mean that you sit on your hands till God hits you over the head with an event. That's determinism."

"I have an idea . . . a plan. It should tell me the truth, and, at the same time, gradually make it clear to Gayle where his affections really are."

"If it doesn't work, try another plan."

Her face grew somber. "Padre, I want to bring the truth home gently to Gayle. After he knows, I'll be able to leave." She was silent for a moment, her thoughts going forward to the drear prospect the future held. She spoke again:

"What do you suppose he will do then?"

"I don't know if he has made plans covering that eventuality."

"On the night of the party at the Desert Moon, he spoke about living alone, the joys of single-blessedness. I may be selfish, but I would like to see him stay single."

"Why?"

"Under the circumstances, I think it's the only way he could be happy." The Padre did not gainsay her and she stood up. "I feel better now. You always help, Padre."

" 'Against hope, believe in hope,' " he quoted. "Let go, abandon yourself, like a child in its mother's arms. I don't like to see that drawn, worried look in your face, Ruth. Despite the moil of circumstances let yourself rest in the arms of that Supreme Design. It's a tide of loving power and will carry you safely, surely to happiness. Nothing can be sent, nothing permitted to happen to you that is not a source of good to you. Believe that."

"I do, Padre," she said, her face clearing.

"You can't see that now, but you will in retrospect. It's like the stones in a mosaic. The colors are all different. Some bitter dark, others laughing bright. Fitted together they produce a thing of beauty. The events of our lives are like that."

"My trouble, I guess, is that I judge the picture before it's finished," she said with sudden insight.

The Padre's face lighted up. "Ruth, you have just spoken like a prophet." He smiled at her, and her own face came alive with laughter at his compliment. She left him then, her mood completely changed.

Back in her room Ruth unlocked the trunk containing her sister's belongings. There was an album of photos. She laid out dresses and began to study the pictures. For hours she sat with half-closed eyes, calling up pictures of Marilyn as she had known her.

That evening at the supper table Gayle was fixing up Bucky's plate when Ruth came in hurriedly from the kitchen. As she took her place she cast a quick glance at

Gayle. He seemed to have completely recovered from the dejected mood that had enveloped him when he left the house that morning. She marveled at it. "Did you say grace, Bucky?" she asked.

"He sure did," replied Gayle.

Ruth closed her eyes and her lips moved, whispering the words of her prayer before meals. Gayle watched her absorbedly. She made such a picture that way. Her eyes opened and she spread a napkin.

"Bucky said grace for all of us, didn't you Buck?" remarked Gayle, reaching forth a hand and touseling the boys hair affectionately.

"Yuh betcha sweet life!"

Ruth looked at the boy with an amused little frown. "You have been talking with your daddy again, I see. I like to say my own prayers, Gayle. — Some potatoes?"

He glanced at her dress. "You're wearing one of Marilyn's dresses, aren't you, Ruth?"

"Yes. I went through her trunk today. Bucky, get the food into your mouth. Look out for your clothes!"

Bucky's napkin had slipped and some gravied potato was decorating the front of his suit. Gayle's voice rose in dry recitative, "When the mush begins to rush down father's vest."

Ruth cast him a reproving look and he subsided.

She got up and adjusted Bucky's napkin, and Gayle's eyes followed her movements. A reminiscent look came into them as he gazed at her dress. Then, with an effort, he shook himself free of the mood, and was charmingly gay and genial. But Ruth detected his eyes, repeatedly straying to her flower-patterned dress.

Toward the close of the meal, Ruth made an irrelevant remark. "Today is Saturday, Gayle," she said.

Gayle looked up. "And tomorrow is Sunday. So what?"

"Don't you ever go to church?"

"Oh!" It was a long, falling inflection. "I used to . . ." he admitted.

[206]

"Don't you think it's about time Bucky got some idea how Sunday should be spent?"

"Hm . . . yes." His eyes had a dubious look as they roved over her. The unaffected grace of that comely head, its smooth blondness, the soft luster of the coronet of hair. A strange imp of roguishness quirked to life within him. His voice was a languid cool drawl as he teased her. "I don't know if anyone ever told you, Ruth, but you are put together just right. And your face and hair . . . well, they make the picture perfect. In plain words, you're an eyeful."

Ruth's face and neck blossomed into a delicious rose, and she cast a vehement glance of warning from Gayle to Bucky. Gayle looked at Bucky.

"Eye-full," mouthed the boy.

There was amusement deep in Gayle's eyes. "You see, he agrees with me. But I was just trying to tell you, Ruth, that if you walk down that church aisle with me, it's liable to create a sensation."

"You don't escape that easy, Mr. Man," replied Ruth determinedly. "Nora will be with you and Bucky. I'll trail along — after you."

"Tongues will start clacking. The ladies haven't seen you yet, you know."

"They've probably been clacking for months — about you who never go to church."

"That's not a very Christian attitude." Abruptly he dropped his tone of light banter. "I'll be glad to go, Ruth. I'm not exactly a pagan. That is — well, there are a lot of things I believe in now."

"You will really come then?"

"Yes. I want to go."

* * *

It was eight-thirty the next morning. Gayle came into the living room. He had on a light gray suit. His turbulent black hair was reduced to order. He gave his tie a final check-up.

Nora was stuffing a handkerchief into Bucky's pocket.

"He's got a touch of hay fever, the poor dear," she explained.

"I 'neezed, daddy," corroborated Bucky.

"Yeah? Well, if you feel it coming on," he pointed to the handkerchief, "haul out that muffler and cover it up. Here's a small bit." He gave him a dime. "A man will come around with a box. Put that in it." He took a turn up and down the room then finally went to the corridor that led to the rear of the house. His voice rose in a loud call "Let's go."

Nora escorted Bucky to the door. Ruth came hurrying in, her hands doing airy feminine nothings to invisible wisps of hair at the back of her neck. Gayle's eyes were suddenly appreciative. She had on a dark suit with a fluff of lace in front. She poised trimly on her high-heeled shoes. There was a pleased happy look about her.

"I . . . I feel triumphant," she said.

Gayle's glance went swiftly from her shoes to her hat. "It's the hat," he declared. "You look good enough to eat."

Her face was radiant. She picked up her purse and gave her skirt an adjusting pat. Gayle fumbled in his pockets. "Got any change, Ruth? Bucky got my last dime."

She opened her purse, and he peered over her shoulder as they went out of the door. "Let's have four bits for the box, Ruth. I'll pay you back tomorrow."

In the car, Ruth sat up front with Gayle. He drove with an occasional glance at the road. "The hat is perfect, Ruth, and it goes right along with the suit . . . that's one of Marilyn's Sunday-go-to-meetings, isn't it?"

"You don't mind, do you?" she said, and her voice was somehow different.

"Your wearing it? No; not at all. Why should I?"

Why should he? And yet he did. There was something funny going on. Just there in the living room, talking about the hat . . . that was Ruth. Now there was a subtle change. He could not put his finger on it, but it was there and it was irritating. He listened to her voice talking to Nora and Bucky. The final consonants were so delicately drawn, reminding him of Spencerian penmanship with those hair-drawn flourishes at the end. It was reminiscent and disturbing. Was she trying to put on the dog? Nonsense. Maybe she figured herself too poor for him. Maybe this dressing up was all an attempt to build herself up to an acceptance. To demonstrate to him that she could wear good clothes correctly. Inferiority complex? Well, if she had one, he had been partly responsible for it by being so stupid about her wages until it was too late. He would not let her see his puzzlement or irritation, though. He would be all the more pleasant and attentive. She was talking to him more freely but somehow this seemed just a new phase of her cool, indifferent attitude. He wondered if they were connected.

When the Wade entourage filed into the church, there was a general craning of necks by the congregation. Ruth had given directions before leaving the house, and she entered the pew first; then Nora and Bucky. Gayle held down the section on the aisle.

Bucky made himself immortal by letting off a succession of shattering sneezes in the midst of the sermon.

The minister stopped his discourse and the heads of the congregation swiveled toward the focus of disturbance. Gayle snatched the handkerchief from Bucky's pocket. There was a sudden metallic clink, and a thin dime ran wildly down the long length of the church floor, desecrating the solemn stillness with its hollowing iniquitousness as it wavered around and around in gradually shortening circles of sound till it finally lay quiet. Bucky had cached his small bit in his handkerchief. Gayle's complexion assumed a Burgundian tinge.

When order was finally restored and the services again under way, Gayle leaned forward a trifle and looked toward Ruth, petitioning for a glance of comfort and condolence. Her profile, singularly pure and other-worldly under that frivolous little hat, was turned upwards in absorbed prayer. He wrinkled his brow and almost muttered something.

Gradually his feeling of annoyance faded and his thoughts drifted away into a quiet abstract little world of reverie. He felt content and peaceful. It was here that he and Marilyn had been married. How blurred and distant that event now seemed. What a world of experiences he had lived through since then! How much he had changed. Change! That was part of life too. Nothing stood still, everything was in flux, everybody was changing, daily, hourly, for better, for worse. His very presence here was an indication of the fundamental change that had taken place in his own being, for he had come here, not as he had formerly come, to please Marilyn, neither was it because he intended to humor a whim of Ruth and so gain her favor. He was here because he had wanted to come. He realized how his outlook on life had changed in many respects. It was easy enough to look down on the beliefs of others with quiet contempt, to be superior to them, passing judgment on the validity of their hopes and faith, saying to one's self: this belief I'll accept, that one is impossible; I reject it. Immutable truths do not change because one rejects them. He saw now that his mistake lay in the shallowness of his appraisal of a truth that was depthless. There was always so much of personal accomodation mixed up with one's way of thinking that one was prone to accept whatever gave one the greatest individual independence. Too easily one made the mistake of glossing over a solid truth because of the restraint upon one's liberty which the acceptance of that truth would necessarily cause.

The congregation stood up to sing. Gayle rose mechanically and his gaze wandered across Bucky and Nora and came to rest on Ruth. He kept looking at her, noting with pleasure the delicate movement of lips, the clean lovely line of neck and throat. . . . She turned her head ever so slightly and her eyes met his. Her right index finger moved up slowly from her hymn book, transfixing him with its pointed gracefulness, and then dropped authoritatively to the book. Gayle's eyes lowered abruptly to discover a hymn book in his own hands and he paged hastily through it till he had found the place. He began to sing.

After the services, Nora deposited Bucky in the back seat

of the car and excused herself to Gayle. There were some ladies who wanted to see her. She billowed away toward an expectant group.

"There," opined Gayle drily, "goes the star reporter of the Back Fence Gazette." He got into his seat and looked at Ruth, demurely seated beside him. "Bet they're talking about you."

"And you!" she added.

Gayle's gaze fixed on the wagging chins surrounding Nora. "I'm probably being ripped from Genesis to Revelations."

Ruth gave him an indulgent smile. It suddenly recalled something to Gayle's mind. "Say, what was the idea of bringing Bucky along when he's got the sneezes?"

"I lost my small bit," complained Bucky from the depths of the car.

"As you were, cowboy," chided Gayle. He looked at Ruth, waiting her reply.

"Was it embarrassing, Gay?" There was laughter in her eyes and a curious expression about her lips.

Gayle turned his baffled gaze away from her. That "Gay" . . . that was what Marilyn used to call him.

That night, in the privacy of her room, Ruth added up the results of her experiment. It seemed such a childish thing she was doing, and yet it was producing results. Gayle was a trifle puzzled, she could see. There was a need for more caution, or he might blunder on to her whole plan, and spoil it. One thing stood out with undeniable clearness: his growing gentleness, his ever-increasing eagerness to be near her, his dependence on her. And that, of course, was bitter medicine for her to take. The more she acted like Marilyn — the more loving he became. It was an indication of the soundness of her fears.

And so the days went slowly by, and, each evening, Ruth added up the day's findings. They mounted steadily and sadly to an overwhelming conclusion. She denied the results, struggled against the inevitable, and drew out her attempt longer and longer. But one evening she placed her head in her arms, and let the tears come. Bitter, burning tears. She could no longer blink the truth. There was no need to carry on the masquerade any longer. The experiment had reached a definite conclusion.

There but remained the task of opening Gayle's eyes to the hard reality, that he could never break free from his loyalty to his dead wife. It would not be easy. Ruth was certain now that Gayle was genuinely fond of her. It was not love, just fondness. She could see that. When she slipped back into her own character, he was very much the joyous comrade. When she acted Marilyn, he was all gentleness, all effort to please, very much the lover.

She dried her eyes and went out into the garden. The peace of evening was all about her as she tiredly walked down the path. She stopped before the palo verde tree. In the shadowy silence of the dusk, its slimness drooped forlornly. Her fingers reached out and passed lightly over the tiny buds knitted to the boughs. They were softening, pulping out, readying themselves to throw wide their petaled loveliness. The chirring of hidden crickets rose on the air. There was a vast aloneness in the sound. It was so impersonal, this growing dusk. There was no friendliness in it. She stood alone.

Her thoughts went back to Gayle. He was well now, carrying on his work daily at the clinic, but he must not be shocked back into his old moodiness and despondency. She would let the truth disclose itself to him. That would be the gentlest way, coming from his own consciousness, but she would see to it that the reality was made undeniably clear.

Slowly, she turned back toward the house. Although her decision had put an end to her doubts and questionings, yet it brought no peace, no joy. Her mind had resigned itself to doing the right thing, but that resignation warred with her love. What a blessing to get the whole thing over with! She could leave then and try to forget. She entered the darkened house.

Several days later, Gayle, unknowingly, set the stage for

the carrying out of Ruth's plan. He came in late one evening from a visit to the Padre. There was no light in the
living room.

"Ruth?" he called out.

"Here, Gayle," came her voice from the sofa.

He snapped on the lights. "What are you mooning in the
dark for?" he asked. "Weaving spells?"

"I was tired. It was restful just sitting here."

"You need a little whoopee, Ruth. How about going to
a surprise party Saturday?"

"No. I think not."

"This is for the Padre."

"Oh . . . for the Padre?"

"Jessie just told me. Saturday is his golden jubilee . . .
fifty years a padre. She is getting a little supper ready. That's
all he wants. But you and I are going to barge in on it —
in formals. I'll wear my tux. You get yourself one of those
Oh-my-gosh evening dresses. I'll pay for it."

"I'll provide my own dress. Thanks anyhow, Gayle. What
about a present? We should bring him something."

They put their heads together over the selection of a gift.

The next day Ruth made a call on Jessie. They took a
long walk into the desert, and Ruth unburdened her mind.
She held nothing back and, at the conclusion, told her what
she planned doing as the final act. "I hope you don't think
me silly," she said. "It seems the kindest way to break the
news to Gayle. Does it look like a school-girl's giddy fantasy?"

"No, Ruth. It's a woman's way. A woman in love seldom
makes a mistake about such matters. It will shock him at
first, but that is inevitable. I know your kindness will soften
it. Of course, you will have to have Nora's help on this.
Would you rather that I explained matters to her?"

"I'd be so grateful. Nora is priceless. I think her old eyes
haven't missed anything these past weeks. She probably
suspects what has been going on. I trust her but I dislike to
talk of this — this masquerade. It makes me feel like an
intriguer."

"I understand, dear, and I'll take care of everything."

They talked over the details and settled on the timing, and Jessie made a note of everything for Nora's information.

*   *   *

It was late Saturday evening when Gayle got home. An unexpected call had come in, requiring immediate attention. He came up the walk with a hasty, impatient step. The setting sun filled the garden with a tired golden light. With a hurried glance he noticed the palo verde drifted deep in golden blossoming. He had spent a musing moment before it that morning, but he had no time for it now. There was a vague irritableness in him, a nervous impatience. The unexpected delay at the clinic, his late homecoming, were partly responsible for it.

He met Nora in the living room. "Where's Ruth?" he asked.

"She's got a whisper of a headache, so I made her lie down for a bit," replied Nora.

"It won't keep her from the party, will it?" asked Gayle anxiously.

"Oh, no; I'm sure it won't. But just to be on the safe side I told her to lie down. I'm to call her at seven-fifteen."

Gayle glanced at his watch. "It's almost that now. Better call her. I'm going to start dressing, myself. We're supposed to be there at eight."

Nora gave him a curious intent stare, which he missed as he turned and hastened into his room. He shaved hurriedly and dressed. The tuxedo fitted him to perfection. The Padre's face would be a study when he marched in. He came into the living room. It was empty. He dawdled a bit, went back into his room and got his gift. Still no Ruth. He went to the rear of the house and tapped gently at her door.

"Ruth?"

"Yes, Gayle?"

"Head all right?"

"Yes, Gayle, I'll be ready in a minute. Got your gift?"

"All set. Hurry or we'll be late."

She did not reply.

He went back to the living room and opened the front door. The night was stealing away the last patch of roseate glory from the Catalinas. He watched it fade, that curious, unearthly color, as he had done so many times — the mystery of its beauty stirring him. Beauty into blackness. A thin little star shivered hesitantly in the darkening sky.

Some slight noise, a whisper of silk, made him turn. His whole body grew rigid, his eyes drinking in the vision of delight. There on the other side of the table stood Marilyn. Just as she had looked on her wedding day. An ethereal creature of gossamer and cloudy lace. Virginal, lovely, resplendently white. Only the veil was missing. It was not needed. For no veil should cover the glory of that cloud of flowing gold-red hair.

Like a man in a trance he walked across the room. His right hand came up, reverently slow, and touched her shoulder, his left arm, hesitantly gentle, enfolded her waist. Then he gazed steadily, knowingly, into the eyes of this woman. A smile of uttermost tenderness came slowly to his lips as they drew near to hers.

And then, through the peace in his face, there tore a sudden contortion. Reality was abruptly gone. His eager arms were stricken dead in the midst of their embrace.

There was no kiss. Only a sudden broken sobbing. The girl stood still as marble.

"Oh, God, I've lost you, Ruth, I've lost you!" And his head came down on his right arm still rigid over her shoulder.

Gently her fingers found his face and put up his head. She looked into his pain-racked eyes. "What is it, Gayle?" Her voice was filled with a vast sadness. "You find that Ruth is too little like Marilyn."

He gazed at her stupidly. "The perfume," he mumbled.

She nodded, lost in her own misery.

"You . . . you notice it?" he asked.

"Yes. Mignonette."

"You *do* notice it?"

There was patient weariness in her voice. "Of course. I'm wearing it."

His hands clenched convulsively in the flesh of her shoulders.

"Wearing it?" His eyes were flaming intensities. "You're sure?"

"I found it among Marilyn's things." She moved slightly. "You're . . . you're hurting me, Gayle."

He did not hear her. His brain was exploding with lights. He wanted to shout, to laugh. Across his face raced a tempest of emotions, but Ruth saw only the superabounding one of joy, and it engulfed her with despair. Like the cold white line of a scalpel, the pain of his bruising hands cut through the misery of her soul.

"Gayle," her voice was quivering, "you're hurting —"

His hands unflexed and fell away. He finally found his voice. A shaky voice, but audible. "Take off . . . those things, Ruth. Put on another dress. I've got to tell you something." Her slow-moving step had the faltering tempo of a dying man's breath, as she made for her room. He came suddenly to her door. "That perfume . . . the mignonette . . . give me what's left."

She gave him the small frail vial. He held it in his hand, looking at it happily. Weariedly she closed the door.

This was sickening fulfillment. She slid out of the white daintiness of the gown. It lay like a crumpled chrysanthemum on the floor. The perfume had been the final touch. He knew now who it was that he loved.

She came back into the living room slowly, the weight of her loss dragging her steps. Gayle was still staring happily at the perfume bottle he held. Swiftly he came to her, took her hand and led her to the sofa. The words rushed forth now. "Ruth, Marilyn has spoken to me, several times. I don't mean with words, but through her perfume."

Ruth raised troubled eyes to his.

[216]

"I'm not off my rocker. The Padre knows all about this. He will tell you. The perfume would appear, but it wasn't perfume. I had it tested by a psychiatrist. He said it was preternatural. When I noticed the perfume on you just now, I didn't know it was real perfume. . . . I thought it was the other thing. I thought Marilyn was warning me away from you. She did that once before — with Sheila." He poured out the whole story of the perfume, his doubts, questionings and gradual understanding of its significance.

"You see, Marilyn said her love for me was deathless," he concluded, "and tonight I understand what she meant. The earthly bond is broken, but there is still a spiritual one. That one goes on . . . always."

"She is still protecting you, watching over you . . . is that what you mean?"

"That's it. Bucky and I both need love. She sent the one who was to take her place."

"A substitute?"

"No; a successor. It took me a long time to learn that earthly love for her ended when she died. I'm kind of — thickskulled. She had to use something tangible to teach me."

An icy hand seemed to unclasp its fingers from about Ruth's heart. She stood up. "Oh!" she said in a choked voice, and went swiftly to the door and out on the porch.

The night was wondrously still, the sky reeling with crowds of stars. She breathed deeply of the crystal clean air that flowed in from the vast dead wastelands of the desert.

Gayle came up close. His hand reached down and found her fingers. He began to speak. "These past weeks, Ruth, what was it? Half the time you weren't you. What were you doing? I had found love again, and, suddenly, it was slipping away. It was tearing me all up inside. I was so afraid to lose you. You are not Marilyn, and her clothes were making you like her. It was you I loved."

Her eyes came up to his then, mistily soft. "*That* was what I had to know, Gayle. It wasn't deceit. I had to know not only for me — mostly for you."

[217]

She put up her hand in a shamefaced way, as though to push the dyed hair out of sight. And suddenly it was all clear to him. His voice was very low and gentle. "There's no blame, Ruthie. It was the right thing." He took the bottle of perfume and poured its contents on the ground. The mignonette's flowery fragrance rose up about them, clinging to their clothes, caressing faintly their faces.

Ruth turned her face up to his, "Gayle, dear, I've loved you so." He gathered her into his arms. The night was warm, mysterious, dark about them.

Gayle's lips were close to her ear, murmuring. "Ruthie, a man seldom finds love twice. I have . . . and it makes me feel very small, and humble, and grateful. — Why are you trembling?"

Her speech was well-nigh incoherent with the burden of her feelings. "It's sweet . . . oh, it's sweet, Gayle, dear. I was afraid I had lost you. I'm so afraid that I may yet lose you."

Gayle spoke with unaccustomed eloquence. "There's nothing to fear. I've learned from loss. We must take the joy of the present moment, Ruthie, knowing that it will not be all joy. Sorrow and separation have a place in the pattern too. But what does that matter? There is something bigger than us that has care of us. It will find for us what we've lost. It's always about us, like a loving embrace, through shadow and sun. It gives and it takes away — but always it gives again."

Ruth snuggled up confidently to him and Gayle's arms tightened about her, but his eyes were filled with a hazed thoughtfulness; for of a sudden the real design had unrolled itself before his mind's eye with startling clarity. It was not just to lead him back to present happiness that all these extraordinary events had befallen him but to find for him a wider vision of life and more lasting values. How futile were personal strength, wealth, individual knowledge and ability! There were chinks in that armor. Man was small and weak when left to his own resources. It was only in admission of that fact, and submission, that his real strength lay; for by submission he identified himself with the will of the infinite power that drew the design of creation. He could ride on it as on the crest of a wave, partaking of its power, filled with the patience of its strength, gifted with the vision of its far-seeing plans, interpenetrated with the divinity of it — as completely as the sponge that floats on the ocean wave and is supported and carried by it and is at the same time one with it.

"What are you thinking of, Gayle? You're . . . you're far away."

He looked down at her, his eyes soft with the confiding nearness of her. "I was thinking, dear, how few answers I had to the riddle of life. But it's different now. I am no longer lost, I am no longer alone."

The white blur of her face was tilted up toward him understandingly. She knew that it was not only of herself and of her love for him that he spoke. Slowly Gayle's hand stole inside his shirt-front. When he withdrew it he put up his palm. On it restfully, easily, glowed Marilyn's little gold cross.

"Now will you wear it?"

She took it and kissed it, smiling her acquiescence.

There was a sound of footsteps before the gate.

Gayle peered into the deepening dark. "It's Jessie," he said.

"Shall we go, dear?"

"Yes, we are late."

She nestled her arm in his and they walked down the path. A shadowy silence loomed up ahead of them.

"The palo verde," murmured Ruth.

"It's in blossom again."

They stood in silent stillness before the vague, swelling mysteriousness of the tree, and when Ruth finally spoke, her voice was the voice of another woman, dream-filled with love and memories. "Like a house of gold . . . all day today . . . I kept looking at it . . . dreaming, wondering, praying."

"Spring has come, Ruth." The urgent exaltation of a great fulfillment sang in his words, and to Ruth came the deeper meaning that underlay them.

"Yes, Gayle," she whispered, "the night is passed."

They drifted on past the tree, and as they walked the haunting fragrance of the spilled mignonette went with them, breathing about them like a blessing.